MISSIONS OF SECURITY

Bjorn Hasseler

Missions of Security Copyright © 2021 by Bjorn Hasseler. All Rights Reserved.

All rights reserved. No part of this book may be reproduced in any form or by any electronic or mechanical means including information storage and retrieval systems, without permission in writing from the author. The only exception is by a reviewer, who may quote short excerpts in a review.

1632, inc. & Eric Flint's Ring of Fire Press handle **D**igital **R**ights **M**anagement simply: We trust the *honor* of our readers.

Cover Art Illustration by Vladimir Shvachko
Cover Art Concept by David Monath
Cover Design and Layout by Jeff Carrico

This book is a work of fiction. Names, characters, places, and incidents either are products of the author's imagination or are used fictitiously. Any resemblance to actual persons, living or dead, events, or locales is entirely coincidental.

Bjorn Hasseler
Find out more about him at https://ringoffirepress.com/authors/hasseler-bjorn/

Printed in the United States of America

First Printing: May 2021
1632, Inc.

eBook ISBN-13 978-1-953034-77-9
Trade Paperback ISBN-13 978-1-953034-78-6

Dedication

To the ROTC cadre at Gettysburg College, especially Colonel John Tartala, Major Collins, Captain Terry Briggs, Sergeant Major Steven Hoffman, Master Sergeant Alex Anderson and Professor/Lieutenant Commander Bruce Bugbee. What you taught me is showing up in all of this year's stories.

Acknowledgments

Thank you to Eric Flint for creating the 1632 universe and making it a shared universe.

Thank you to Jim Baen and Toni Weisskopf, who have supported the 1632 community from the beginning and gave us a place on Baen's Bar.

Thank you to Walt Boyes and Joy Ward, editors of Ring of Fire Press, who made sure this novel got better along the way. Thank you to the Ring of Fire Press staff. There's a big difference between hearing about all the steps of publishing a novel and watching people make your novel happen.

Thank you to Dave and Aaron for their good advice along the way.

Thank you to everyone who has read the Neustatter stories. Thank you for asking for more.

CONTENTS

Chapter 1: Winter Plans 1
Chapter 2: The Spring Rush 47
Chapter 3: *Bibelgesellschaft* 89
Chapter 4: Now Hiring 107
Chapter 5: Blood in Erfurt 145
Chapter 6: Babies 175
Chapter 7: The Battle of Flieden 191
Chapter 8: Home 267
Cast List 286

MISSIONS OF SECURITY

CHAPTER 1: WINTER PLANS

Saturday, October 8, 1633

"It's been just over a year since we met the up-timers at Alte Veste," Edgar Neustatter said. "We worked the winter in Grantville, went home, and brought our families back to Grantville. We went to Basic Training and formed our own outfit. This attack by the League of Ostend is just the next step. Give it a little time, and we will have wagons and trucks to guard."

News of the Battle of Luebeck Bay had arrived yesterday. NESS could not afford to linger at the Thuringen Gardens day after day, but there was a radio at the high school broadcasting Voice of America. Big crowds were gathering in Magdeburg, moving toward the palace. No one really seemed to know what would happen next.

They waited anxiously all day, getting nothing done. Neustatter stationed Ditmar in the high school, and the others took turns as messengers, bringing news back to everyone else in the refugee quarters. When Otto returned and rattled off a whole list of names of people who were being cheered by the crowd in Magdeburg, everyone was relieved.

Astrid recognized President Stearns and Princess Kristina. She did not know the rest of them—yet.

Sunday, October 9, 1633

NESS awoke at dawn on Sunday to someone pounding on their door. The men literally rolled out of bed and reached for weapons. Karl headed for the fireplace, slow matches in his hand.

"Neustatter! NUS Army! Open up! We need you now!"

Neustatter motioned Ditmar into position next to the door, then he unlocked it and swung it open. A soldier in uniform stepped in, and Ditmar hastily lowered his clubbed musket. The soldier winced but did not step back.

Instead he asked, "Do you know about the Battle of Wismar Bay? And the crowds in Magdeburg?"

"*Ja.*"

"John George says Saxony is leaving the CPE."

"Bastard," Neustatter pronounced.

"He has to pass orders before Saxony can do anything."

"It is, what, eighty miles from Magdeburg to Leipzig, *ja*?" Neustatter asked. "A dispatch rider could cover that in two days, reach Leipzig tonight."

"Exactly. Saxony might do something stupid. Your personnel records say you can ride."

"They do?"

"Somebody checked that box. Can you ride a horse without falling off?"

"Ride, *ja*," Neustatter answered. "Cavalry charge, *nein.*"

2

"We need patrols on the border, and we need them tomorrow. You are to report to Sara Carroll for a check-out ride, and then you will be given your sector."

The men were out the door in minutes. Neustatter took a minute to tell Astrid, "Miss Schäubin, you will have to watch the office. If any clients come in, tell them we have been *called up* but will return when we can."

Tuesday, October 11, 1633

After the men left, the women and Johann went to Sunday services at the Lutheran congregation Ursula had found. Now that they had moved to the high school refugee housing, they were probably just as close to St. Martin's in the Fields, but Ursula was insistent. Anna was inclined to agree. Astrid figured a Lutheran church was a Lutheran church. Neustatter later called it her charmingly naïve phase.

Astrid sat in the office each day they were gone, except Sunday. *Frau* Ennis came by on Tuesday to check on the workmen's progress. Astrid scrambled to her feet.

"How are you all doing?" *Frau* Ennis asked.

"Anna and Ursula and I wish the men were not going to be gone for so long," Astrid answered. "It will be for no longer than their mission to Halle, but it seems like it."

Leigh Ann nodded in understanding. "I don't like it, either, when James is gone."

Then she looked around the room. "Miss Schäubin, you need a desk and a chair if you are going to sit here all day," she stated. "And you need a phone."

"*Ja,* we do," Astrid agreed.

"Then let's go shopping." Leigh Ann said that like it was all settled.

"Someone has to be in the office."

"Is everyone else out with Neustatter?" *Frau* Ennis asked.

"*Nein*. Ursula and Anna are in our quarters."

"How 'bout they watch the office?"

"I think that would be all right." She hoped.

"If you don't mind my saying so," *Frau* Ennis continued, "it says something that you are the secretary."

"Ursula is quite normal," Astrid explained. "She has a child and is a good cook. Anna is simply quiet and sews very well."

"And you're the one who is getting a job. Does Neustatter trust you to make decisions?"

"For some decisions, he must."

"Are you and Neustatter . . . ?" Leigh Ann's question trailed off.

"Are we what?"

"You know. Together."

"*Nein!* Why does everyone think that?"

Leigh Ann shrugged. "Sorry. It just seems . . . natural."

That sounded more like a question than a statement to Astrid, but she let the matter drop.

Ursula and Anna were initially hesitant but agreed to stay at the office. *Frau* Ennis and Astrid walked into Grantville. Astrid learned a lot as Leigh Ann told her about each business they passed by or the family that lived in each house.

"So that is the Historical Society." Leigh Ann pointed to a building on right side of the road.

"*Ja, Frau* Haun," Astrid responded.

"Please, Miss Schäubin, save the '*Frau* Haun'—or better, '*Frau* Ennis, since I took James' name—for when we are signing the rental agreement," she said. "I'm Leigh Ann."

"Then *I bin* Astrid."

Leigh Ann smiled. "Amideutsch?"

"*Ja.* Our village says, '*Ich heet.*' It is *Plattsdeutsch. Hochdeutsch* is *Ich heisse.*"

"That piece of Amideutsch is our fault," Leigh Ann told her. "It sounds like President Kennedy's speech. *Ich bin ein Berliner.*" She told Astrid what she remembered learning about the Berlin Crisis up-time.

"But use 'Miss Schäubin' at work," Leigh Ann advised. "Was 'Miss' your idea?"

"Neustatter's. When the men came home from the war in April, he called me *Fräulein*. I told him not to say that where *Herr* Augustus or *Frau* Sophia might hear. Or anyone who might go tell them. Our men had been in Grantville from Alte Veste until good traveling weather came in the spring. They started talking like you do here."

Frau Ennis—Leigh Ann—raised an eyebrow. "I'd heard that. I don't get outside of Grantville much, and when I do, it's usually one of the towns right outside the Ring of Fire. I hadn't realized the nobility would take offense."

"Some certainly will." Astrid smiled. "I understand some of the *adel* near Grantville have gotten used to you up-timers."

"Been contaminated by our ideas, you mean. Absolutely. Let me tell you some stories . . ."

Leigh Ann led Astrid to a *furniture* store. It sold chairs, couches, desks, beds, and so on, all down-time-made but incorporating up-time designs. At least, Astrid *thought* they were up-time designs. She had never seen anything like them before.

"I know what you down-timers call a desk is what we up-timers call a lectern," Leigh Ann told her. "But that is not what you want. You want to be able to sit comfortably with all your paperwork within reach. Besides, I've seen the movies that Neustatter talks about. I gather you're the gorgeous blonde dame who's going to be sitting behind the desk, so pick something you like."

Astrid examined the desks on display one by one. Several featured intricate woodworking on the front panel and around the edges. She looked at the cost of one of them and blanched.

There were simpler designs, though. She spotted a plain wooden desk and checked the price. NESS could probably afford this one.

Leigh Ann raised an eyebrow. When Astrid nodded, she looked for the sales clerk.

Astrid saw only one drawback. "I do not think it will fit in the door."

The sales clerk knelt down and pointed to something underneath the desk. "There are heavy pegs here, here, here, and here." He pointed them out. "They slide. It comes apart."

"That's ingenious!" Leigh Ann exclaimed. "Do you have those on the fancier models, too?"

"Some of them."

"I will definitely mention these to my mother-in-law. She works in real estate."

Astrid got talked into two desks and two chairs. She suspected they would need more chairs, but she wanted to talk to Neustatter first. Leigh Ann helped her arrange delivery and payment. Then they started back.

"What's next on NESS's list?" Leigh Ann asked.

"Up-time firearms and horses," Astrid answered.

"I might be able to help," Leigh Ann said slowly. "Where are you going to keep the horses?"

"I do not know."

"It's a shame there's no bridge across Buffalo Creek right there," Leigh Ann mused. "If there were, you could keep them in my parents' barn. Of course, if there were a bridge, the two halves of our property wouldn't be so cut off from each other. I wonder if we could put up a bridge . . ."

Build a bridge, Astrid marveled. *Just like that.*

"Might even help Julia get back to the farm more often."

"What do you mean?" Astrid asked.

"My mother works at a day care in Grantville. She stays in town during the week and comes home on the weekends. It's not far as the crow flies, but it takes quite a while, and it's almost impossible in winter weather. My kids and I moved in with my parents while my husband is with the Army."

"Is he at Camp Saale?" Astrid asked.

"No, he's with one of the new units, but he'll be back next month. For a while, anyway."

Sunday, October 16, 1633

The men arrived home in time for dinner.

"We rode horses for a week and made camp every night," Hjalmar told Astrid. "Guarding the salt wagons was more dangerous that patrolling the border with Saxony. The salt mission at least had a brawl." He was going to say more when Neustatter called everyone together.

"Circle up! Sit, stand, whatever."

"Basic," Hjalmar whispered to Astrid as they all gathered around. Most found seats at the table in their quarters.

"The Confederated Principalities of Europe is now the United States of Europe. Captain-General Gars will still be the emperor. President Stearns is going to be the prime minister."

Neustatter looked around to make sure everyone understood. Astrid nodded. She had heard that at her classes while they were gone.

"The New United States is going to be called something else, and Ed Piazza will be the new president."

The women had heard that, too.

"The dragoon unit that Tom Simpson organized replaced us. The Army said they want their best riders on the border and us guarding wagons. The USE and Sweden are going to try to hold Luebeck and Wismar. They'll be under siege by the League of Ostend soon. That is the French, the Danes, the Spanish, and the English. The NUS Army is rushing supplies to those two cities. They are using trucks—and using up a lot of fuel. So supplies they might have moved elsewhere by truck are going to be carried by wagon. Even when the trucks get back, they are going to conserve fuel as much as possible. They need us."

"Us, NESS? Or us, all the mercenaries and security services?" Stefan asked.

"All of us," came Neustatter's answer. "Some of the Albernians are out on a mission, so they will probably not take as many convoys as they otherwise could. We will be allowed to take our Reserve weapons. Our first priority will be cold weather clothing and range time." He looked at Astrid. "Have any clients shown up yet?"

"*Nein*. But the office is almost ready. I believe *Frau* Ennis will find a way to get us a telephone. I need to talk to you about up-time weapons and horses, too."

Astrid could tell Neustatter was interested, but he held his questions for later. With dinner, discussion of the new Lutheran congregation, and the political situation, later became the next day.

Monday, October 17, 1633

Neustatter turned in place, studying the NESS office from the inside. The two desks were set up to the left of the door.

"I like this," he said. "How much did this cost?"

Astrid told him.

"Not bad," he said. "Not bad at all. *Und* you mentioned telephone, horses, and guns?"

MISSIONS OF SECURITY

"Leigh Ann—that is *Frau* Ennis—said she had some ideas. She said if there were a bridge over Buffalo Creek here, we could keep the horses in her father's barn."

"That would really help," Neustatter agreed.

He smiled. "You do realize, do you not, that the reward for doing well is more work? I need NESS's secretary at the desk, answering the door and the phone. If there is nothing else to do, do your school work."

Astrid nodded. That made sense to her.

A mounted courier arrived before noon with assignments for NESS. They were needed in Erfurt right away—so much so that the Army was sending a pickup despite the fuel shortage. He handed over written orders, which Neustatter read and passed to Astrid.

The Committees of Correspondence had been recruiting, and ever since the Battle of Wismar Bay, volunteers had poured in. Several hundred were gathered in Erfurt, and the new USE Army wanted them at Camp Saale for basic training.

"Do not ask me who stays with the NUS Army and who moves to the USE Army," the courier warned. His weary tone said he'd been asked that question a lot already. "They do not tell me who or why."

"They are probably making it up as they go," Neustatter agreed.

"How are eight of you going to guard hundreds of men?" Astrid asked.

"Oh, we are not. Look at the end of the orders," Neustatter told her.

"Supply wagons."

"Food," Neustatter explained. "This would not be the only group coming to Camp Saale. Thousands of soldiers will need a lot of food. We are really there to guard the food from the recruits."

Thursday, October 20, 1633

The men returned home Thursday night. The women had already gone to bed, and the knock at the door awakened them. Astrid quickly dressed and went to the door.

"Who is there?"

"Neustatter."

Astrid hurriedly unlatched the door.

"*Danke*," Neustatter said. He stepped out of the way as the rest of the men filed in. "Long march, new recruits, and Camp Saale is really busy."

"More groups like the one you brought in?"

"*Ja.* There are more new volunteers at Camp Saale than there were men in the entire NUS Army just a month ago. I ran into Sergeant Wolfe from Bretagne's Company. They just brought in two food convoys from west of here and are headed back out in the morning."

"Do you have an assignment?"

"We are to meet a *Herr* Schrödinger downtown tomorrow. On Saturday, he has a shipment of goods going to Magdeburg. He is going, too."

Astrid frowned. "He did not come to the office."

"*Nein*, we got this assignment through the military."

"Why?"

Neustatter grinned. "They did not tell us. You may draw your own conclusions about the nature of his cargo, of course."

Friday, October 21, 1633

Neustatter decided they had time to talk to Leigh Ann before the men were due to meet with *Herr* Schrödinger.

As they took the long way around—the only way around—Neustatter muttered, "*Ja*, I want a bridge, too."

MISSIONS OF SECURITY

Leigh Ann welcomed them in. She was holding a baby who could not have been more than a few months old.

"I did not know you have a newborn!" Astrid exclaimed. "I am so sorry for keeping you the other day!"

Leigh Ann tucked a lock of hair behind her ear. "Pffft. I needed the break, and my father is perfectly capable watching Carrie for a couple hours and breaking up the occasional argument between Julia and James. Those are the two you hear in the next room. What do you think of the office furnishings, *Herr* Neustatter?"

"Just Neustatter, *bitte*. The desk and chairs are just what we need."

"Good. Come, sit down."

Leigh Ann led them to the same room as before. Once they were seated in the armchairs and had drinks, she got down to business. "We are having phone lines run to two of the offices. We'll add the other if I can find a phone for it. You're getting an old sit-on-the-desk rotary phone. I hope that's okay."

"Any telephone is more than we expected," Neustatter assured her.

"Astrid said you needed up-time weapons and horses."

"*Ja. Und* I agree that a bridge would be helpful, but I have no idea how to do that."

"Let me ask my husband about that," Leigh Ann told them. "He's always been good at building stuff and put in a simple bridge on the back road to his hunting camp. It was a ways away and didn't come through the Ring of Fire."

"A hunting lodge?" Neustatter asked. "That is something the *adel* have."

"And a lot of West Virginians. James belonged to a hunting club. A few dozen people got together and paid membership dues to keep up the camp building and rent the land from one of the big companies."

"What was this camp building like?" Neustatter asked.

"I think we have a picture around here somewhere. Excuse me a moment, please." Leigh Ann returned with a photo album and quickly leafed through the papers before stopping at a page with a couple pictures of her husband standing next to a buck.

"I have not seen that kind of deer before," Neustatter said. "Up-time?"

"Yeah. Whitetail. But there are plenty of 'em over in North America right now." Leigh Ann frowned. "Up-time, we had game laws. You had to get a license from the state, and that let you hunt during a certain season. There were special days you could use bows or muzzleloaders or hunt doe. The game laws kept the deer from being hunted out. There were seasons for other animals, too." She paused for a moment. "I don't know if there are any whitetail left in the Ring of Fire or not. We may have hunted them all that first winter, trying to keep everyone fed. I hope there are still some out there, but . . ."

Neustatter nodded. "We have hunting rights, too, but they are limited. *Und* we understand—you could not let people starve that first winter. The building behind *Herr* Ennis is very large. Is that the hunting lodge?"

"Yeah. It's got a big kitchen and dining hall and a couple rooms with rows of bunks. People can join the club, pay their due and a certain number of days' labor, and hunt on the land the club rented from one of the big companies."

"Hjalmar's description of the barracks at Camp Saale sounded something like this," Astrid said.

"*Ja.*" Neustatter smiled. "Until we went off to the war, I thought *Herr* Augustus lived in a *schloss*. It is really just a hunting lodge. The family divided their lands so much that there was not a real *schloss* left for each son and grandson." Then he shook his head. "*Und* up-time commoners had something much closer to an actual *schloss* that they shared by subscription."

"We had an upper class, too," Leigh Ann said. "They didn't have titles—not in the United States, anyway—but they had a *lot* of money. But there weren't many of them around Grantville. Their hunting lodges were really fancy and had employees to find the game for them. In West Virginia, we hunted to put meat on the table. That means we had a fair number of guns, for deer, small game, birds, even bear."

Neustatter nodded his understanding.

"Right after the Ring of Fire, the Emergency Committee asked everyone to donate any weapons they didn't need. We kept what we needed and donated the extras."

Neustatter nodded. "We are issued up-time weapons when we are on an assignment for the Army."

"We Americans had a jillion different calibers," Leigh Ann continued. "The Army picked a few to make ammunition for. The rest have just been sitting there for a while now. They are starting to return those. If something like the Croat Raid happens again, they want those weapons being used. And quite a few of us up-timers have a lot of land and personal possessions but are cash poor. So, once the weapons are returned, some folks will sell them."

"*Adel*, bürgers, and security services will be happy to buy them," Neustatter said.

"We've had some returned, and we'd like to give you the first opportunity to buy."

Neustatter appeared just as stunned as Astrid felt.

"*Danke*. We truly appreciate this," he said. "What kind of weapons?"

"Pistols. A couple thirty-eights and a twenty-two. And a twenty-two rifle."

"Those would be very helpful. *Danke*."

They got down to haggling. In the end, *Frau* Ennis got a good price. On the other hand, if NESS were ever attacked, these weapons could literally be the difference between life and death.

When the men left to meet with *Herr* Schrödinger, Neustatter, Ditmar, Hjalmar, and Otto were carrying the up-time weapons.

Hjalmar, Wolfram, and Stefan came back to NESS's quarters at dusk.

"Astrid, *Herr* Schrödinger did not just want to meet us. He wants us to guard the cargo tonight. So, you ladies and Johann are on your own until we get back. It will be three days by wagon, then we move the cargo to boats with engines. Whatever the cargo is, it is important. The mission will be two weeks, but if it turns into sixteen days, do not worry."

"I will protect them," Johann stated.

Hjalmar nodded solemnly. "You have the matchlocks if you need them. Do you remember how to load them?"

"*Ja.*" Neustatter, Hjalmar, and Ditmar had drilled it into her often enough.

Hjalmar crossed the room to pick up one of the weapons. "Show me."

Astrid pantomimed loading the matchlock.

"*Gut.* I have to get back."

Astrid hugged her brother. "Stay safe."

"Always."

* * *

While the men were gone for two weeks, Astrid kept working on her English. Her class was learning up-time English, but in the hallways and around town people spoke a blend that was part English and part German. She heard someone call it Germlish, but it seemed like more people called it Amideutsch. Most people did not worry about what it was called. They just spoke it and felt no need to do so in exactly the same way that everyone else did, although there did seem to be a particular "flavor" of Amideutsch at Calvert High School. People could understand each other—that was what mattered. Astrid liked it for that reason.

One day Astrid asked Anna to stay in the office while she went downtown to the *polizei* office. She wanted to let Chief Frost know how NESS was doing.

"Miss Schäubin," Dan Frost greeted her. "On your own today?"

"The men are still out on that mission."

Frost nodded. "How are you all doing?"

"Well, *danke*," Astrid replied.

Chief Frost leaned forward, elbows on his desk. He interlaced his fingers and rested his chin on them. "I have a question for you, Miss Schäubin. Are you and Neustatter seeing each other?"

Astrid tried to figure out the idiom. "Do you mean do we pay attention to each other? Of course. Neustatter runs NESS, and I am the secretary."

"No, I mean romantically."

Astrid's head jerked back in surprise. "Of course not. Neither one of us has enough money saved up to marry, and it would not be to each other."

"Just checking."

Once outside—she didn't want to insult Chief Frost—Astrid shook her head in bewilderment. Then she went by their old quarters in Spring Branch and Murphyhausen, just in case anyone had been looking for NESS there.

She could tell at a glance that a new family had moved into the refugee housing. There were a few plants on either side of the door, and a different set of cooking irons stood over the fire. When she knocked, the door was opened at once.

"*Gut morgen.*"

Since the woman had greeted her in Amideutsch, Astrid replied in the same dialect. "*Gut morgen. I bin* Astrid Schäubin. My brother and cousin and I and some others from our village lived here when we came to Grantville."

A short man looked out at her warily. "Dietrich Kluth, tinsmith from Brandenburg. Did you leave something?"

"*Nein.* I thought someone might look for Neustatter's European Security Services here. Has anyone asked for us?"

"*Nein.*"

"*Gut.* We have an office on the other side of the Ring of Fire, out past the high school." She noted his blank look. "How long ago did you come to Grantville?"

"A few days."

She heard children inside. "Have you found the schools yet?"

An apprehensive look crossed his face. "We were not sure who could attend . . ."

"Everyone," Astrid told him. "The schools are very good. Stefan and Ursula's son Johann is learning a lot. I attend the adult education classes. They help with learning about Grantville."

"Come in, *bitte.* You should meet my wife Margareta and my sister Maria."

Astrid answered their questions about Grantville and showed them where the school bus stopped. She thought about stopping by the office of the Grantville Ecumenical Refugee Relief Committee, but a different idea occurred to her.

MISSIONS OF SECURITY

Astrid backtracked to the last row of housing and checked to see if Maria and Wilhelm Rummel and their group were still there. The door opened at her knock.

"Astrid!" Maria exclaimed. "We did not know where you went from Murphyhausen."

"You can find us at the high school refugee housing." Astrid gave Maria a short account of what had happened. "Do not tell strangers we live there, *bitte*. NESS has an office out past the high school if anyone needs to find us."

"We will not tell anyone," Maria promised.

"How are you doing?" Astrid asked.

"All of us are working. Except for the children. They go to school. Some of us have found positions, but others are still doing day labor." Maria frowned. "We have started to talk about moving out of the refugee housing. Wilhelm thinks we would need at least three rowhouses. He claims that if we can get three next to each other, we can turn the ground floor of one of them into additional bedrooms."

Astrid smiled. "That is a good idea. I do not know if you will be able to find three in a row."

"I have heard talk that the new row of houses will be have three stories. I am trying to convince him to get two of those."

"Also a good idea," Astrid said. "Have you met the families in our old quarters?"

"*Nein*."

"They are new here. Do you think you could show them around?"

"Like you did for us? *Ja*. What do they do?"

"Dietrich is a tinsmith."

"Oh, he should have no trouble finding work. . . ."

Monday, October 31, 1633

NESS received a strange request from the Marion County Tax Assessor's Office, inquiring about guards. Astrid read it carefully, twice. Something did not seem right. Over lunch at Cora's, she caught up on Grantville gossip, including a dispute over the Stones' geodesic dome which had spilled over into a fight right there in Cora's.

Astrid soon learned enough to realize that someone at the tax assessor's office had overstepped his bounds, quite badly. She wanted no part of this, and Neustatter had authorized her to accept or decline assignments.

Back at the office, she declined the request. She also wrote a memo for Neustatter explaining why and promptly lost it. Astrid never did realize that she'd accidentally attached the memo to her letter to the assessor's office.

Saturday, November 5, 1633

The men returned after fifteen days. Neustatter, Ditmar, Hjalmar, and Astrid gathered around the table after diner.

"It was a quiet mission," Hjalmar told Astrid. "We had a chance to see some of Magdeburg. It is bigger than I remember it in May,"

"Any news?" Neustatter asked.

"The Kluth family moved into our old quarters in Spring Branch. They are from Brandenburg. He is a tinsmith, and the two families have half a dozen children. The Rummels' group is doing well. No one has asked for NESS there. I did have one inquiry at the office, though."

"Oh?"

"One of the machine shops needs extra security from time to time. NESS was not available this time, but there will be more chances. They have our telephone number."

"*Gut, gut.* Anything else?"

"'James Ennis is home."

"We will not be, not for long," Neustatter told her. "I do not know when it will be, but we heard talk in Halle and in Magdeburg. The USE is building an army of these volunteers. Lennart Torstensson is in command. They are preparing to fight the League of Ostend in the spring. They are pushing hard to have everything where it needs to be before the snow comes. We will not travel as much during the winter. Then in the spring there will be a lot of shipments before the campaign starts."

"Will you be *called up*?" Astrid asked.

"I do not think so. There are a lot of the new volunteer regiments. Really a lot. But there will be plenty for us to do. For now, we need cold weather clothing. On Monday, I would like to discuss our finances with you."

Monday, November 7, 1633

On Monday, Astrid showed Neustatter how she was tracking NESS's income and expenses.

"I have everything since we left the village," she told him. "Just not all in one place."

"It is a good thing you can keep track of it." Neustatter looked at her suspiciously. "Are you about to tell me that there is an up-time solution for this?"

"It is funny you should use that word 'solution,'" she returned, "because it is something I heard about in math class—an account book."

"If the cost is reasonable, buy it," Neustatter told her. "Buy paper and folders, too, *bitte*. We should start writing a report of each assignment. It is something up-time detectives did, and those are all men who claim to hate paperwork."

Next, they figured out how the telephone worked. Neustatter called the Hauns. After a brief conversation, Neustatter reported that James Ennis would be by the next day.

The men were taking a day off after their two-week mission. But Astrid soon realized Neustatter had two purposes for that. One was indeed rest. The other was buying winter clothing. Once he knew exactly how much money they had available, Neustatter took everyone downtown. They bought heavy coats and trousers, gloves, and hats. The hats were something the up-timers called *fedoras*. The coats were blue, of course. Neustatter insisted that Astrid, Anna, Ursula, and Johann needed them, too.

Tuesday, November 8, 1633

Astrid wondered if James Ennis approved of all of Leigh Ann's decisions. It was not something they could, or should, ask. It would be like Ennis asking if Neustatter approved of the decisions she had made, except worse because James and Leigh Ann were married.

She recognized James Ennis from the picture Leigh Ann had shown them. He was a tall, strong-looking man with close-cut hair. He shook hands all around, appearing to study them carefully.

"Heard you were in the Reserves."

"*Ja.* Basic in July and August and mostly guarding convoys since then."

Ennis nodded. "I've been building stuff. Buildings mostly, but some bridges, too."

Neustatter nodded.

"Let's go take a look at it."

They walked east from the office, turned up Riverfront Park Road, and descended downhill through a strip of woods to where Deborah Street had been extended since the Ring of Fire. All of this was the Hauns' land. Further north, deeper within this loop of Buffalo Creek, the land flattened out, and Deborah Street and Riverfront Park Road merged. From Deborah Street they could see across Buffalo Creek to the rest of the Hauns' land.

"I don't think we can do this," Ennis said at length. "We'd need someone with more experience, and that would cost. And permits. Maybe more than one. Lots of labor."

"We can handle that," Neustatter told him.

"That's all details." Ennis ran a hand over his short hair. "The problem is the steep hillside. Could I build a footbridge across Buffalo Creek that we could use with a hard climb up? Sure. But something a couple horses could use without falling off? No." He shook his head. "It'd help you, it'd help Leigh Ann get over here, it'd help Julia get home more often. But I can't build what you need. And I'm not sure it'd be a good idea."

Astrid was surprised. Why wouldn't it be a good idea? But she didn't say anything. Ennis would get around to explaining.

After a few moments, he did.

"Neustatter, how much do you know about the Croat Raid?"

"When we were in the siege lines before the Battle of Alte Veste, we heard stories that Wallenstein had sent a couple thousand Croats at Grantville and that less than half of them had come back. Once we got here, we walked the town square and the high school parking lot. I have talked to Dan Frost about it."

James Ennis pushed his cap back. "So, you have the details of the main battles. But there were little skirmishes all over, too."

Neustatter nodded. "Miss Schäubin found the memorial for the tree-trimming crew."

"I was at Eisenach. Leigh Ann and her dad were out here with our oldest two kids. Julia was five, and James was two. Frederic went out to check on the cattle and came across a few Croats killing a couple of them just because. He got back to the house, grabbed a rifle, and took care of business. He and Leigh Ann tossed the kids in a dry bathtub with paper and up-time crayons and lots of snacks. Then they spent the next couple hours moving from window to window, keeping watch. They could hear the battle at the high school."

James Ennis looked out over Buffalo Creek, then concluded, "I don't know that I want to build an invasion route right to the family farm, y'know? Even if I could."

Neustatter nodded slowly. "I understand."

"The livery stable across from the high school—or the one at the high school—you could board your horses there. I think it would be simple enough to build something on the east side of the building where you could keep them if you were coming and going throughout the day."

"Unless we find housing with stables even closer by, I reckon that will do," Neustatter agreed.

James Ennis laughed. "You reckon? That's some three-quarters German with a Western drawl you got there, Neustatter."

"I watch the movies." Neustatter added, "It helps me understand you."

Ennis stuck his thumb through belt loops on his trousers. "What are you doing for housing?"

"We just moved from Murphyhausen to the high school refugee housing," Neustatter told him. "We would like to find something else as soon as possible."

James Ennis nodded in understanding. "Leigh Ann and I had to sell our place in town. We just weren't making enough money to hold onto it. It's looking like I'll probably be assigned to the USE Army and stationed in Magdeburg. I think we'll probably wait a bit before seeing if Leigh Ann and the kids should join me."

"First time they come up for a visit, we'll make sure they get there," Neustatter told him.

"You don't have to do that," Ennis protested.

"You did not have to sell us the firearms," Neustatter replied.

Ennis shrugged. "We gave those up in '31. Kept enough to protect ourselves, of course. When the Army gave 'em back . . . well, you need the firepower, and the cash isn't going to hurt us any. In fact, I could probably spare one more—a forty-five pistol."

Neustatter nodded gravely. "I sincerely appreciate that."

The price they settled on meant Astrid had to recalculate NESS's finances the next day, but Neustatter quietly told her that Ennis had asked significantly below market value and that the Colt M1911 was a truly significant increase in NESS's firepower.

Saturday, November 19, 1633

The men got one more mission in, to Suhl, Schleusingen, and Schmalkalden, before the winter storms started. NESS bought four flintlock rifles from U.S. Waffenfabrik in Suhl.

The day after they returned, NESS marched downtown to the *polizei* office. Astrid's job was to trail a distance behind and see how people reacted. They drew a lot of attention, of course. Not all of it seemed positive, but being in step with uniforms, blue coats, yellow *halstücher*, flintlocks shouldered, and the old matchlocks slung gave NESS a professional appearance. They even had business cards. Maneuvering around passersby instead of forcing them out of their way went a long way, too.

Chief Frost came out front of the police station to review the troops.

"Looking good, NESS," he pronounced. "I do believe you guys have pulled it off, Neustatter."

Neustatter simply nodded, but Astrid could tell he was pleased. "I think we can turn in these matchlocks now, Chief."

Chief Frost nodded. "We keep a stash of them in town. It's probably unnecessary, but we're still twitchy from the Croat Raid."

※ ※ ※

After moving forces on short notice in September and October, the NUS Army was able to reestablish a regular schedule in November. The men were assigned to Camp Saale for a week—Eagle Pepper week for some of the new volunteers.

They also started going to the range regularly. Astrid did not know much about shooting, but she did frown at the ammunition expense more than once. At least they used black powder ammunition, even for most of the up-time weapons. That made cleaning the weapons messier, and those supplies added to their expenses. At the same time, she understood how important it was for them to hit what they aimed at.

Neustatter sent Hjalmar and Astrid to find out who the leading citizens of Grantville were. By then, Astrid was in the library research class at the high school. They soon found many other people had wanted exactly this information, and a new book had been written to provide it: *Grantville Genealogy Club's Who's Who of Grantville Up-timers*. Neustatter made sure all of them studied the book. Otto seemed particularly taken with it.

A lot had happened in the last three months, and everyone agreed it was time to send another letter to Pastor Claussen. Astrid did most of the writing, sometimes taking dictation from the others. Neustatter read it over and had her strike a few items.

"Written down in our files is *okay*. But anything sent to the village could fall into the wrong hands."

Astrid's initial annoyance faded as she thought about that. In the morning, she wrote a clean copy without certain information and sent it off.

✳ ✳ ✳

Neustatter took the opportunity to continue learning martial arts. Gena Kroll had a handful of other students, too, and one Saturday afternoon she had just about finished throwing them around the thick blue wrestling mat at the high school when an up-timer a few years younger than Neustatter walked in.

"Gena!"

"Hey, Eric. Give me a couple minutes."

As soon as Gena dismissed the class, the man approached her. "What would you say to dinner and a movie?"

"That depends—on where dinner is," Gena told him. "I'm not going to the Club 250."

That name registered with Neustatter. It was the small tavern across from the Thuringen Gardens and was frequented by the relatively few up-timers who did not like down-timers. He decided to take longer than usual to gather up his things.

"No, no, dinner and a movie," came the quick response. "It's at the Rawls' tonight."

"What's the movie?" Gena asked.

"*Citizen Kane*."

"And you waited until this afternoon to ask me?" Gena stood on the mat with her hands on her hips.

"The Army—National Guard—whatever we are this week—had us on a big project, Gena. Wasn't sure we'd get done in time. I know how much you like being stood up."

Gena looked more-or-less mollified.

"Excuse me," Neustatter ventured. "May I ask a question?"

"If you're going to tell me I shouldn't hang out at the Club 250, save it, down-timer," the man growled.

"Eric!" Gena objected.

"Who cares about that," Neustatter responded. "Movies?"

"Yeah, the dinner-and-a-movie club watches movies." Both men grinned at his sarcasm. "Usually the more sophisticated ones that wouldn't be appreciated by a wider audience on WVOA. Do you watch movies?"

"*Ja.* Chief Frost showed me *She Wore a Yellow Ribbon*. I like westerns and detective movies."

"Eric, this is Edgar Neustatter. Neustatter, this is Eric Glen Hudson. You guys can talk movies for a few minutes. I'll go shower and make myself presentable, Eric."

After Gena left, Neustatter asked, "What is *Citizen Kane* about?"

Eric Hudson gave him a thumbnail sketch of the movie, then watched his expression. "Not enough action for you?"

"Would it help me understand Grantvillers?" Neustatter asked. "It sounds like it is about people from other places up-time."

Hudson continued his study of Neustatter. "Now that is a very good observation. That's what you're doing with the movies, isn't it? Learning about up-timers."

"*Ja.*"

"Yeah," Hudson corrected. "Short A."

After a moment, Hudson mused, "Westerns and detectives . . . Neustatter, have you seen a movie called *The Big Sleep*?"

"*Nein.*"

26

"Do you know you can request movies? There's a request list at the front desk in the library. We've got time to put *The Big Sleep* on the list before Gena gets back. Maybe we can get it shown in the auditorium."

Friday, January 13, 1634

One day in early January, Astrid was sitting at the desk in the NESS office when the phone rang. She jumped and banged both knees against the underside of the desk. As she winced, the phone continued to ring.

"Hello. Neustatter's European Security Services. Miss Schäubin speaking."

"This is Eric Hudson. Tell Neustatter that *The Big Sleep* is showing in the high school auditorium Friday night at seven."

"I will do so."

"Make sure you do. He'll enjoy it. Tell him to meet me out front at quarter of."

The caller hung up before she could say anything else. Astrid told Neustatter but did not point out that some up-timers considered Friday the thirteenth unlucky.

That evening, Neustatter and Eric Hudson found seats in the auditorium next to a short down-timer with light brown hair and an equally light Van Dyke beard. Neustatter commented later on how serious the young man looked.

"*Guten Abend.*"

"*Guten Abend.*" Neustatter shook hands with him.

Hudson did not. He more or less ignored the other down-timer.

"You're going to like this one, Neustatter. The screenwriter was Leigh Brackett, the same woman who wrote *Rio Bravo*, *El Dorado*, and *Rio Lobo*. She was called the Queen of Space Opera before she started writing scripts.

A lot of people don't know this, but she wrote the first draft of *The Empire Strikes Back*, too."

"This sounds promising."

"All the same, I'm surprised *The Big Sleep* got enough votes to be shown this month. I was starting to think I was going to have to suggest it to the dinner-and-a-movie group."

The other down-timer spoke up. "Excuse me, did you also request this movie?"

"Sure did," the up-timer stated. "You requested it, too?"

"Yes. I was told it is a detective movie. I wish to learn about detectives."

Eric Hudson laughed. "Well, you're in luck then. You're sittin' next to one."

"Edgar Neustatter. My men and I retired from the wars. Now we are security consultants."

The up-timer laughed again. " 'Security consultant' just means that Neustatter's figured out how to be a cowboy and a detective at the same time."

"A 'cowboy'?"

"One genre at a time, okay?"

After the movie, the young down-timer ventured, "So that is a detective."

"That is one style of detective," Neustatter said. "The up-time movies are full of action. Sometimes a detective's work is long hours of asking questions and standing around that all comes to nothing."

"Hm."

"*Dank*, Eric," Neustatter continued. "I do enjoy Leigh Brackett's work. I saw some things I will adopt and others that I will avoid."

"Yeah, well, do yourself a favor and never take a divorce case."

MISSIONS OF SECURITY

Neustatter handed the other down-timer a NESS business card. "If you should ever need a security consultant . . . My men and I do a lot of guard duty and escorting shipments. We do take detective cases, but as Eric says, no divorces. And if what you want is written information, you are better off hiring a library researcher."

"I *am* a library researcher."

"Then you should give me your card."

"I, ah, do not have cards yet."

"Have some made up," Neustatter told him. "Many people need library researchers. I even hire one from time to time. I will look for you next time I need one, *Herr* . . ."

"Casimir Wesner. *Danke.*"

❉ ❉ ❉

Throughout the winter, goods intended for Magdeburg piled up at the machine shops and other businesses in Grantville. NESS picked up assignments standing guard duty at warehouses. Whenever the weather improved, a shipment went out. Often it went by train as far as possible before switching to wagons or sleighs. NESS guarded a couple of those shipments and got snowed in for a week in Halle on one of them. The men were working steadily, and on days they did not have an assignment, they were able to find day labor, clearing away snow after storms if nothing else. Neustatter even found time to arrange for NESS to join the Grantville Chamber of Commerce.

During the winter, the men spent less time away from home. Some of them occasionally went out to taverns, and Lukas occasionally disappeared until very late. But what they spent came out of their personal shares. NESS's overall *cash flow*, as Astrid's math class called it, improved. That was welcome. Buying weapons had used up most of NESS's savings.

Whenever NESS did not have a mission, five of the men would find day labor. Neustatter always left one man available. Wolfram would report to Leahy Medical Center, and Karl found a blacksmith's forge that would be happy to have him whenever available. Still, there were times that several NESS agents were in the office at the same time, so Neustatter bought more chairs.

Karl brought in little pay, preferring to be compensated in metal and working it on his own time. Any objections to that vanished when he finished a poker and tongs for the Franklin stove. Trivets for the cooking pots soon followed. Late in the winter, Karl moved to a foundry, expanding his skills and then making his own pour. He presented NESS with a large cast-iron skillet.

* * *

Soon both Ursula and Anna were pregnant. Both were inclined to find a midwife until Wolfram had a long talk with Anna about up-time medicine. After that, both of them went Leahy Medical Center and saw a Doctor Shipley. And neither of them wanted their children born in refugee housing.

The apartment buildings on Kimberly Heights were completed midwinter. Everyone wondered why places to live that were attached to each other were called apartments. Each had a central room with cooking facilities, a bathroom, and two bedrooms. Joel Carstairs contacted Neustatter as soon as Building Two was finished, and NESS moved on February 1. They put the married couples in one—Wolfram and Anna in one bedroom, and Stefan, Ursula, and Johann in the other. The rest of them took the other apartment. Hjalmar, Ditmar, and Astrid were in one bedroom, and Neustatter, Otto, Karl, and Lukas in the other. The tables, chairs, and beds were relatively inexpensive but sturdy. Astrid thought whoever was building the furniture should probably hire NESS to guard him on his way to the bank.

They had accumulated some household goods since they had come to Grantville, so it took two trips in the cold to carry everything from the high school refugee housing to the apartments. The apartments were even closer to the NESS office than the refugee housing was. More importantly, they were *their* apartments. NESS were renting them, of course, but they finally had their own place.

That news went in the long letter they wrote to Pastor Claussen. Everyone just kept adding to it throughout the winter, and they would send it in the spring.

All of them quickly agreed it made more sense to continue to eat their meals together. Anna was having morning sickness, badly enough that she did not want to be around meat, so the other apartment became the main place of cooking. Ursula, who claimed not to be feeling any discomfort at all, organized it to her satisfaction. By now, each of them had his or her own plate, bowl, mug, knife, fork, and spoon—although Ursula occasionally muttered about forks being an affectation. Astrid spent more time helping prepare meals. So did the men. They had survived six years in the war eating their own cooking. Hjalmar and Ditmar were reasonably good cooks, Neustatter, Stefan, and Wolfram were passable, and Otto, Karl, and Lukas needed to be assigned other duties. They became responsible for the beer kegs.

Downtown Grantville was closed to vehicles during the day, so it was difficult to buy kegs of small beer and carry them home. Apparently older up-timers remembered when milk was delivered just like mail or newspapers, and most of the brewers in town had gotten together and set up routes. The area NESS lived in—Route 250 and side roads east of Deborah Road—got deliveries on Monday. They paid a *deposit* for each wooden keg and then got that money back when they turned it in the following week. It took a couple weeks to figure out how many kegs they needed. They had water, of course, and Leigh Ann assured them it was safe. They knew that by now but preferred small beer.

One of the reasons they cooked together was that often all eight men were not needed to guard a building. Sometimes it was four at a time, and stew could be warmed over the fire for those coming off a guard shift. Ursula also sent them to guard duty with meat and vegetable turnovers. Everyone started collecting different names for them. Depending on whom you asked, one of these was either a strudel, a pasty, an empanada, or a stromboli. Apparently, every country had something like this. The big differences came from what you put inside. For NESS, that usually meant whatever was available—although Ursula did *not* believe in tomato sauce. At first, they did not want to eat potatoes, either, thinking they were just for livestock. But then some of Astrid's classmates dragged her to the Freedom Arches, where *fries* were one of the expensive choices on the menu.

That was still not enough to convince Ursula. But then Leigh Ann came out to the new apartments to check on them. Half the men were out on guard duty. The others were asleep—they had guard duty that night.

"How are you ladies doing?"

"We are well," Ursula answered. She pointed at Astrid. "Even if that one keeps pestering me to cook animal food."

Leigh Ann looked very confused.

"She means potatoes," Astrid supplied. "I had fries."

Leigh Ann snickered. "Another victim of the Freedom Arches, I see. Best fries up-time, if you ask me."

"Even if any of us wanted to eat them, boiling them in fat and oil sounds dangerous," Ursula stated.

"It can be," Leigh Ann agreed. "But you can bake fries. There're a lot of other things you can do with potatoes, too. You can bake the whole potato. You can also bake the meat and potatoes together. If it's chicken or fish or even beans, with potatoes or noodles and stock or wine then it's a casserole. But if it's red meat, potatoes, and cream of something-or-other soup, then it's a hot dish." She smiled. "Some people get worked up over the difference."

Astrid reached for her notepad, quill, and inkwell, but Ursula reach out a hand to stop her.

"I understand this," she said. "It is like the strudels, but the whole meal for everyone is in a single pan."

"Close enough," Leigh Ann agreed. "And if you've got a little bit of butter or lard, you can cut potatoes up and fry them in a pan. James and I had some in a fancy restaurant up-time once. They called them potatoes julienne. He calls 'em 'hunting camp potatoes' because that's how the guys made them at camp."

"Jäger fries," Anna murmured. "We should try this."

Ursula did not look impressed.

"Anyway," Leigh Ann said, "I need a 'girls' day,' and I thought you ladies might need one, too." She paused and looked at Astrid. "And you need to get your hair cut and styled, Astrid."

Astrid gave Leigh Ann a very wary look. She did not like how many up-time women wore their hair.

"Secretaries don't wear a long braid and a kerchief. Or whatever you call it."

❋ ❋ ❋

After dinner, Astrid asked, "Neustatter do you have a minute?"

"*Ja.*"

"*Frau* Haun—Leigh Ann Ennis—had an idea." Astrid explained.

Neustatter shrugged. "I do not see why not. Keep it reasonable. Something your brother won't glare at me about."

"Oh, Hjalmar would glare at *me*," she assured him.

So, one Saturday, Leigh Ann, Ursula, Anna, and Astrid went to the Curl and Tan Beauty Shoppe. Astrid approached cautiously when one of the women beckoned her to a chair.

"Hi. I'm Desiree Reynolds. What would you like?" She seemed friendly enough.

"Just a *trim*." Leigh Ann had explained that term earlier.

The woman nodded in understanding. "Just enough to even everything up, right? Standard down-time cut? Two, maybe three inches?"

"I want to look respectable," Astrid explained. *Frau* Reynolds kept nodding. "I am a secretary for NESS." She told the beautician a little bit about Neustatter's European Security Services.

"Honey, if you just want a trim, I'll do that," *Frau* Reynolds said. "But if you're the secretary for private eyes, you really ought to go for glamorous. Because you could really pull it off."

"That's what I told her," Leigh Ann contributed from the next chair.

"Tell me about this *glamorous, bitte.*"

"You have such pretty hair. You really shouldn't braid it all the time. What if we brought some of it in front of your shoulders"—she demonstrated—"and gave it a wave? Trim a few inches here, but just a couple in back. You could still wear a kerchief, if that's what you want."

From the next chair, Leigh Ann was signaling her approval with the V sign. Ursula was frowning. Anna's face held a mischievous expression Astrid hadn't seen on it in years.

"I do not want to make a mistake," Astrid said. "Would you explain that to me again, *bitte*?"

After the beautician did so, Astrid nodded. She must have looked apprehensive, because *Frau* Reynolds said, "You can trust Desiree. I won't steer you wrong."

On the way back toward our apartments, Anna nudged her. "Those two young men over there are looking at you," she whispered.

"*Nein*," Astrid said. But she checked, using a reflection in a store window. She had read about that in a mystery book. The two young men were indeed staring in their direction, but it could have been at any of them.

The three of them thanked Leigh Ann when they reached Deborah Road. Leigh Ann turned off to go to the Ennis farm.

When the men got home, Neustatter's comment was, "Good balance." Astrid gave him a quick smile to show she understood that he had spoken first and approved so that no one could criticize.

Hjalmar just sighed dramatically. "I am going to have to beat off your suitors now."

Astrid poked him in the ribs.

Tuesday, February 7, 1634

Just as manufactured goods had been piling up in Grantville during the winter, newly made firearms had accumulated in Suhl, Schleusingen, and Schmalkalden. The National Guard wanted to pick up what it had ordered before any of those weapons found their way into the increasing unrest in Franconia, which was just on the other side of the Thüringerwald. The plan was for a major shipment before the roads were clear—using sleighs. Someone without a solid grasp of the weather picked March 1.

Not two full days later, early in February, the researcher Neustatter had met at the movies called NESS. Casimir Wesner wanted to consult

NESS on the safety of someone who was about to visit Grantville. Neustatter met with Wesner. He did not tell Astrid what they discussed, but he did have her rearrange a couple guard shifts at a machine shop in Grantville to leave him and Ditmar free on Tuesday.

While the Higgins Hotel was the fanciest place to stay in Grantville, it was outside of town. Neustatter checked it and then ruled it out. By early afternoon, he'd determined that The Inn of the Maddened Queen would suit his client's purposes much better. Ditmar later told Astrid and Hjalmar that Neustatter had stationed him along the main street to watch for Wesner. At first, Ditmar thought that was an excessive precaution. However, when Wesner got off a tram at the nearest stop, Ditmar quickly spotted two other people who disembarked and followed him. One was a tall, broad-shouldered man built along the same lines as Neustatter himself. The other was a blonde-haired woman. Both were down-timers.

Ditmar fell in behind them. They were doing a reasonable job following Wesner, who apparently had no *situational awareness*. That was a term all the men knew from basic training. But the two *tails*—that word came from the movies—were not looking around, either. Ditmar was able to follow them in turn, and he *was* looking around to see if there were any other players in the game.

Neustatter saw them coming, of course. He sent Wesner into the inn, while he stepped forward to confront the pair.

"Why are the two of you following my client?"

"Uh . . . uh . . ." The man obviously could think of nothing to say.

"Why do you think we are following him?" asked the woman.

" 'Cause you kept the same distance behind him all the way down the street. Not a whole lot of situational awareness, though." Neustatter pointed behind them.

The man knew enough not to fall for that. "You look," he muttered to the woman.

She did. "There is another man behind us, dressed just like him, coming this way."

"So why are you following *Herr* Riedel?"

"Who?" the man blurted out.

"Oh, so you know his name isn't Riedel..."

The man realized he'd just been outsmarted. "What do you want with him?" he countered.

"When he comes back outside, he can share as much or as little of his business with you as he pleases," Neustatter told him.

The man tried again. "And who are you?"

"Edgar Neustatter. I run Neustatter's European Security Services."

The man fidgeted until Casimir Wesner exited The Inn of the Maddened Queen.

"Mathew! *Frau* Boekhorst!" Wesner immediately exclaimed. "What are you doing here?"

"Following you," Neustatter stated.

"Why?" Wesner asked.

"You have been leaving school quickly every evening, and you are obviously up to something."

Wesner glanced around and appeared to consider his words carefully. "You know I was sent to Grantville by Saxe-Altenburg," he began, "to look for banking and investment opportunities. But the bank can pay only part of my salary. My supervisor pays the rest. He asked me to arrange lodging for an army officer and his wife."

"Saxon?"

"USE Army."

"Could we not have helped you with this?" the man he had called Mathew asked.

Wesner's gesture encompassed the three of them. "Do you know where to seek safe and reputable lodgings for *adel*?"

Both of the others shook their heads no, more than a bit grudgingly.

"My thoughts were the Higgins Hotel or somewhere in Castle Hills," Wesner continued, "but Neustatter pointed out that lodging within Grantville itself is more convenient and safer because they will not have to cross open country every day."

"If safety is a concern, they ought to have bodyguards," Neustatter stated. "However, . . . May I discuss the details?"

"Yes, of course."

Neustatter studied Matthew and *Frau* Boekhorst for several seconds. "Very well. If my men and I guarded an army officer, people would wonder why. It would attract more attention to him. I assume a USE officer can handle himself?"

"*Ja.*"

"Then you and Mathew ought to be enough. Perhaps *Frau* Boekhorst can accompany his wife."

"We are not bodyguards," Mathew stated. "Or detectives."

Neustatter shrugged. "As I told *Herr* Wesner, I have a contract that will take both my teams out of town that week."

"*Danke.* Is there anything else I should do?"

Neustatter started to shake his head, but then grinned. "*Ja.* Take them to the movies."

Friday, February 10, 1634

"Neustatter, I've got something to tell you," Chief Frost announced.

Neustatter and Astrid waited expectantly. Chief Frost had called the office a couple days ago and asked them to come in sometime in the next few days.

"I'm resigning next month. It's time somebody started sharing with other cities and towns how police work developed up-time. I'm going to be doing that full-time, basing out of Magdeburg. The military police have done a pretty good job here in Thuringia, but somebody needs to teach police procedure from a civilian perspective."

Neustatter grimaced. He sat there for a long moment before speaking. "We would rather have you here, but I understand what you are saying."

"This boom town is pretty well under control. Press Richards will be the new police chief, and he'll do a great job. There are good people working on Magdeburg already, but Grantville and Magdeburg aren't the only growing cities. When a city gets big enough, everyone doesn't know everyone else, and that brings in a whole different kind of crime. I want to get ahead of it in this universe." He touched a button on his phone. "Mimi, ask Press to step into my office, please."

Preston Richards shook hands with them readily. While Dan Frost had accepted that mercenary companies and security agencies simply existed, Astrid thought Richards had not completely come to terms with it. Her impression was that he'd rather there not be a need for them. In the books, movies, and television shows, the polizei never wanted private agencies around. So it would not surprise her if Richards followed the up-time tradition. But unlike private detectives, NESS did not actually get in the way of the *polizei*.

On their way home, Neustatter told Astrid, "With Chief Frost leaving, we will not have someone to give us advice. We will have to learn more up-time history. Let's stop at the State Library and find out what they have about security contractors, unions, and labor disputes—since we already know the Pinkertons were involved in those."

At the library, Astrid quickly found that there were some published research papers on those subjects. They purchased a copy of "The Mining Wars." Soon Neustatter was finding out about Matewan and Blair

Mountain. A reference to a Battle of Athens intrigued him. With Astrid's help, later that week, Neustatter had enough information to satisfy himself.

"A narrow victory," he told Astrid, Ditmar, and Hjalmar. "No one seized the initiative and pushed an attack all the way through. Next time we are part of the Eagle Pepper exercise, we need to get the recruits to include the villagers right from the beginning. We will learn from Athens."

Saturday, February 18, 1634

Astrid was not the only one in classes during the winter. Neustatter had all the adults who had not yet taken the citizenship class enroll.

"I want everyone to pass the class," he said. "If anyone needs help, go see Astrid or come to me or your team leader. If you need time to study, ask and I will rearrange guard shifts."

An election was coming up on February 22. Franconia was voting on whether to join the State of Thuringia. Even though Grantville would not be voting, that date made an excellent deadline. Lukas and Karl passed the citizenship the week before. Then on Saturday, February 18, 1634, all of NESS, even young Johann, walked downtown to city hall and took the loyalty oath.

Grantville City Hall was even less imposing that the *polizei* station. While the police building could pass for a modest *schloss*, city hall seemed to Astrid to be not much bigger than one of the *mobile homes*. It was brick, and the roof had a very shallow pitch. Thin metal posts painted white held a smaller section of roof over two low sets of brick steps that led up to small landings at either end of the front of the building. It was a small building for as large a city as Grantville was these days.

The parking lot was equally modest, just an extension of the pavement on Mead Avenue. Yellow stripes divided it into a row of nine parking places for up-time vehicles. That was it.

Today the parking lot was full. Several dozen people were about to become citizens, and most of them had family and friends in attendance.

Mayor Henry Dreeson administered the oath. He made a point of reminding everyone they could swear or affirm. Astrid saw one family nodding solemnly.

All of them raised their right hands. "I do solemnly swear that I will support and defend the Constitution of the State of Thuringia . . . So help me God."

NESS celebrated with lunch at the Thuringen Gardens.

Then they went home.

Sunday, February 26, 1634

The men left on Saturday, February 25. If all went well, they would reach Schleusingen two days early. Neustatter did not trust the sleighs.

Sure enough, on Sunday afternoon, the lead sleigh suddenly slewed sideways, and the driver quickly halted the horses. The sleigh was tipped to the right. Neustatter quickly jumped out and peered underneath.

"Looks like we lost a runner!" he called to the others.

The other three sleighs coasted to a stop, and Karl piled out of the third one. It took him only a minute to assess the situation in Amideutsch.

"Aw, crap. A strut gave way. When it shifted, the second strut twisted from the stress until it snapped."

"Can you fix it?" Neustatter asked.

"In a blacksmith's shop, *ja*. Out here? I cannot really fix it. See this metal coupling?" Karl pointed to where half a strut was dangling from an iron sleeve. "That has to be unbolted to get the broken strut out. Then we can put one of the spares in."

He got to his feet and dusted snow off his trousers. "I think I can refit the front strut. Then if we splint the back one, we can probably limp into the next village."

"What do you need us to do?" Neustatter asked.

"Empty the sleigh, unhitch the horses, and tip it up on its side," Karl directed.

They emptied the sleigh, and then with everyone lifting, they flipped it up on one side. Karl put the runner back on and splinted the broken strut. Then they eased it back down. One of the other sleighs broke trail ahead of the damaged one. With just the driver on board, and him sitting as far left as he could on the bench, the horses were able to slowly pull it to the next village.

They had to stop once and redo the splint. By the time they reached the next village, everyone was cold and damp. Then the local blacksmith refused to work on the Sabbath. So they paid arguably too much to crowd into a spare room.

The blacksmith took a look at the sleigh in the morning. He confirmed what Karl had said. The two of them worked all day repairing the sleigh, drawing in some of the other men when needed. They stayed a second night and arrived in Schleusingen on Tuesday. NESS went to Suhl on Wednesday, Schmalkalden on Thursday, and started back to Grantville just in time for a thaw on Friday.

Saturday, March 4, 1634

Just ten days before, Franconia had voted to join the State of Thuringia, which was what the NUS had changed its name to. It was now going to change again, to the State of Thuringia-Franconia, and there were those who did not like that. And NESS was guarding four sleighs full of weapons that could barely move.

MISSIONS OF SECURITY

They made it into Suhl before the gate closed on Saturday.

"Head for the garrison," Neustatter directed. "The sleighs will be easier to guard there."

Once the sleighs were as safe as they were going to get, Neustatter put Hjalmar's team on guard duty and sent Ditmar's team to an inn with the sleigh drivers.

"Drivers, get a good night's sleep," Neustatter directed. "Team One, eat, but don't drink too much. You will be switching places with Team Two so that they can eat, too."

"And where will you be?" Stefan asked.

"I am going to find a radio and see if anyone can tell me when it might snow again."

It took a good while and more money than he wanted to spend, but Neustatter found out it would not be worth switching to wagons. NESS was stuck in Suhl until a storm came Monday night. It was the kind some up-timers called "wintry mix": some snow, some sleet, and some rain. It was miserable weather, but produced just enough accumulation for the sleighs to run on.

By the time they straggled in Thursday night, the men were cold, wet, tired, and most of them were getting sick. Soon everyone was sick. Next, they were all visiting doctors' offices.

Between a longer mission than anticipated and the fact that Neustatter declined missions until he had at least a team healthy enough to carry them out, NESS earned next to no money for a couple weeks and had higher expenses from medical visits. Astrid's adult math class had covered this situation. Not making money you expected to make was not the same thing as losing money. Nevertheless, NESS's available cash dwindled.

Wednesday, March 15, 1634

On the next Wednesday, Neustatter, Wolfram, Stefan, Ursula, and Johann were more-or-less recovered. That meant one apartment was on the mend, except for Anna. The other apartment was miserable, except for Neustatter, who was just plain too stubborn to stay sick. But the machine shop needed guards, and Neustatter, Wolfram, and Stefan stayed up all night. In the morning, they handed off to Bretagne's Company.

A couple days later, Neustatter made a point of dropping by Bretagne's Company's headquarters to thank them for picking up that shift. He ran into Guilo Bretagne himself.

The wiry, dapper Italian sized him up before shaking hands.

"So you are the *cowboy*," Bretagne observed.

"*Das bin ich*," Neustatter responded. "That is me. *Dank* for taking that shift for us. Most of my men are sick after a mission to Schleusingen."

"Do not take this the wrong way, but I will always be pleased to take one of your shifts. I do not understand how a small company like yours gets so many." Bretagne stroke his mustachios and evidently swallowed his pride. "How are you doing it?"

Neustatter grinned. "I go to the Chamber of Commerce meetings. Those businesses will call who they know."

Bretagne stumbled over the words. "The Chamber of Commerce? We are not *bürger*."

"*Ja*, we are—in the up-timers' eyes," Neustatter stated.

"Strange folk. But they pay many of the bills, *sí*?"

"They certainly do." Neustatter considered something. "Come to the next Chamber of Commerce meeting with me."

It was mud season, but that did not really explain why manufactured goods were piling up at the Grantville machine shops again. Some of the major roads were graveled, and while they would certainly be muddy, up-time trucks could usually make it through. The following week, a now-healthy NESS guarded a big shipment to Erfurt, but not much was going north yet.

Bjorn Hasseler

CHAPTER 2: THE SPRING RUSH

Friday, March 24, 1634

NESS had better food, clothing, and shelter than they'd had in the village. Anna and Ursula had medical care at Leahy. The men had the weapons they needed. In late March, they finally got to the last item on NESS's list: horses.

Astrid had been over the books several times, and NESS simply could not afford to own horses. But Neustatter and Karl went over to the livery stable anyway to see what they could learn. They found the manager working with a horse in the paddock beside the stables. His rangy, well-muscled appearance suggested this was his regular practice.

He handed the reins to an assistant and shook hands with Neustatter and Karl.

"Johann Mestermann."

"Edgar Neustatter."

"Karl Recker."

"What can I do for you?"

"I run Neustatter's European Security Services. We escort wagons, guard buildings, that sort of thing. We need horses for some of our missions."

"Horses are expensive." *Herr* Mestermann smiled. "Of course, you already know that. How often do you need to ride?"

"Usually it is a week or two at a time. Sometimes it is that long again until the next mission. Other times, it is only a couple days."

"So, you would not actually need your own horses all that often." The manager quoted a number. "That is how much it costs me to care for one horse for one month. The average, you understand. Plus, there is the initial purchase price."

"Eight times that is out of the question," Neustatter agreed. "Even four times that."

"You are not the only business in this position," the manager went on. "You could simply rent horses from us." He held up a hand. "You will, of course, object that when you need horses, you absolutely must have them, and what if I am out? So we have other options."

"I think I want my secretary to hear these," Neustatter told him. "Karl, go get Astrid, *bitte*. You can run the office for a while, *ja*?"

"*Ja.*"

Astrid soon arrived, and the livery stable manager showed them into his office. The walls were rough wood and bare other than few sketches of horses in inexpensive wooden frames. Astrid noted that he had the same model desk as she and Neustatter did.

Mestermann summarized their situation. "Lots of people want horses, Miss Schäubin. There simply are not enough for everyone who wants one—or who wants eight. But NESS will not be riding every day, so why not split the cost with someone who needs to ride on the days you do not?"

"You mean rent horses from you," she said.

"Sort of. I am thinking of a *timeshare*. A group of people buy a horse, and each has shares according to how much money he puts in. Then each signs up for the days he wants that horse. NESS would be able to sign up for certain days and add others later."

"It sounds like a library of horses." Astrid observed the drawings hanging on the office walls and wondered if those were some of Mestermann's horses.

The manager's face lit up. "I had not thought of it like that, but, yes, it is."

"What if other . . . owners? . . . wanted the horses on the same days?" Astrid asked. "What happens?"

"If one party has bought in at a higher level, that party gets the horse that day. If they are at the same level, first to request gets the horse that day," he explained.

"So, this places the customer in a group with a better chance of getting that particular horse," Astrid observed. She looked the drawings again, wondering this time if they represented the *timeshare* groups.

"Yes, of getting that particular horse—that chestnut whose drawing you are looking at is one of them, although most of the rest are simply my favorites over the years. It might be a horse you have accustomed to gunfire, for instance. And on some days, it might be your only opportunity to get a horse at all. Once all the regular horses are rented for a given day, you could still get a timeshare horse—if you have bought in."

"What if someone already has the timeshare horse? Would we get one of the other timeshare horses?"

"You could get another horse in that same pool," the manager explained, "but not one from a pool you do not belong to."

Neustatter raised an eyebrow.

"*No offense, Herr* Mestermann, but I would like a second opinion about this concept," Astrid said.

The manager smiled. "None taken. My too-smart daughter thought of timeshare horses as a project in *Herr* Christopher Onofrio's business class in the Tech School."

"May we see her project?"

Herr Mestermann was only too happy to brag about his daughter. He pulled the professional-looking report from a desk drawer and handed it to Astrid.

She started flipping through it. *Frau* Mestermann had charted the number of horse rentals per day for 1632 and most of 1633, indicating the days when the stable had rented all its horses. She had then designed a timeshare for a group of four horses for one steady client, two frequent clients, and two occasional clients. Astrid could see that the arrangement would have worked out. The clients' higher costs were balanced by the fact that they would have been able to rent horses on more of the days they had wanted to. It looked solid, so Astrid nodded to Neustatter. She would still ask *Herr* Onofrio, of course.

Wednesday, March 29, 1634

Late in the evening of March 29, someone banged on NESS's apartment door.

Neustatter opened the door with his left hand. His right was at his holster.

"I am looking for Neustatter's European Security Services," announced an earnest young man in a National Guard uniform.

"*I bin* Neustatter."

The soldier spoke in quick Amideutsch. "The railroad reached Halle today. They beat their schedule by two days. We received the radio message a couple hours ago. The first supply trains are leaving in the morning. They need guards. You did not answer your phone."

MISSIONS OF SECURITY

"The phone is in the office, not here. How many guards?"

"All of you. The seven, eight, and nine o'clock trains are covered. We need you at ten."

Neustatter nodded to Ditmar, who stepped past the messenger to go tell Stefan and Wolfram next door.

"*Danke*. We will be there."

"MPs and a supply sergeant will meet you at Schwarza Junction and assign you National Guard weapons. Be there by nine."

"*Danke*."

"It is an express to Halle. That means it is not stopping, so bring food if you want lunch. You can stay over in Halle and catch a train back in the morning."

After the messenger excused himself, and Ditmar, Wolfram, and Stefan came in, Neustatter whistled.

"Trains on the hour. This is the big push. Circle up. I will make this quick."

"This would be a good time for the League of Ostend to try to disrupt the supply line," Ditmar pointed out.

"*Ja*, it would," Neustatter said. "If they know about it. Even if they do not—yet—seeing trains passing every hour ought to tip off any spies out there."

"If they do not already know, it will take them time to report, receive instructions, and act," Hjalmar stated.

"That is true, but if they do know, they might know all the details. So take your NESS weapons, too." Neustatter patted his holster. "Our pistols hold more rounds than most rifles and shotguns. That could be a nasty surprise for someone."

✳ ✳ ✳

The 10:00 express reached Halle without incident. At Halle, the cargo was transferred to boat to be taken the rest of the way to Magdeburg. The men came home the following day—and left again the next. They were so busy for the next couple weeks, guarding trains north to Halle and coming back the next day, that Neustatter missed the dinner and a movie gathering.

Astrid remembered how long it had taken them to get from Halle to Grantville that first time, and here her brother was eating breakfast in the Ring of Fire and dinner in Halle.

The men discussed the news at length when it was announced that Admiral Simpson's fleet had sailed from Magdeburg. It was heading down the Elbe, of course. Not long after, aircraft were reported over Hamburg, and then Simpson's fleet attacked the city. They apparently crushed the defenses quickly; the next news they heard stated that General Torstensson had an army outside the city—a *USE* army, not a Swedish one—and that the Captain-General had sent Prime Minister Stearns to take charge of Hamburg.

※ ※ ※

As the war heated up, the nature of NESS's missions changed. It was interesting to see which of the warehouses they had guarded during the winter emptied first. The NESS agents assumed those were military goods. It took no more than two weeks to ship the stockpiles north by train and boat.

But as true spring replaced the muddy season, civilian assignments started to come in. Other businesses had stockpiled goods in the winter months, too. They understood that priority military goods were going out first, but they wanted to deliver their products as soon as possible. So right after the two weeks of military shipments, there was a burst of civilian deliveries. Most of these used smaller guard forces. Some companies did not even use guards from Grantville to Jena or along the Thuringian Backbone. NESS got hired for a long-distance mission guarding an industrial shipment to Kassel. Neustatter left with Hjalmar's team on April 14. Ditmar's team stayed in Grantville and worked a couple shorter missions.

* * *

During all of this, Neustatter and Astrid had talked to *Herr* Christopher Onofrio at the tech school.

"Oh, right, right. The horse timeshare project. I don't give A pluses easily, but Hippolyta did a great job. As I understand it, her father hasn't made more than a few minor adjustments to her proposal."

"Then you are convinced this will work out? That if we *buy in*, we will have horses when we need them?" Neustatter asked.

"Look, it probably won't be perfect. But just renting horses from the stables isn't perfect, either, is it?" Onofrio pointed out. "Some days, they're all out."

Astrid nodded. It was true enough. "Our chief concern is what happens when the timeshares are already signed for on the days we need horses."

Onofrio nodded. "You get first choice of the regular rentals. There is a formula—in fact, it's an excellent piece of logical programming in a computer spreadsheet. The bottom line is that if conditions in 1634 are similar to 1633, you will get horses ninety-five percent of the times you want them."

"What is a spreadsheet?"

By the time Astrid understood *Herr* Onofrio's answer, she thought if she could do something like that, even though she would most likely have to use paper, they could forecast when NESS could afford to buy an additional weapon and when they should save up money.

"*Danke, Herr* Onofrio," she said. "Once I have learned more math, I will see about taking a business class."

"Good idea."

"*Danke*," Neustatter added.

After dinner that night, Neustatter called everyone together and explained what they had learned.

"We will have to care for the horses," Stefan pointed out.

"I will help with that."

They all turned to Anna. It was the first time she had spoken in the discussion, and she met everyone's gaze.

"I like horses. I always have."

"Me, too," Johann piped up.

"You may both help," Neustatter stated. "We will not be making you do all the work. Especially not Anna."

Astrid had to agree with Anna. She was not going to mind occasionally being around horses, either.

The next day, Neustatter, Anna and Wolfram, Stefan and Johann, Karl, and Astrid walked over to the stables. Neustatter signed the agreement, and NESS became part owner of four horses.

The up-timers had a few horses, of excellent stock. They were breeding them with the best down-time horses they could obtain. Two of horses in NESS's pool were Oldenburg/quarter horse crosses, both mares—fillies, properly, since they were not yet three years old. The third was a Dutch warmblood colt. His characteristics were apparently not ideal for breeding, which is why he hadn't been sold to one of the *adel*. But he was calm for a male—so far at least—and suited to being ridden by nonexperts. The fourth was a horse found after the Croat Raid. The Grantvillers had nursed it back to health, although it was not considered fit for strenuous cavalry service. But it could carry a rider just fine and was accustomed to gunfire.

So, when Neustatter, Hjalmar, Otto, and Karl left for Kassel, they did so mounted. Neustatter had his cavalry.

Tuesday, April 18, 1634

Four days later, Astrid was sitting in the NESS office wondering if anyone was ever going to come through the door when someone did just that. It was the same National Guardsman who had come to their apartment the day the railroad reached Halle. He had dark hair and was of medium height, although he seemed taller because he carried himself professionally. Astrid saw now that he wore a lieutenant's insignia, a single silver bar.

She greeted him in Amideutsch. "*Gut tag, Leutnant.*"

"Moser, Ma'am." His eyes flicked toward the nameplate on the desk and back to her. "Uh, Miss Schäubin."

"What can we do for you?"

"I have an assignment for Neustatter. Is he nearby?"

"*Nein.* He and my brother's team are on an assignment to Kassel."

"This is another assignment to Schleusingen, but it is not until July. *Und* it is a convoy from there to Erfurt."

That seemed odd to Astrid. It was no secret that tempers were running hot in Franconia, and Neustatter and the men thought that their frequent trips to the three gunmaking towns were meant to keep the available supply low.

"If you do not mind my saying so, *Leutnant* Moser, that lets four months of new weapons pile up there."

"Funny you should mention that." A look passed over Moser's face, either disapproval or exasperation. "The gunmakers told us that their April and May production is already spoken for."

"I see." Astrid waited a couple seconds, but Moser did not add anything else. "I will put it on the schedule and let Neustatter know as soon as he returns."

"*Danke. Gut tag,* Miss Schäubin." Lieutenant Moser smiled and was gone.

Friday, April 21, 1634

Ditmar and Astrid were in the office when a short, light-haired man came in. He held out a NESS business card.

"Is *Herr* Neustatter here?"

"*Nein,* he is out on an assignment," Astrid answered. "May I help you?"

"I met him at the movies some time ago. I understand he takes detective cases, *ja*? My name is Casimir Wesner, and I need a background check on someone."

Astrid rose from her chair behind the desk and indicated the chairs arranged around the Franklin stove. "Please have a seat."

Once *Herr* Wesner and Ditmar were seated, Wesner explained what he needed.

Ditmar looked at him in bemusement. "You want us to do a background check on a village farmer and his wife?"

"*Ja.*"

"Why? Everyone in a village already knows each other. Probably still have grudges left over from childhood antics."

"They have already convinced the *gemeinde* to grow up-time crops. The background check is for the *adel* who are investing in the project."

"Surely the *lehen* holder can give the *adel* a character reference."

"They want a character reference from Grantville," Casimir told him.

Ditmar shrugged. "Okay. What are their names?"

"Heinrich Kraft and Helene Olbrichtin. They claim to have trained under a master gardener."

"That should be easy enough to verify," Ditmar told him.

After Casimir left, Ditmar looked over at Astrid.

"You heard?" At her nod, he asked, "Who are the master gardeners?"

"I will find out."

Monday, April 24, 1634

On Monday morning, Ditmar was out on that mission when a tentative knock sounded at the door. Astrid looked up in time to see the door slowly swing inward. The man who paused to look at the outside of building before he tentatively stepped inside was an up-timer, and he appeared to be middle-aged. Astrid did not think she had ever seen him before. Nor did she have any idea at the time how important this meeting would prove.

"May I help you?"

He studied her for a moment and seemed wary. Astrid wondered if any of that were disapproval, and if so, whether it was because she had gotten the image of up-time secretary wrong—or because she had gotten it right. It was part of the image, as was the long, wavy blonde hair that spilled over her shoulders in an up-time style.

He glanced at her nameplate and spoke politely. "Miss Schäubin, I am looking into hiring an armed escort to Jena."

"Jena is not very far, and it is not a dangerous ride," she observed. "Our services can be expensive."

"Oh, I agree. If it were just me, I would tag along with a larger party. But there are a number of teenagers. We wish to meet with the theology faculty at the University of Jena." His German was good, although Astrid was not familiar with his dialect.

She frowned. "Still, up-time teenagers . . ."

"I'm not explaining this well," Green stated ruefully. "My name is Al Green. I am . . ."

"The Baptist pastor in Grantville." Astrid smiled because that told her a great deal.

Al Green blinked. "You're very well informed."

She shrugged, trying to bring off up-time casual. "We try to be."

Pastor Green gave her a very sharp look.

"As an employee of NESS, I am supposed to know who the leading citizens of Grantville are," I told him.

Pastor Green objected. "I'm hardly a leading citizen."

She looked him straight in the eye. "You are the pastor of an up-time church. This makes you important. NESS thinks so, anyway."

Green cocked his head. "Ness? That's the second time you've said that."

"Neustatter's European Security Services."

Green laughed. "Oh, that's good. Not just an acronym, but making it sound like a famous federal agent. *Herr* Neustatter sounds like a shrewd man."

Astrid nodded. "You are taking teenagers to Jena?"

Pastor Green came back to the subject at hand. "Yes. A group of students at the high school wish to catalogue Bible manuscripts. They are all down-timers—some Anabaptist, some Catholic, and some Lutheran. We need to talk to the theology faculty at the University of Jena and see if they can smooth the way for us."

"Ah! I see why you require an escort. The Lutheran students may riot as they did last April. As soon as they discover some of your students are Anabaptists and Catholics, there will be trouble."

"Exactly."

She gave him her best earnest-but-innocent expression. "Surely the town watch . . ."

Pastor Green wasn't having any of it. "The town watch would be hard-pressed to maintain order. And it would be a bad example for a religious quarrel within the State of Thuringia-Franconia to require intervention."

"How long will you and your students be in Jena?"

"I don't know. This trip will not take place until summer. I just want to be prepared and to make sure that there will be guards available."

Astrid nodded, all business. "Of course. If you put a deposit down now, we can reserve a number of guards for you. I will make sure that *Herr* Neustatter knows that a steady team leader will be needed. He is away this week, but I will have him call you when he gets back."

"Thank you." Pastor Green paid the deposit and left.

Tuesday, April 25, 1634

Ditmar investigated Heinrich Kraft and Helene Olbrichtin. Within a few days, he had an appointment with a Staci Ann Beckworth.

"Heinz and Helene?" she asked. "Sweet kids and good gardeners. Heinz worked at the Freedom Arches during the winter."

"They are of good moral character?" Ditmar knew that was important to a village *gemeinde*, and he figured it would matter to *adel*, too.

Staci Ann laughed. "They're just what you'd expect in down-time German farmers. Serious, hard-working. I think the most exciting thing they ever did was sneak off to the swimming hole together—after they got married. What's this all about, anyway?"

"They are apparently involved in a new venture to grow up-time plants, and the *adel* want to know if they can trust them before they invest."

"Absolutely. Those *adel* can write to Arnold. He's the head of the Grantville Grange, you know."

Thursday, April 27, 1634

Astrid Schäubin looked up from her paperwork when she heard footsteps on the front porch of the building. The steps paused. He—it sounded like a man—was probably reading the sign that read "Neustatter's European Security Services" and then the hand-painted decal below it that read "Member of the Grantville Chamber of Commerce." The porch creaked again, and the door opened.

The man gave the Franklin stove along the back wall a quick glance as he stepped into the room. It was lit against the cool spring day. After a moment, he turned toward the desk. He was older, lean, and still fit. Everything about him—haircut, posture, clothing—showed he was an up-timer. Besides, Astrid recognized him.

"How can I help you, sir?" Astrid asked in accented English.

"Ah, Miss Schäubin, I am looking into hiring an armed escort to Naumburg."

Since this seemed to be a replay of her conversation with Al Green, Astrid gave him the same answer. "Naumburg is not very far, and it is not a dangerous ride. Our services can be expensive."

"Oh, I agree," the man assured her. "If I wanted to go to Naumburg myself, I wouldn't think anything of it. But I need some goods delivered unobtrusively. They absolutely must get through in time for planting."

Miss Schäubin frowned slightly. "Are you planting crops in Naumburg?"

"I'm not explaining this well," he stated ruefully. "My name is Willie Ray Hudson. I am . . ."

"A consultant to the Grange who just turned down appointment as Secretary of Agriculture," she supplied with a smile.

Willie Ray blinked. "You're very well-informed."

She shrugged. "You are one of the leading citizens of Grantville, and before you claim otherwise, I will point out that you were nominated to the Emergency Committee by Mike Stearns himself."

Willie Ray laughed. "All right, all right."

"So you have something that needs to be delivered to Naumburg in time for planting? Seeds?"

Hudson came back to the subject at hand. "Yes. There are some people doing some good work. But they cannot be seen to be associating too closely with us."

"Naumburg is in Saxony."

"Yes. The people who need the seeds are in that area that Gustav transferred to us from Saxony. Supposedly temporarily. Kinda without asking." Willie Ray grinned. "As you've just demonstrated, I'm a little too recognizable. The delivery needs to take place without being noticed."

Astrid's face brightened. "Ah! I see why you want us. Make the delivery but blend in." She tried her best earnest-but-innocent expression again. "Of course, the USE and Saxony are currently at peace. Perhaps you could simply publicize it as a gift . . ."

Willie Ray shook his head. "John George wants his land back, and there are people who are loyal to him. As far as Gustav is concerned, John George turned his back on him *after* the Ostend War started. Things are tense. And if anyone supports us too publicly, John George's supporters have ways of making life difficult for them."

Astrid nodded, all business. "Of course. If you put a deposit down now, we can reserve a number of guards for you. I will make sure that Neustatter knows a full team will be needed. He is on an assignment today, but I will have him call you when he gets back."

"Thank you." Hudson paid the deposit and returned to Grantville.

Friday, April 28, 1634

Astrid Schäubin listened to the riders outside and knew without looking out the window that Edgar Neustatter, Karl Recker, Otto Brenner, and her brother had returned from their assignment. The horses were being led around to the day stable for feeding and grooming. It would be a while before anyone came in. They would probably bring lunch inside—unless there had been trouble on the road, in which case they'd be cleaning weapons first.

Astrid went back to the books. Assuming the just-finished job had gone well, Neustatter's European Security Services should have enough money to buy another up-time weapon. It wasn't so much the actual purchase price but the perpetual expenditure of ammunition. Up-time ammo was expensive—more so if you were shooting from the saddle and couldn't recover your brass. Then you didn't get your deposit back.

Edgar Neustatter came in first, taking off his up-time fedora as he came through the door.

"Good morning, *Herr* Neustatter," Astrid greeted him with a hint of mischief.

"Good morning, *Fräulein* Schäubin." That was Neustatter's regular response to any sort of title, even *Herr*. She knew it was deliberate, too, because Neustatter made a point of always referring to her as "Miss Schäubin" in front of clients.

"Did the assignment go well?" she asked.

"*Ja*, no problems at all. Just like assignments are supposed to be. Are there any new jobs?"

"Only three."

"Three is good. What are they?"

"The Strategic Resources Board has more shipments that need to be escorted from Schleusingen to Erfurt. They do not want the escort to be actual troops. They want us for the July shipment. Pastor Green has a Bible society of young men and women from the high school who are going to Jena to confer with the university professors in June. They include Catholics and Anabaptists. Willie Ray Hudson has seed to be delivered near Naumburg before spring planting."

"Very good. I have an assignment to add," Neustatter said. "*Herr* Schrödinger will be traveling to Magdeburg again in a few weeks. This time he is taking his family along. This makes it difficult for us," he mused. Neustatter sat down at his desk and thought for a moment. "Do we ride to Halle or take the train and then rent horses?"

"Renting horses would increase our expenses, and you would also have to buy train tickets," Astrid offered.

"I could pass the expenses on to our clients," Neustatter said. "But I would really prefer not to. It is very helpful to have the client know we will not add costs for one thing and another."

Astrid frowned. "The up-time detective agencies you had me read about charged a set fee plus expenses."

"Yes," Neustatter agreed. "They did. But other up-timers, what they called defense contractors, often overcharged. In some ways, our firm is closer to a defense contractor since we actually know very little about being detectives. It is a fine image for clients, but we must not confuse image with reality."

Astrid suggested an alternative. "Meeting the client in Halle is the least expensive option, but that does no good if something happens before they reach Halle."

"No one has hit a train so far." He shook a finger like a school teacher. "Tell me why that reasoning is flawed."

Astrid frowned. "It is unprofessional to trust the railroad people to protect our clients. You always say, 'Stay with the client.'"

"Very good. But that is why it looks bad. That is not why it is a Really Bad Idea."

Astrid flashed a quick smile as she recognized the capital letters. A "Really Bad Idea" was Neustatter's polite way of saying a disorganized, dangerous mess. There were many American expressions for that sort of thing, few of which either Neustatter or her brother Hjalmar would share with her.

"People say the train is well-defended," Astrid said slowly. "But they do not really know, do they? Because no one has ever attacked a train."

Neustatter agreed. "Eventually some bandits will be smart enough—or stupid enough—to realize that."

Astrid thought that over. Neustatter said such things with the assurance of a prophet all the time. He usually turned out to be right, too.

"You could have some men on the train while a couple of others lead all the horses to Halle."

"A good idea," Neustatter said. "It gives us the most options. However, it ties up all of us when *Herr* Schrödinger is paying only four of us. I think we will take the train and hire horses later if we need them."

Neustatter broke off as the back door opened and Astrid's brother Hjalmar came in. He had food with him. Astrid rose to hug him.

"Welcome home."

"It's good to be back." Her brother glanced at Neustatter who shook his head. "Astrid, why don't you go with Neustatter for lunch? I will answer the door and the telephone."

Astrid gave them both a very sharp expression.

"I have no romantic intentions," Neustatter assured her.

Astrid nodded slowly. She had figured that out already. Neustatter was a very focused man, all business. This was an admirable quality, and in Astrid's opinion he would make a fine husband for some woman—for some *other* woman. If he were interested in her, Neustatter would have brought his considerable focus to bear. Subtle, the man was not. That was fine with her. It made him an easy boss to work for, once she had gotten past his often-gruff manner. As far as romance, Astrid secretly liked the American ideal. She wasn't entirely sure what to do about that, but . . .

Hjalmar was grinning. She gave him her best sisterly glare.

As they waited for the tram, Astrid asked, "Where are we going? Cora's? You have sent me there to meet with prospective clients." The Thuringen Gardens was not only out of their everyday price range but also noisy. She had already figured out that Neustatter's purpose behind lunch was privacy, including from the rest of his employees, but he didn't say anything else until the tram pulled up. Once they were seated and the tram was in motion, Neustatter adjusted his fedora and looked at her.

"Anyone out of the ordinary at Cora's draws attention," Neustatter pointed out. "If a prospective client is not interested enough to come out to the office, then they are not ready to discuss destinations and times. So Cora's is safe enough for that type of meeting. Plus, the busybodies there know who you are and where you work, so it is free advertising." He watched Astrid digest that information.

When the tram pulled up in front of the hotel, Neustatter offered Astrid a hand down, and they went inside. Astrid looked around curiously. "What is this place?" she asked. The tables were almost empty, but quite a few people were crowded together in front of some blackboards, all talking at once.

"Table for two?" a waitress asked. Neustatter nodded, and she seated them.

"What is everyone doing?" Astrid asked.

"The stock market is open," the waitress answered.

"May we observe?" Neustatter asked.

"Yes, but do not buy unless you have the money with you."

"Indeed?" Neustatter asked. "We will just watch from the table, I think. What is today's special?"

"Amideutsch stew, red cabbage, and small beer."

"My favorite kind," Astrid said.

"What is in Amideutsch stew?" Neustatter asked.

"A little mutton, a little beef, spätzle, onions, carrots, celery, and some seasonings."

"How is that Amideutsch?" Neustatter asked.

"German stew has mutton. American stew would have beef and potatoes," the waitress told him. "Amideutsch has both."

"*Dank.*"

After Neustatter had watched the stock market for a few minutes, he took out his pad of paper and added a note to his ongoing list. Astrid gave him an inquiring look, and he slid the notebook over. It read:

45. Do stock people need security consultants?

"Good question," Astrid acknowledged.

"Miss Schäubin, how many kinds of stew are there?" Neustatter asked.

"Everyone makes it a little differently. There must be hundreds of variations."

"There are seven mercenary companies in and around Grantville. All different. We chose to be security consultants, and we use the up-timers'

Wild West and detective images. I think it is time to add something else. A female agent."

After a moment, Astrid realized that her boss was quite pleased with himself for leaving her speechless. "You want *me* to be a soldier?" she finally asked.

"A security consultant," Neustatter corrected. "Or a defense contractor, if you prefer." He paused. "You may join the army if you wish, but I would rather you continued working for me."

"Am I not a good enough secretary?" Astrid asked, dreading the answer.

"Miss Schäubin, you are a fine secretary. I want you to be able to act as a security consultant for two reasons. First, one of the assignments you obtained for us is escorting students to Jena. Some of them are young ladies. I would like a security consultant who is able to accompany them to whatever quarters they might find. And one who can talk to them."

"This sounds like what the up-timers call a liaison officer," Astrid noted.

"Liaison." Neustatter spat the word out. All of the military contractors got regular visits by liaison officers from the SoTF army. Some of the other outfits were definitely mercenaries and had typical mercenary attitudes toward requisitioning everything that wasn't nailed down. Periodic crackdowns made for a lot of extra paperwork—mostly for Astrid. "No, I want you to be a security consultant who can stay with the female principals and convince them to follow orders should something happen."

She considered that. "What do I have to do?"

"You can already ride. You need to learn how to shoot."

"Have you talked to Hjalmar about this?"

"About learning to shoot? Yes. He is in favor of it and offered to teach you himself. But I thought you might want to attend the free classes at the police station."

Astrid wasn't having any of that. "No, about me being a security consultant."

"He is not entirely in favor of it," Neustatter said very dryly.

"I did not think so," Astrid said.

"Hjalmar understands why we need at least one woman security consultant. He would simply prefer that it not be you."

Astrid smiled. "That sounds like Hjalmar."

"It is time to hire more men," Neustatter said. "We will still be the smallest of the seven companies, but I want to be able to take two jobs at once. If things go well, someday add an office in Jena or perhaps even Magdeburg."

Astrid blinked in surprise. She hadn't realized that Neustatter was planning that far ahead. She took a minute framing her words. "Hjalmar told me that you survived in Wallenstein's army by keeping the men from the village as isolated as possible from everyone else."

Neustatter nodded. "We knew many of the other men in our *tercio*. But they were associates, not friends. The men of the village stuck together. But now we need more men, and obviously we cannot get them from the village. Here in Grantville, unlike in Wallenstein's army, there are men we can trust. And it will be good practice for Hjalmar and Ditmar as team leaders to do some background checks. It would be easier if you were a security consultant first. If you are one before they are hired, it will be harder for the new men to complain."

"Who is going to be the secretary?"

"You are, much of the time," Neustatter answered. "I will hire someone for when you are on an assignment. You will be training her. Or him. Maybe Anna."

Astrid gave a firm nod. Her standards of organization were considerably higher than those of any of Neustatter's men.

"You do not have to give me an answer now," Neustatter said. "You and Hjalmar talk it over tonight. Let me know what you think."

"Okay."

*　*　*

After dinner that night, Hjalmar asked Astrid to go get something from their room. She was still looking for the book when her brother came in.

Astrid looked up from where she was a running her hand underneath the edge of his bed. "I do not think your English book is here, Hjalmar."

"*Nein*, it is not." Hjalmar tossed her the book.

"You left it in the *living room*?"

"*Nein*. I wanted to talk to you about something without telling everyone else."

"Oh?" Astrid wondered what her brother wanted.

"Today, when Neustatter said he had no romantic intentions . . . What would you think about that?"

Astrid wasn't quite sure what Hjalmar was trying to ask. "What do you mean?"

"You and Neustatter."

Astrid frowned. "I read mysteries, Hjalmar. I know not to *date* the *boss*. You do not need to remind me."

"That is not what I mean." Hjalmar paused. "People do get married, Astrid. What about you and Neustatter?"

Astrid started to laugh, then she stopped and looked at Hjalmar.

"Are you serious?" She studied him and realized he was. "*Nein*. Just because Neustatter and I work well together does not mean we should get married. He is looking for a female agent, not one more person to protect in the field."

Hjalmar gave her his own steady look. "He said he had no romantic interest in you."

"I was there."

"*Nein.* Earlier. The two of us talked on the ride home. I asked Neustatter if making you an agent was his approach to courting you."

Astrid cocked her head and thought about it. "*Nein.* I think Neustatter would ask a woman directly. Not hint around. He would not be oafish about it, but he would not be subtle, either."

Hjalmar gave her a wry look. "You are probably right."

"What did Neustatter say about me?" Astrid sighed. "If you talked about this . . ."

"All right," Hjalmar conceded. "Neustatter likes that you keep track of everything. Where everyone is, how much money NESS has, what we need more of. That is a good quality in a—"

Astrid interrupted her brother. "It is the same thing you and Ditmar do, is it not? That is why you are team leaders. You do what you know Neustatter wants done, but you take action if you need to."

"Hm. I did not think about it like that," Hjalmar said. "*Initiative*, the National Guard calls it."

"I am not saying I should be a team leader like you. I usually keep track of things rather than people." Astrid smiled. "I have heard you and Ditmar and Neustatter got in trouble in the army—Wallenstein's army—for too much of this *initiative.*"

Hjalmar laughed. "*Ja.* Us for initiative. Lukas for . . . drinking. The others usually got overlooked. Especially Otto. And I have heard that you were the unruliest of the girls working for *Frau* Sophia, always trying something without asking."

"Not always. Once in a while," Astrid protested. She smiled again. "But see—those are qualities Neustatter wants in an agent, not in a wife. Neustatter needs a wife who challenges him. Not one who is unruly, but one who has . . ." She circled with her hand several times, looking for the word.

"You mean a woman with a great deal of confidence."

"*Ja.*"

"An up-timer?" Hjalmar asked.

Astrid shrugged.

Her brother smirked. "*Adel?*"

Astrid laughed. "I do not know how a family of the *adel* would allow it." Then she thought of something. "Maybe you are right, Hjalmar. In the mystery books, the *boss* does not *date* the secretary. Or if they do, they later believe it to be a mistake. But the detective often pursues the heiress. I think that is the closest the up-timers had to *adel*."

"Who does the secretary marry?" Hjalmar wanted to know.

"A nice guy."

Monday, May 1, 1634

Astrid was at her desk at eight on Monday. Some of the men were milling about. Neustatter came in five minutes later. He flipped through some paperwork and then looked up at his men. "Hjalmar, your team is on the range this morning. Ditmar, you have the desk."

"*Ja*, sir," Hjalmar answered. "Karl, Otto, Astrid."

They got up and started toward the door.

"Miss Schäubin." Neustatter pulled the ninth *halstuch* from his desk and tossed it to her. She caught it and tied it around her neck.

Astrid thought it was very neatly done. It was apparent from Karl's expression that he had absolutely no idea what was going on, but Karl didn't question Neustatter's orders. He was just as easy-going as the up-timers—which was probably a good thing in a man who had once been made a blacksmith's apprentice because of his build. On the other hand, there was a reason he was not a team leader.

As soon as they were outside, Otto Brenner did ask questions. "Hjalmar, why is Astrid coming with us?"

"Because Astrid is part of our team now," Hjalmar explained.

Otto stopped and looked back and forth between Hjalmar and Astrid. "Why?"

Hjalmar explained. "Astrid is going to go with us on some assignments. Sometimes we escort women. Astrid can be in their quarters. And sometimes we need more than eight men."

"Okay."

Hjalmar looked over at his sister and shrugged. Apparently, Otto was fine with it, too.

Astrid smiled back. She had been nervous about the men's reaction.

❋ ❋ ❋

Hjalmar's team returned to the office after range practice and lunch. They entered to find that Neustatter and Ditmar had their heads together at the desk working on upcoming assignments. Ditmar's team was sitting around the Franklin stove.

"Good shoot?" Neustatter asked.

"Good shoot," Hjalmar confirmed.

Otto began stacking his brass on the desk. Astrid stepped up next and put her brass in a single line.

"Why is Astrid on a team?" Stefan Kirchenbauer demanded.

Stefan liked to complain, Astrid reflected. It was annoying.

MISSIONS OF SECURITY

"Because we have an upcoming assignment where some of the principals are women," Neustatter answered. "And you are not going to be close coverage in their quarters."

"Of course not." He switched objections. "Why does Hjalmar get a bigger team?"

"Because he is going to keep an eye on his sister anyway. I will put Wolfram with your team."

"But we have been soldiering together for years."

"I am going to hire more men soon," Neustatter stated. His tone left no doubt that he was telling them, not asking them. "Anyone I hire will be someone we did not soldier with. You all know Astrid."

"We could go back to the village."

"No, Stefan, we cannot. Not unless we want a battle."

"We can take them," Lukas Heidenfelder stated.

Neustatter had a remarkably repressive tone. "No, Lukas. We are not going to go fight people we have known all our lives and get them and maybe some of us killed."

"But . . ."

"Lukas. Shut. Up." That was the end of it.

Neustatter stood up. "The next time *Herr* Schrödinger goes to Magdeburg, Hjalmar's team and I will take the assignment. Ditmar, you will be in charge here. Lukas and Stefan, you have security. Wolfram, you have class."

"Why does Wolfram not have to work?" Stefan complained.

Wolfram Kuntz grinned. "If you think I am not working, you may sit in on my classes."

Neustatter continued. "Lukas and Stefan, keep an eye on the houses and the office and get to the range at least once. Stefan, you are welcome to take up medicine after that.

"Now, the assignment is to escort *Herr* Schrödinger to Magdeburg. He is taking his family by train to Halle and then taking a barge the rest of the way. They plan to remain in Magdeburg for several days. Astrid and I are close cover. Hjalmar is the lookout. Otto is the invisible man. Karl, I have not decided your role yet. Take your regular weapons and three days of food. We will buy more in Magdeburg.

"Ditmar, I will telegraph you if we run into any trouble. Make sure there is someone here to receive an emergency message and check for messages at the AT&L office every day.

"Questions?"

"How do we know an emergency message will get delivered?" Stefan asked.

Astrid smothered a smile. He was definitely their resident cynic.

"Because I make sure to take the telegraph offices things from Grantville. Newspapers, gossip, small items. In our line of work, it pays to have friends."

"How do you know you will reach Magdeburg?" Stefan pressed. "There is a war on."

Neustatter picked a newspaper up off the desk and held it out. "The same newspapers. The navy's battle group shot its way past Hamburg, and Prime Minister Stearns has taken command of the city. General Torstensson has some of his forces there and the rest in Magdeburg. If the papers are right—and I think they are—Torstensson will be the one pushing the attack. The League of Ostend will not be coming for Magdeburg. They are still trying to take Lübeck. We will be safe enough in Magdeburg.

"Now, Ditmar and Hjalmar, I have an assignment for you."

Friday, May 12, 1634

The train coasted up to the platform at Naumburg Station.

"Naumburg! Train leaves for Weissenfels in thirty minutes! You have time to disembark if you want to. Naumburg Station has restrooms and a food cart. Keep your ticket stubs with you and show them to me to get back aboard."

Neustatter, Ditmar Schaub, Stefan Kirchenbauer, and Otto Brenner filed off behind several other passengers. They moved to the back of the train where a porter was handing down baggage marked for Naumburg. Neustatter caught the first bag and passed it to Stefan. In just a few minutes they had a small pile of bags at the end of the platform.

"Now what?" Stefan asked.

"Now I go buy lunch," Neustatter said.

He looked at the menu posted on the side of the food cart while he studied the three men running the cart. One of them was a typical German farmer. He looked fit, well-fed but not fat. Clearly his village was doing more than merely surviving. The second was a young man who resembled him—probably his son, perhaps a nephew. Some might have passed over the third man as just another villager who ran a food cart, but Neustatter noted how he carried himself with confidence.

Neustatter addressed the leader. "Sausage, onions, and sauerkraut on a bun. Fifty-seven of them." But he handed over money for only four.

The man handed him four sausage buns. "After the train pulls out, I will come get you," he said quietly.

Neustatter took the food back to his men. After making sure they were out of earshot of anyone else, he said, "He will talk to us after the train pulls out."

While they ate, they watched the food cart do a brisk business.

"There are more people buying food than arrived on the train," Neustatter pointed out quietly. "Some of them came from Naumburg and are going back into town with their lunches."

"It seems odd that he does not take the food cart into the town," Ditmar remarked.

The train pulled out on schedule. The men at the food cart took care of a few more customers, and then the one in charge clapped the other on the back.

"You take it from here, Peder," he said loudly. "Stay for a couple of hours, then check with the station master and find out if there are any locals coming through. If not, come on home. I will see you there."

Then he harnessed one of the horses tied up beside the station to a plain farm wagon sitting near the tracks. As the wagon rolled slowly by, he called to Neustatter, "Are you men waiting for someone?"

Neustatter called back, "We were headed to Freyburg but the man who was to meet us has not arrived."

"My village is part way to Freyburg. I will give you a ride for a couple of coins. Perhaps you will meet your man along the way."

"*Danke.*"

Neustatter and his men piled the bags into the wagon and then climbed in themselves. Neustatter sat on the front bench beside the man from the food cart. Once they were out of sight of Naumburg, the man said, "I presume you are Neustatter?"

"I am," Neustatter confirmed.

"Heinrich Kraft. Call me Heinz. Thank you for bringing the seeds."

"This seems like a lot of trouble just to deliver seed for planting."

"I do not think Duke John George would like what I am planting," Kraft stated.

"More than just food," Neustatter said.

"This area was pillaged in '31. Many of us fled. My wife and I ended up in Grantville. Our village has always provided food for Naumburg, but in Grantville we learned how to grow more vegetables. We came back here last spring. At first the up-time vegetables were just something extra. We convinced the *gemeinde* to grow more of them this year. When Gustav Adolf put this area under Thuringian jurisdiction last fall, Naumburg refused to let us enter the town any more. So now we have the food cart at the train station every day. Even the market is held at the station Tuesdays and Saturdays."

Neustatter decided to trust Kraft. "My men and I were drafted into an army. We surrendered to the up-timers at Alte Veste. Well, to Germans who had joined them. When we got home, it did not work out. We are security consultants in Grantville now."

"They have that effect on people," Kraft observed. "The code you were given? To order fifty-seven? Up-time, a very large company made that many food products and sold them across the up-timers' country. If villages here work together and grow more food than we need, we can sell it. Spread the new foods across the Germanies. Maybe use the railroad. Not be held down by the towns."

Neustatter nodded. "Freedom to control your own affairs."

Friday, May 26, 1634

Herr Schrödinger's party disembarked from the Grantville-Schwarza Junction local. *Herr* Schrödinger and Neustatter already had tickets to Halle in hand. The train was waiting at the platform. The engine was a converted pickup truck with a natural gas tank in the truck bed. It had three cars behind it—two of the short, stubby passenger cars and a boxcar.

"All aboard!" the conductor shouted.

"Miss Schäubin, what can you tell me about the other passengers?" Neustatter asked quietly.

Astrid watched the line ahead of them. She was nervous about her first mission and wanted to answer Neustatter's questions correctly. Two finely dressed men wearing swords were first aboard the lead car with a pair of less ostentatious but still well-dressed men behind them.

"Two *ritter* with servants," Astrid whispered back.

"*Ja,* and the shorter servant has a concealed dagger," her boss added. "They've taken the front seats on both sides with the servants behind them."

Astrid eyed the next bunch. Two of them were also finely dressed, but not in the same style. The three younger men with them wore robes.

"*Bürgermeister* and assistant clerks, I think," Astrid surmised.

"*Ja.*"

Astrid saw that the next group was similar but wearing less-expensive fabrics.

"Two masters with their apprentices?" she guessed.

"Possible," Neustatter allowed. "But they look soft. Merchants, I think."

Astrid was annoyed with herself. Yes, now that Neustatter had pointed it out, she could see that they were probably merchants rather than craft masters.

Then, as pre-arranged, Karl Recker boarded the first car and made his way to the back seat.

"And now we know those *ritter* will be useless for anything other than a frontal assault," Neustatter pronounced. "Man's got a rifle slung over his shoulder, and they just let him take a seat at their backs." The security consultant's disgust was obvious.

The conductor waved the rest of the passengers to the second car. First aboard were a pair of men, one old and the other in his late teens or early twenties. He was dressed almost as finely as the *ritter*.

"A tutor and his student?" Astrid ventured.

"I think so."

Astrid was glad to have gotten one right after her earlier mistake.

Herr Schrödinger's group boarded next. Otto was first aboard and swung into the front left seat across the aisle from the tutor. Astrid saw Neustatter tense and realized why when she reached the top of the three stairs—four men were already seated in the back of the car. The two in the back left were soldiers—one in USE gray and the other in SoTF blue. Halfway back on that side was an older man in up-timer clothes. He was seated sideways with one leg stretched out across the seat. The fourth man was seated between him and the soldiers. Astrid was pretty sure that one was what the up-time detective novels would describe as "a seedy-looking character." His rather wild hair and worn clothes contrasted with how he had a cloak neatly folded up in his lap with his hands tucked inside the folds as if it were a muff.

Unfortunately, she had no choice but to sit across the aisle from him. Neustatter had dropped into the seat ahead of the up-timer, and *Herr* and *Frau* Schrödinger took the seat behind the tutor and his student. Their two sons sat behind their parents and ahead of Astrid. Hjalmar was the last passenger aboard and sat behind Astrid, across the aisle from the soldiers.

"Look me up in Halle," the unkempt man told her.

Astrid studiously ignored that. Not only did she find him personally repellent, but his position across the aisle from her made him a potential threat. He could have anything hidden in that cloak. Astrid assumed he was carrying at least a knife. Fortunately, Hjalmar was right behind her.

The conductor swung himself aboard, pulled the door shut, and the train pulled out at 8:00 AM sharp.

* * *

Astrid marveled at how little time it had taken the train to reach Jena. It was not long after noon, and they were already north of the university town. She understood that the up-timers considered this slow. The stops seemed to be as much of a limiting factor as the actual speed of the train. If the railroad could lay enough track and cut out all the stops—what the up-timers called an "express"—they would be able to reach anywhere in the USE in two or three days.

Astrid sniffed in amusement. Well, if *she* could see that, so could anyone else. It was possible that one of the Ostender powers would strike at the Grantville-Halle line—although with the USE Army marching north, that did not seem very likely. She saw nothing out the window but open ground and occasional small stands of pine. She glanced over at Neustatter and nodded.

Neustatter returned the nod. His side of the train was clear, too. Astrid turned her attention back inside the train. She didn't particularly like the situation, but it hadn't changed much. The train had picked up a couple of passengers in Rudolstadt but they had disembarked in Jena. She went back to scanning outside and hoped that her month of training was enough to allow her to see everything she needed to.

The unkempt man leaned toward her. "How about . . ."

Astrid flinched away. The older man suddenly caught him by the collar and tossed him back against his seat. "Leave the lady alone," he growled.

Neustatter whirled around, and Hjalmar lunged up out of his seat. But each of the soldiers already had the man by a shoulder. Astrid flushed. She should not need five men to come to her aid.

"Easy now," the older man said. He tugged his overcoat aside, and Astrid glimpsed the six-pointed star pinned to the jacket underneath.

So did Neustatter. "Shouldn't you have cuffs on him, Officer?" he asked.

The older man pulled the unkempt man's cloak away. Astrid and Neustatter saw that his hands were indeed handcuffed together. "Sorry, there's no way to cuff him to the seat."

Neustatter nodded.

"Oh, and it's marshal," the man added. "Harley Thomas." He and Neustatter shook hands.

Their client's two children were staring at him. "What's a marshal?" one of them asked his father. That was nine-year-old Franz.

The master craftsman shrugged. "I am not sure, son."

Franz turned around. "Miss Schäubin, what is a marshal?"

"Do you know, girl?" the unkempt man hissed at her.

Astrid turned to face him. "Yes. A marshal is like a city watchman, except he works for the Supreme Court of Thuringia-Franconia."

"Stinking city watch. Stinking courts." The man spat in the aisle.

Harley Thomas ignored it. "You're pretty well-informed for a governess."

Astrid ran her fingers across her vest, momentarily disarranging it so that Thomas could see the strap of her shoulder holster.

Thomas's eyes may have widened ever so slightly, but that was it. His prisoner seemed to miss it completely.

"A watchman?" their client's other son, seven-year-old Josef, piped up. "You do not look like a watchman."

"The only uniform a marshal has is his badge and his gun," Harley Thomas stated. "I don't work for a city. I work for the State of Thuringia-Franconia. Chief Justice Riddle assigns me and the other marshals a list of criminals to bring in. Some of them ran out on their bail. Others are fugitives. The other marshals and I find them and take them to the city or county where they broke the law."

That led to more questions. Marshal Thomas seemed to spend a lot of time staring at his prisoner while he explained "bail" and "fugitive." "No," he answered a follow-up question, "we do not beat or torture suspects. If I catch any town watch doing that, I'll be arresting *them*."

Astrid noted that the tutor up front whipped around so fast his neck would probably regret it later. His student was rubbernecking, too.

"How do you know where to find the bad men?" Josef asked.

Marshal Thomas looked relieved by the question. "Well," he answered, "part of what I am is a detective."

"What is a detective?"

"Franz, Josef, stop bothering *Herr* Marshal Thomas," the children's mother directed.

Harley Thomas smiled. "It's no bother, ma'am. A detective figures out what happened. Look at your fingers. See the little patterns there? Do you know every person's are different? Now, have you ever touched a window or a glass and left it smudged?"

"Many times," their mother confirmed.

"If I sprinkle powder on the fingerprints, then I can lift them up with tape and take them with me," Marshal Thomas explained. "And then someone can check them against our files and match them to the person who left them."

"Wow!"

"Detectives can do the same with other things, too. Now, are your names really Franz and Josef?" Having been assured by the children that they were indeed, the marshal said, "There are books about two up-time detectives with your names. Well, they have American names—Frank and Joe—but they're the same as Franz and Josef. Their last name is Hardy. A lot of us up-timers read Hardy Boys books when we were your age or so. I assume there are some in the school library."

Astrid mostly hid a smile at Franz and Josef's rapt attention. They were kneeling on the seats, facing Marshal Thomas. Their mother was frowning and likely to reprimand them at some point.

But that wasn't Astrid's concern. She noted that the prisoner seated between Thomas and the soldiers looked distinctly uncomfortable. Perhaps he is wondering where he left his fingerprints, she mused. Neustatter was also paying attention. She assumed Otto and Hjalmar were, too, but didn't want to point them out by looking at them.

Harley Thomas looked over at Astrid. "There's another series of up-time detective books about a girl detective named Nancy Drew. There should be some somewhere in Grantville."

"*Dank*," Astrid responded. She was surprised that the marshal had passed that along.

The man across the aisle from her wasn't having any of it. "So you think you could be a watchman, do you?"

Astrid ignored his sarcasm.

"I said, so you think you could be a watchman?" the man hissed. He reached out and grabbed at her hair in spite of the cuffs.

Astrid jerked away from him. *Should I go for my gun?*

Hjalmar, the USE soldier, and Marshal Thomas all hit the prisoner at the same time. Neustatter was a split second later, only because he'd started from further away.

"Slow learner, this one," the soldier commented.

"Sure is," the marshal agreed, looking down to where the man had fallen into the aisle. He left him there until they pulled into the station at Bad Kösen.

Astrid sighed. She had had to be rescued again.

* * *

"Naumburg Station!" the conductor shouted. "Train leaves in thirty minutes! Keep your ticket stubs if you want to reboard!"

Neustatter turned from the window and said, "*Herr* Schrödinger, there is a food cart at this station. Marshal, Sergeants, it is good food."

Since the platform also had restrooms, everyone aboard disembarked. While they were eating, Astrid knew she needed to talk to Neustatter.

"I am sorry I *screwed up*, Neustatter."

"You did not *screw up*, Miss Schäubin," he told her.

"The master craftsmen who are really merchants. Not drawing my gun on the prisoner."

"The first takes practice. And it is good that you did not draw on the prisoner. I believe he still thinks you are the children's governess."

"But . . ."

"You are doing fine, Miss Schäubin," Neustatter told her.

The restroom door opened. The prisoner stepped out and lunged back against the door, slamming it against Marshal Thomas. Then he dashed across the platform.

Neustatter saw it from ten yards away. "Karl!" he shouted.

Karl Recker looked up and stuck his foot out as the prisoner ran by. The man tripped, fell off the platform, and faceplanted.

Thomas limped over. "*Dank*."

"*Bitte schön*."

Neustatter and Karl helped Thomas haul the prisoner back up onto the platform. His nose was bleeding.

"Thanks," Harley Thomas said. "You're one of Neustatter's, too, eh? I owe you guys one." He winced. "Slammed it into my bad knee, too."

"I am curious. Where are you taking this prisoner, anyway?" Neustatter asked.

"Magdeburg. We picked him up in Grantville for breaking and entering. While he was doing his time on a road crew, we got a wanted notice from Magdeburg. More breaking and entering up there."

"Is that worth trying to escape?"

"I would like to keep all my fingers, *danke*," the prisoner spat.

"They don't cut off fingers anymore," the marshal told him. "Legally abolishing that is the only way they can get extraditions from Justice Riddle. Nope, if found guilty you'll probably get assigned to a night soil detail."

That seemed to upset the prisoner even more. "But . . . but the status . . ."

"Well, then you should probably stop taking other people's stuff."

※ ※ ※

Herr Schrödinger's party left the train at Halle. After collecting a bundle from the baggage, Neustatter motioned to Astrid, and they entered the station.

"What are we doing?"

"Meeting someone," Neustatter answered. "The schedulers' office is over here." He held the door for her.

The cramped room had a sturdy table against one wall with several pieces of equipment on it. One piece was chattering away. One of the three men in the room was transcribing the message. The second—this one in uniform—was reading over his shoulder.

"Tell the northbound he's cleared to Teutschenthal. Then tell Jena to hold that southbound local until we hear back from the track crew." He looked up and saw them. "Neustatter!"

"Sergeant Hudson." Neustatter handed over a bundle. "Grantville newspapers and some liquor from Tip's. And the movie schedule."

"You're a lifesaver."

"This is Astrid Schäubin, first of my new agents."

"Pleased to meet you, ma'am. So, Neustatter, what movies have you seen lately?"

"*The Hunt for Red October* and *Maverick*. Both at the high school."

"Popular, but quality," Eric Glen Hudson admitted. "Now if I could just get you to watch *Citizen Kane*."

Neustatter shuddered. Astrid sensed this was some sort of running joke between the two men.

"Ha. When are you coming back through?"

"Next Friday."

"See you Friday. Who knows? The war might be over by then."

* * *

Herr Schrödinger's cargo got delivered to the Navy Yard even before he and his family took a room in what had to be the nicest inn in Magdeburg. That said certain things about the nature of cargo NESS had been guarding, although the guarding had taken little effort on either the train or on the riverboat they'd boarded in Halle.

The Neustadt Gasthaus had flush toilets, hot water, and electricity. NESS got to stay there, too, although Astrid spent most of her time following *Frau* Schrödinger around Magdeburg, usually with Franz and Josef in tow.

One day Neustatter and Karl had accompanied *Herr* Schrödinger to a meeting. *Frau* Schrödinger and the children were shopping. Hjalmar was looking like an obvious bodyguard. Neither Otto nor Astrid were wearing *halstücher*. Astrid was supposed to look like a governess, and gawking at the many newly built and opened shops in Magdeburg wasn't hard at all. Otto meandered around, seemingly unconnected to the party. He and Hjalmar were using signs to convey information without being seen talking with each other.

Frau Schrödinger was looking through a market. Astrid was scanning the crowded streets. People were talking about the Baltic War—that seemed to be the name everyone had settled on. The War of the League of Ostend was running a distant second, at any rate. By the time they had reached Magdeburg, the USE Navy had defeated the Ostender fleet in Luebeck Bay, and the USE Army had defeated the French army at Ahrensbök. Prime Minister Stearns had even taken a *timberclad* to rescue? . . . pick up? . . . the embassy that had been imprisoned in the Tower of London. At almost the same time, the situation in Franconia erupted. The newspapers were calling that the Ram Rebellion.

Church bells started ringing—and not on their regular schedule. It did not take more than a couple days in Magdeburg to learn their regular patterns.

"Back to the inn," Hjalmar snapped.

"But—"

Astrid cut *Frau* Schrödinger off. "We do not know what the bells mean. If it is an emergency, that is where *Herr* Schrödinger and Neustatter will look for us."

Frau Schrödinger considered that and took Josef by the hand. Astrid took Franz, and they started toward the inn. Everyone else had similar ideas, and the streets were full. They had gone only a couple blocks when they heard someone shouting news on the next street corner. Astrid saw Hjalmar give Otto a sign.

Otto wormed his way through the crowd, stayed just long enough to get the news, and hurried back to the rest of them.

"What news?" Hjalmar called when he got close.

"Peace!" Otto shouted. "A peace conference in Copenhagen!"

Hjalmar's "*Dank!*" blended in with murmurs of "*Danke Gott!*" from the crowd around them. People were starting to cheer.

"Hjalmar, I think we can go back to the market," Astrid suggested.

"*Ja*," he agreed.

They returned to Grantville with no incidents. Astrid barely had time to reflect how much shorter this trip took than their first journey from Magdeburg to Grantville, just over a year ago.

CHAPTER 3:
BIBELGESELLSCHAFT

A couple days after they returned home, Neustatter sent Hjalmar to the high school to gather information about one of the upcoming missions.

Astrid waited until the men had left. "Why are we investigating our clients? Do you not trust them?"

"I want to know what the other students at the high school think of this *Bibelgesellschaft*. Who thinks well of them and who does not will tell us a lot."

Hjalmar spent the better part of a couple days at the high school. On the third day, he gave his report to Neustatter and Astrid.

"The *Bibelgesellschaft* is complicated," he began. "It is actually students—Lutheran, Catholic, and Anabaptist—with the Catholic priest Athanasius Kircher and the up-time pastor Albert Green as their advisors. I actually found a couple papers members wrote." He handed those to us. "They're available for purchase in the library, just like any other research paper. I figured it was worth the money."

Neustatter nodded absently. He skimmed one paper, while Astrid skimmed the other. Her English was steadily improving. She recognized *canon*, but *textual criticism* meant nothing to her.

"So, they are trying to find the original text of Scripture," Neustatter drawled. "Less Indiana Jones, lots more painstaking research."

Astrid nodded in agreement. From what she had been able to understand, that seemed a good summary.

"What is strange," Hjalmar continued, "is that there are at least two, and maybe more, beliefs about this that have nothing to do with Lutheran, Catholic, Calvinist, and so on. That seems to be how they all get along well enough to keep working together."

"What do you mean?" Astrid asked.

"If their chief differences were Lutheran, Catholic, and Calvinist, they would get caught up on the larger arguments. They have their own disagreements that almost no one else understands. So there is no outside pressure against them working together."

"Did you find any problems?" Neustatter asked.

"Besides escorting Catholics and Anabaptists to the University of Jena? *Nein*. Oh—I did find one problem for them, but not for us. Some of them are not able to travel to Jena. I think their parents will not allow it."

Neustatter shrugged. "Based on what I found out about the riot at the Rudolstadt Colloquy last year, that does not seem unreasonable to me."

Friday, June 9, 1634

Neustatter and Hjalmar were waiting in the office when a knock sounded at the door. It swung open, and a man in black clerical robes stepped in, closely followed by a young man in his teens. A girl about the same age followed. Pastor Al Green brought up the rear.

Astrid rose from behind the desk, and Neustatter and Hjalmar both stood. Astrid saw the girl was eyeing Neustatter's gunbelt.

MISSIONS OF SECURITY

"*Guten Morgen*, Magister Kircher, Magister Green." Neustatter considered the young people for a moment. "And Master Felke and Miss Meisnerin, if I'm not mistaken." He shook hands with all of them. "I am Edgar Neustatter. I will be commanding your escort today."

Neustatter was speaking English with an Austrian accent. He had been playing with it ever since seeing *Terminator 2*.

"I don't recall mentioning the names of any of the students," Al Green commented.

"You did not," Neustatter confirmed. He switched back to German. "I am training my men in investigation. I sent one of my team leaders to Calvert High." He gestured toward my brother. "May I introduce Hjalmar Schaub? I assure you, he is older than he looks. Hjalmar has been in the field just as long as I have, since 1626."

Miss Meisnerin and Pastor Green exchanged glances. They both looked unsettled at Neustatter's words.

"I apologize for seeming to investigate you," Neustatter said smoothly, "but sometimes my clients are not aware of something that affects their safety. As a security consultant, I dislike surprises."

"Did we surprise you with any safety concerns?" Athanasius Kircher asked. The Jesuit scholar hadn't blinked an eye at Neustatter's explanation.

Neustatter gave them a wry grin. "I have learned more about church politics than I ever wanted to know. I understand enough to know that your BGS would like to find the most accurate Greek Bible so that you can make better translations."

Neustatter was still speaking. Astrid wondered if any of their clients had noticed that the Austrian accent had vanished as soon as he got down to business.

"I also understand that collaboration between people from several different churches alarms the more extreme members of all of those churches. Which is why you came to us, *ja*? Hjalmar, would you assemble your team out front?"

After he left, Neustatter gestured toward Astrid. "May I introduce Miss Astrid Schäubin. Miss Meisnerin, you and Miss Kellarmännin will be her principals."

Katharina shot Neustatter a surprised look and examined Miss Schäubin. Astrid's long, blonde hair was swept forward over one shoulder and curled inward at the ends. Her blouse was the latest Grantville fashion, a more or less up-time style made of heavier down-time fabric. She wore riding skorts, leather boots, and a gunbelt, although her was the neat black *polizei* type, not a gunfighter's rig like Neustatter's.

Neustatter was *very* perceptive. "She is quite good." He didn't sound offended.

"I am sorry, Miss Schäubin," Katharina apologized. "I have never met a lady soldier before."

Astrid returned the observation. "I have never met a lady theologian before."

Katharina smiled. "Fair enough. But that is not really what I am."

"Me, either. As *Herr* Neustatter said, you and Miss Kellarmännin are my principals."

"Does it bother the men?" Katharina blurted out. "That you are a bodyguard?"

"Sometimes. It worries my brother, and some of the men have their doubts."

"Me, too. Being in the *Bibelgesellschaft*, I mean. Some people do not take us seriously. Come meet Barbara. She is outside."

The two of them left, still comparing notes in being a woman in what was usually a man's profession.

Once outside, they saw that the rest of the *Bibelgesellschaft* members who were going to Jena had arrived.

"Barbara!" Katharina called. "This is Miss Astrid Schäubin. She is our bodyguard."

"Miss Kellarmännin," Astrid said.

Barbara giggled. "I am not anyone important. Only teachers call me *Fräulein*. I am Barbara."

"And I am Katharina," Miss Meisnerin put in.

"Then you must call me Astrid." She smiled at the two of them.

"I do not think I have met anyone named Astrid before," Barbara said.

"It is Danish. My family settled in Holstein long ago. We lived there before the men went off to war."

"Did you go with them?"

"No, after they first came to Grantville they came back and got their families. We all came to Grantville then."

Katharina and Barbara seemed to expect more, but that was everything Astrid intended to say on the matter.

Hjalmar reappeared with Karl and Otto, and Neustatter introduced them. Father Kircher introduced the other *Bibelgesellschaft* members.

Katharina's brother Georg had loaded everyone's baggage already, so they climbed aboard the wagon. Kircher and Green seated themselves on the bench next to Georg, while the students sat on the benches along the sides of the wagon. Katharina was right behind Georg with Barbara next to her and then Markus Fratscher and Guenther Kempf. Horst Felke, Johann Speiss, and Mattheus Beimler were across from them on the right side. Astrid knew the Meisners and Barbara were Anabaptists, and Horst Felke was Catholic. She was a little hazy about the others, but the two next to Horst were probably the other Catholics. The one with dark hair— Johann—wanted to be a priest, and Mattheus was sort of a protégé of Athanasius Kircher. That meant the other two were the Lutherans. She thought Guenther was the one in the Young Crown Loyalists, and Markus was the one who wanted to attend the University of Wittenberg. On the one hand, it was a little unsettling how much information Hjalmar had been able to learn, just by asking around at the high school. On the other, it meant that the students generally did not have deep, dark secrets and did not hide their ambitions from students of other creeds. She supposed on the whole that was reassuring.

The NESS agents were riding horses today. Hjalmar and Neustatter were out in front of the wagon while Karl, Otto, and Astrid followed it. Traffic was heavy enough that right now flanking guards would just get in the way.

The wagon rolled steadily along. Occasionally it slowed. Astrid realized that Georg Meisner was a skilled teamster who planned ahead for what might happen so that he rarely had to bring the horses to a complete halt. Plus, he did not seem to have any problem letting his sister take the lead on the *Bibelgesellschaft*.

So, when the wagon slowed at the base of the hill leading up out of the Ring of Fire, Astrid wondered why. Any momentum the wagon had would be useful. Then she saw the men blocking the road.

Neustatter and Hjalmar had already turned around. Hjalmar spurred to a gallop as soon as he reached level ground. Neustatter's horse ambled back to the wagon, giving every sign of being bored.

"It seems there will be a slight delay," Neustatter drawled.

"Who are those men?" Horst Felke demanded. "They have no right to block the road!"

"I believe I mentioned extreme factions in each of the churches," Neustatter reminded him.

"But we've accounted for everyone. Catholic, Lutheran, Methodist, Disciples of Christ, Church of Christ, Baptist, and Anabaptist," Green protested.

"Ah, but if I'm not mistaken, Master Fratscher and Master Kempf are from Pastor Kastenmeyer's Lutherans. The men in the road are from

MISSIONS OF SECURITY

Pastor Holz's Lutheran church. That is the church my men and I belong to as well."

Astrid saw Katharina tense, but got diverted by Pastor Green's question.

"Did you know about this, Neustatter?"

"I had my suspicions," Neustatter acknowledged. "I suspect that Pastor Holz assumes he can block the road because the place he is doing it is outside the Ring of Fire. He might think it is outside Chief Richards' jurisdiction."

"It seems Holz has outthought us," Kircher said.

"Not entirely," Neustatter said. "I sent Hjalmar to find an SoTF marshal. This is within the marshals' jurisdiction."

Katharina's jaw dropped.

Neustatter noticed, of course. "Don't worry, Miss Meisnerin," he said. "I will get you to Jena."

"I suppose we ought to see what they want," Pastor Green said. "Georg, keep hold of the reins."

Kircher climbed down from the wagon to let Green out. Some of the men in the road started shouting at them as soon as they realized Kircher was wearing his clerical robes.

Neustatter turned to one of his men. "Karl!" The two of them spurred forward on either side of Green and Kircher.

"If you gentlemen are almost done with the road, we would like to pass through to Jena," Green said mildly.

"You heretics will not be going to Jena."

"Why is that?" Neustatter demanded.

"Because they are *heretics*, Neustatter," Pastor Pancratz Holz explained. "They want to change the Bible."

"What I gather, Pastor," Neustatter drawled, "is they're wanting the University of Jena's help in finding old Bibles."

"They are trying to change the Scripture! I have read their books. They questioned *everything* about the Bible uptime!"

"No, we're not!" Al Green burst out. "I'm no liberal! And I'm not a higher critic, either." He proceeded to call the wrath of God down on a couple individuals named Graf and Wellhausen and then loudly pointed out that the *Bibelgesellschaft* had freedom of assembly, and if they wanted to assemble in Jena, they would, thank you very much. Pastor Pancratz Holz retorted that his congregation also had freedom of assembly, and if they wanted to assemble on the road to Jena, they would, thank you very much.

Astrid heard Katharina ask her brother, "What's happening?"

"The Lutheran pastor is shouting," Georg reported. "And Pastor Green is shouting back. And they all look confused and angry." He sighed. "And now the Lutherans are shouting again."

Someone in the crowd threw a rock. Astrid do not know why anyone would think that was a good idea.

Neustatter immediately sent his horse plunging into the crowd, who scattered in all directions. Neustatter wheeled the horse around and pursued a couple who hadn't scrambled quite far enough for his liking. Karl circled in the opposite direction, opening a gap.

"Take the wagon forward!" Astrid shouted to Georg.

Georg glanced between her, the disturbance ahead, and Katharina. Then he flicked the reins.

"Is it safe?" Katharina asked.

Astrid brought her horse alongside the wagon. "I'll watch this side. Otto will watch the other side. Keep moving."

Georg looked rather startled but complied. When he reached Kircher and Green, he slowed not quite to a complete stop, and the two clerics scrambled onto the wagon.

"Holz is rallying his men," Kircher pointed out.

Sure enough, the mob was coming back together further down the road, minus a handful of men whom Neustatter and Karl had driven far to the side of the road. Neustatter turned back toward the road and nudged his horse to a canter. A couple seconds later, Karl did the same.

Astrid wished her pastor weren't trying to forcibly prevent her clients from traveling to Jena. Pastor Holz did have a point—their clients were mostly heretics—Catholics and Anabaptists. On the other hand, their clients had a point, too—they were bound for a Lutheran university to present their case as to why denominations that disagreed with each other should work together to examine and preserve ancient copies of the Scriptures.

One man pitched a stone at Neustatter as he cantered toward the men in the road. It went wide. Neustatter kept going. Astrid saw the men edging backwards, and then the crowd broke. Neustatter and Karl scattered them again.

Georg kept the wagon rumbling steadily forward. Holz was determined, but he and his men had to run to keep pace with the wagon. Neustatter and Karl were able to keep them away from the wagon. They were growing more and more frustrated but fortunately there wasn't much available to throw at the horsemen.

One man made a run at the wagon, and Neustatter wheeled his horse around to head him off. Twenty yards from the wagon he lashed out with a boot and sent the man sprawling. Neustatter gestured at Astrid to take it from there while he turned back toward Holz—just in time to find another man making a break toward the wagon. He stopped that one, too. The third one was on his way in when everyone heard a siren.

A Grantville Police Department cruiser rolled up behind the wagon. One officer got out but the driver stayed in the vehicle.

"This isn't Grantville!" Holz shouted. "You have no jurisdiction here!"

The officer passed the wagon. "Brother Green. Father Kircher."

"He's not Grantville police," Georg observed.

"That's Marshal Thomas. The marshals work throughout Thuringia-Franconia," Astrid told him.

Up ahead, Marshal Harley Thomas was explaining that fact to Pancratz Holz.

"You cannot give orders here! This is Schwarzburg!"

"No, this is part of West Virginia County. But I'm a SoTF marshal. We have jurisdiction throughout the entire state, including Schwarzburg. Pastor Holz, it's illegal to interfere with other people's right to assemble peaceably."

"But it won't be peaceably! They're going to Jena to try to destroy the Scriptures!"

Harley Thomas sighed. It looked like it could be a long morning.

"There's only one of you."

The marshal stepped up in Holz's face. "Yeah. But it looks like you only brought one riot with you, Holz. So get out of the way. Now."

The situation wasn't improved by Neustatter laughing out loud at that point. But Holz very grudgingly got his men out of the road.

They did make a few threats as the wagon rolled by.

"Any Lutheran who consorts with you heretics is risking excommunication!"

Green looked over his shoulder and said, "I'll be sure to warn Johann Gerhard."

Astrid was not at all happy with the situation. Neustatter was shaking hands with Marshal Thomas, and it seemed to her that he was the only one who was not obviously upset. Well, Karl did not seem too distressed, either. Otto was frowning, as were Pastor Green and Father Kircher. Katharina and Barbara looked concerned, but it seemed to Astrid that as Katharina looked around, she was doing the same thing Astrid was—assessing their party.

MISSIONS OF SECURITY

Hjalmar had caught up while Marshal Thomas was dispersing Holz's men. At Neustatter's signal, Karl took the lead, and Georg got the wagon moving. Neustatter and Hjalmar were deep in conversation as they rode behind the wagon, so Otto took one side, and Astrid took the other. About ten minutes later, Neustatter rode up beside Astrid.

"Miss Schäubin, I have sent Hjalmar back to Grantville to talk to the other men and their families. And to keep an eye on Pastor Holz. I know he wanted be along on your second mission, but someone needs to brief Ditmar's team. The men won't care. We all had to pretend to be Catholics in Wallenstein's army. But Stefan and Wolfram's families have been Lutherans all their lives."

"We could all just go to St. Martin's in the Fields," Astrid pointed out. "It's Philippist but it would do until the new Flacian church on the Badenburg Road opens."

Katharina had been listening in. "Excuse me. I haven't studied much about the Flacian-Philippist dispute, but you obviously have strong feelings about it."

Neustatter shrugged. "Flacians follow Luther more closely. It pi . . . annoys the Catholics more. Uh, begging your pardon, Father Kircher."

"Our pastor in Holstein was Flacian," Astrid added.

"And our pastor in Holstein was Flacian," Neustatter agreed.

Katharina started to say something, but did not get past, "Um . . ."

"Yes, of course," Neustatter agreed. "If Miss Schäubin and the others want to go somewhere else or all go to different churches, that is quite all right. Well, no, it probably is not, but they are allowed to. Miss Meisnerin." He touched the brim of his hat and rode off to join Karl in front of the wagon.

After Katharina had recovered, she ventured, "Does he do that often?"

"Read your mind?" Astrid asked. "*Ja*."

"Does it not bother you?"

"I am the secretary. It is quite helpful, actually."

❊ ❊ ❊

The rest of the journey to Jena was uneventful. They hired rooms at an inn and then walked to the university where they were met by the superintendent Dr. Johann Major. Neustatter and his team stood back while Dr. Green made the introductions.

"I am pleased to meet you, Dr. Green. I really should have seen to that before now. Master Kircher."

Major was accompanied by a couple students, Hans and Christoph, and within a few minutes, he had neatly split off Green and Kircher to go meet a colleague. Neustatter fell in behind them.

That left Karl, Otto, and Astrid with the students. Katharina, Barbara, and Astrid quickly became the center of attention.

"Are you from St. Martin's?"

"No."

Astrid could tell Katharina was concerned about where the conversation was going. Barbara was hanging back a little bit, observing.

"Flacian, then."

"No."

"Then?"

"You know the *Bibelgesellschaft* contains students from several denominations?"

"Yes."

"I am Anabaptist."

Christoph deflated. Hans turned to Barbara. "And you?"

"Anabaptist."

He looked to Astrid. "And you are?"

"Armed." She patted her holster.

"You are . . . you are . . . " Christoph stammered.

"A mercenary," Hans finished.

"I work for Neustatter's European Security Services. So does Karl over there." Astrid saw no reason to draw attention to Otto.

Heads swiveled. "Well, yes, obviously," Christoph agreed. "But bodyguards? Here?"

"There was an anti-Catholic riot here last year," Astrid reminded them. "Go ahead. I will watch the flank."

They got the grand tour of the University of Jena, ending up at a display of books.

"*Alchemia*?" Georg asked.

"By Andreas Libavius. He was a student here in the arts and medical curricula," Christoph explained. "He died in 1616. But it is the first systematic chemistry book. These are all books by university faculty or students."

Katharina was reading the titles. *Methodus tractandarum controversiarum theologicarum*.

"That's one of Dr Himmel's books. And *Passionale Academicum*, right next to it."

There was one in English. *Sixe Bookes of Politickes or Civil Doctrine, Done into English by William Jones*.

"Oh, Justus Lipsius was a professor here for a while. He converted from Catholicism. Then when he got hired at Leiden he converted to Calvinism. They say he was really a Stoic all along. But a lot of influential men speak well of these books—Richelieu, Olivares, Maximilian."

"Perhaps those are not the best possible endorsements," Guenther remarked.

"And these?" Katharina asked.

"*Loci communes theologici* and *Meditationes sacrae* are Dr. Gerhard's books," Markus answered. "Some of us *are* Lutheran."

"And this is a draft of the first section of *Confessio Catholica*," Christoph announced proudly. "Dr. Gerhard is demonstrating the catholicness of the Augsburg Confession from Catholic sources."

"Oh, please," Johann Speiss protested. Mattheus just rolled his eyes.

"A draft?" Katharina put in quickly.

"Yes. He has just started it. It probably will not be published for a few years. The book display is to show some visiting students. They are here from Latin schools and from some other universities. It's some sort of up-time idea. They call it 'recruiting.' As if a university were an army."

As if on cue, a number of other students entered the hall. Introductions were made all around, and shoptalk broke out. Katharina edged back out of the crowd and tried to locate Barbara but found herself talking to a student from the University of Erfurt.

They shook hands. "Johannes Musaeus."

"Katharina Meisnerin."

"You are . . . "

"Not a student here, *nein*. I am with the *Bibelgesellschaft* in Grantville."

After the tour, they rejoined Kircher and Green. The *Bibelgesellschaft* had a couple hours on their own before a formal dinner with the theology faculty. Astrid listened to Katharina and hoped she could remember everyone's name. Apparently, the important faculty members were the three Johanns: Johann Gerhard, considered the number three Lutheran theologian ever, after Luther and Chemnitz; Johann Maior, the superintendent who had welcomed them; and Johann Himmel, who had written a couple of the books on the display table.

During the dinner, the NESS agents "held up the wall," as Neustatter put it. That was fine with Astrid. It meant she did not have to demonstrate whether she actually remembered everyone's name.

MISSIONS OF SECURITY

After the dinner, the BGS went back to the inn. Neustatter and his team fell in around them as they left the building.

"You didn't get to eat!" Katharina realized.

"We will eat at the inn," Astrid said.

"That is not fair."

"I would rather be able to just eat than worry about etiquette and professors. What did you have?"

Katharina recited high-class but quite traditional fare.

Astrid smiled. "The main reasons we picked this inn are because we trust the innkeeper, and it is safe. It also has a well-deserved reputation for cheap food. But that is okay—I like stew and fries."

When we reached the inn, most of the BGS elected to stay up for a while. Neustatter pulled Astrid aside.

"Miss Schäubin, you and Otto go ahead and eat."

"But you . . . "

"Will eat later. You have first watch."

Astrid discovered that being on watch was boring. After an hour, she upgraded that to really boring. Finally, a door swung open and Neustatter ambled out, looking ridiculously chipper.

"*Guten Morgen*, Miss Schäubin." His eyes twinkled. "Get some sleep."

Saturday, June 10, 1634

On the next day, the NESS agents spent a lot more time holding up the walls. The theologians and students were seated behind tables. Each row was up a bit higher than the one in front, and the floor was sloped like the one in the Calvert High School auditorium.

The theological discussion was a lot more interesting than nighttime guard duty. Or rather, it was *not* a theological discussion. Pastor Green—*Doctor* Green was actually the title that mattered here—spoke first, followed by Horst, Katharina, Markus, and Guenther. Doctors Gerhard, Major, and Himmel asked quite a few questions.

At one point, Dr. Hummel asked, "But why should we join with you to do this?"

"We will get more done, faster, if we work together."

"I don't think we should work with sectarians and Anabaptists."

Astrid could see people stiffen.

Then Al Green grinned. "You don't think we're saved. Well, fair enough. I'm not entirely convinced about you all, either."

There were gasps throughout the room, and a couple people sprayed their drinks.

Green's eyes twinkled. "I think we both have concerns about our brother Athanasius here. And he about us, no doubt. As for me, I'm more than a little concerned that seventeenth-century Lutheranism seems to value adherence to a body of doctrine more than adherence to Christ. And I can only assume that you in turn are quite concerned that I'm not under any ecclesiastical authority outside of my own church's board of elders."

"That is, indeed, chief among my concerns," Gerhard answered.

Astrid sensed that Gerhard was truly concerned but also just a little bit amused. She decided she liked him. Although she would not able to repeat what the up-timers called the *technical details*, she could tell that the theology faculty's questions were shifting from *if* to *how*. Finally, Dr. Gerhard requested that the University of Jena theology faculty be able to confer amongst themselves.

The NESS team stepped outside with the *Bibelgesellschaft*. Johannes Musaeus joined them, since he was a guest as well.

Once we were all outside, he spoke first. "That was a good presentation. I was not sure what to expect, but now I hope the faculty works with you."

"*Danke*," Katharina said.

"If they accept, I definitely need to attend here. If you will have me, I would like to join your *Bibelgesellschaft*."

"Welcome aboard." Markus was the first to shake his hand. "We can always use more Lutherans. Flacian, I assume?"

"*Ja*, definitely."

They settled down into shop talk. After about an hour, Katharina got up and started pacing. Eventually, Georg joined her.

"Relax, Kat."

"I cannot. What if they do not want to work with us?"

"I think they will."

The morning dragged on. Katharina kept pacing. Astrid was pretty sure some of the *Bibelgesellschaft* were praying. A discussion of whether they should send a few people to get lunch had begun when Dr. Gerhard finally came out. Everyone converged on him.

"One question, *bitte*," Gerhard asked. "Magister Kircher, you did not say anything." The Lutheran theologian studied the Catholic theologian for several seconds. "Rome wants information on the manuscripts, does it not?"

"Yes, of course."

"Have you been ordered to send it?"

"Yes. Dr. Gerhard, I would much prefer not to race you to the manuscripts. Rome wants the information. I have no directives concerning anyone else having the information as well."

"But we would have to work with Catholics."

"And I would have to work with Lutherans." Kircher grinned. "I am willing to make that sacrifice. But I would very much like to study some Sahidic manuscripts."

Astrid found herself holding her breath along with everyone else.

"Magister Kircher," Gerhard said, "I think I would also prefer not to race you to the manuscripts. I might not get as many as I would like." He glanced at Dr. Green. "You two have made this work so far?"

"Well, we're both pretty busy," Dr. Green answered. "It mostly works because the students make it work."

Dr. Gerhard smiled. "I expect that will continue. Very well, ladies and gentlemen, the University of Jena theology faculty will join the *Bibelgesellschaft*."

The students erupted in cheers. Katharina hugged Georg and then sought out Horst and extended her hand. Horst had a big grin on his face as they shook hands.

"If all of you would come back inside?" Dr. Gerhard waved Kircher and Green through the door. "We're going to need some Calvinists. I think we should start with the University of Basel."

CHAPTER 4: NOW HIRING

The rest of the *Bibelgesellschaft* mission went very well. As soon as the team returned to Grantville, Hjalmar and Ditmar told Neustatter that the SoTF National Guard had sent the men's annual training orders. They wanted NESS for June's Eagle Pepper exercise.

The men reported for duty on Friday, June 16 and stayed through Monday, June 26. That left Astrid running NESS for ten days. Most of that was sitting in the office and occasionally explaining to potential clients that Neustatter and the men would not be available until they finished helping with the current basic training cycle. Astrid started another letter to Pastor Claussen. Anna wrote to her family. She had started walking the short distance to the livery stable most afternoons to brush the horses.

The USE had expanded during and after the Baltic War. The Congress of Copenhagen had created entire provinces. Most were *some assembly required*, as the up-time expression went. But the beginnings of industry were starting to spread, and soon NESS had a contract to guard a shipment of machine tools to Frankfurt that summer. It would take at least three weeks, which was going to be lucrative for NESS. The clients were actually a group of businesses which could split NESS's fee.

NESS was doing well as a business. But Astrid realized she was going to bed exhausted. She thought about that the next day, and realized it had nothing to do with NESS. She was spending a lot of time chasing after Johann after work. Ursula was five or six months along, and, although she insisted otherwise, not really able to keep up with an eight-year-old boy.

Astrid rethought her tactics. Johann had been a handful when they lived in the village. Since they'd come to Grantville, he'd been a pretty good kid most of the time, becoming a handful again only recently. Ursula tended to ascribe it to Stefan being gone more. But the longer Astrid thought about it, the more she thought there was more to it than that. Certainly, there had been a change in Johann's behavior since Stefan had come back from the war, but Stefan and the rest of the men had been gone for days at a time since the beginning of spring. *Nein,* this had more to do with *summer vacation.* Johann had a lot of time on his hands.

At dinner that evening, Astrid asked him, "Johann, do the friends you met in Spring Branch and Murphyhausen still live in Grantville?"

"*Ja!* Hans and Fritz live in different places now. Josef still lives in the same place, but it's not the refugee housing. It's down the road."

"Were they in your class at school?"

"*Ja,* of course."

"And school is out . . . Johann, what do Hans and Fritz and Josef do during the summer?"

"Josef plays baseball!"

Aha! "He plays baseball?"

"*Ja,* he is on a team."

"How does that work? Not baseball," Astrid hastened to add. "How does being on a team work?"

Johann enthusiastically explained. Astrid learned all about T-ball and summer leagues and how it all worked. After Johann went to bed, she asked Ursula about it.

"*Ja,* sure, it would be good for him—if we could afford the equipment, and if we had a way to take him to the games."

"What if I found a way?"

Ursula shrugged.

The next day at work Astrid decided that as long as they had a phone, she might as well use it. It took a while, but she learned that the first *season* ended in July, and then there would be a second season in July and August. She also learned about fundraising and sponsorships and team names.

Anna was at loose ends—she often went to visit the horses—and readily agreed to watch the office the next day. Astrid volunteered to watch Johann for the day. She had an idea, and she figured Neustatter was either going to like it, or he was going to think she was crazy.

"Johann, if we go over to Murphyhausen, do you think you can find Josef's house from there?"

"*Ja,* I sure can! But let's go to the refugee housing where we lived at first."

Astrid discovered that Josef lived in Spring Branch, which seemed even more crowded than before. Johann found Josef's house with ease, leading her to believe that he and his friends had ranged over a much larger area than the adults had been aware of.

Johann knocked on the door. It opened moments later.

"Johann!" a dark-haired boy exclaimed. Astrid figured he must be Josef.

Josef's mother was only steps behind him.

"Can I help you? Oh, *gut morgen,* Johann." She looked up at Astrid. "Are you his mother?"

"*Nein. I bin* Astrid Schäubin. I come from the same village as Johann and his parents. Do you have a few minutes? I would like to ask you about the baseball league."

Frau Forster was only too happy to enlighten her. "Josef is a very good player. He is the *shortstop*."

By the end of the conversation, Astrid understood they simply needed a way to get Johann to *practice* and to games—and that the person she wanted to talk to about this was not Stefan or Ursula, but Neustatter.

※ ※ ※

NESS ran into another problem that was not nearly as easy to fix. The first Sunday the men were on annual training was also the first Sunday after they had returned from the *Bibelgesellschaft* meetings in Jena. Astrid saw the dark looks that Pastor Holz and a few others were giving her, Anna, and Ursula.

"Was it like this last Sunday, too?" Astrid whispered to Anna.

"*Ja.*"

After the service, as they were filing out, Pastor Holz took them aside.

"You should warn your men they are treading dangerously, dealing with heretics."

Anna cringed. Astrid grasped for something to say, but Ursula beat her to it.

"If you have something to say to Stefan, tell him yourself, Pastor." After the briefest of pauses, she added, "*Guten Tag.*"

Once they were safely outside and on our way home, Astrid gave Ursula an inquiring look.

"I have not decided if our men acted wisely or foolishly," Ursula declared, "but if you have a problem with a man, go to him directly. Not through his wife."

Tuesday, June 27, 1634

After the men returned from their National Guard training and had a day to get some sleep, Neustatter sat down with Astrid in the office to go over the books and upcoming missions.

"*Gut*," he pronounced. "We have enough money to start hiring additional agents."

"How many?" Astrid asked.

"Four, I think. We will need a weapon for each, of course."

Neustatter allowed himself to lean back in his chair. "The SoTF National Guard has changed Basic training some since last summer, based on lessons learned in the Baltic War. Eagle Pepper—you are more likely to hear it called *Adler Pfeffer* these days—is a lot more . . . professional, I guess I would say. It is not that we were *goofing off* last year, but actual war changes things. Everyone from the drill sergeants on down took it more seriously. Us, too. We still broke *Adler Pfeffer*. But not to prove we could win. To train what we would do to an actual enemy. They have begun teaching MOSS MOUSE, a way to remember the principles of war, even to enlisted men, on the grounds that anyone could find himself in a key position. The two great heroes of the Battle of Ahrensbök—Engler and Hartmann—were both sergeants at the time, so it is not hard to see why."

Astrid nodded. That made sense, even though she was not familiar with the specifics.

"We are going to do *Adler Pfeffer* again in August," Neustatter continued. "By then some veterans of Ahrensbök will rotate to Camp Saale. The training will be the best yet. Quite a few of the recruits we have trained with are very promising. A lot of them are now active duty, of course. But there are a couple Reservists I want to visit in the next few days."

"You are telling me this because you met recruits you want to hire."

"*Ja.* One of them is a Jakob Bracht. He was in our recruit class last year. I think he has been in some tough places in life."

"Do you think he needs another chance?" Astrid was skeptical.

"*Nein.* I think he took his other chance when he joined the SoTF National Guard. But he is in the Reserves, and he is doing day labor the rest of the time. There is another man, Gottlieb Seidelman, who would be a good addition, too."

"And the other two?"

"I think we are going to have to *advertise.*"

Astrid had her doubts about that, but they placed classified ads in the *Times*, the *Freie Presse*, and the *Daily News*.

Tuesday, July 4, 1634

All of them went into Grantville on July 4. It was the up-timers' Independence Day, but most of them just called it the Fourth of July. They had held a parade in 1631, just a little over a month after the Ring of Fire, and now it was what everyone expected. There were flags everywhere—the new USE flag, the SoTF flag, and the up-time American flag. Grantville was crowded. A lot of people had chosen the Fourth of July to visit. Some came for the tech fair. The regular fair—the agricultural one—would be later in the summer. At night there would be fireworks.

Most of all, there was food. Up-timers—*Americans*, Astrid corrected herself, because it might not have been the same in other up-time countries—had specific foods they ate outside in summer. *Hamburgers, hot dogs, barbecue, potato salad* . . . She'd had some of these before. They ate a little here and a little there, and it all added up to a lot.

At the same time, they were walking around Grantville in uniform. Their uniforms were not anything more than tan shirts and trousers (or skorts in Astrid's case), with *halstücher* and hats. But it was enough. Passersby frequently greeted Neustatter.

Some of the other companies were doing the same thing. They saw men from Bretagne's Company and men from Schlinck's Company, even a few Hibernians.

"Some of Schlinck's men are *trash talking*," Ditmar reported when they all met up near the town square.

"Have your team keep an eye on each other. Do not talk back. Not today. But if they follow one of you, the other two trail their guys and involve the *polizei* sooner rather than later," Neustatter directed.

Astrid tried to watch passersby carefully, but there were so many people in downtown Grantville that it was difficult. She certainly noticed that the same group of four of Schlinck's men kept crossing paths with them. She spotted other people more than once, too. One was a striking dark-haired woman who reminded her of Anna, enough so that she did not focus on the man or the two children with her. For a while, Astrid was not sure *why* she reminded her of Anna. Her hair was dark, shorter (but still long), and styled differently. Her face was nothing like Anna's. The third time Astrid saw her, she realized it was her clothes. Unless she was very mistaken, the woman came from peasant stock. Her clothes were simple but well-made, and she had added some color here and there. *That* was what reminded Astrid of Anna. Leigh Ann would say that she knew how to *accessorize*.

The two children—a boy and a girl—also wore simple but neat clothing with small touches of color. The man wore standard workman's clothes.

"What do you see?" Neustatter spoke quietly, which he did not do often.

"She sews like Anna. They are what the up-timers call *working class* but could be mistaken for *middle class*."

"Interesting. We keep crossing paths, and it is the husband who is choosing their way." Neustatter studied the family.

The man returned his gaze.

"Do you want me to intercept the wife?" Astrid asked.

"*Nein.*" Neustatter turned and scanned the crowd. He quickly caught Wolfram's eye.

"You want me at the interview," Astrid realized.

The man approached them near the middle school.

"*Guten Tag.*" He paused and seemed to gather his words. "*I bin* Phillip Pfeffer. I know you are *Herr* Neustatter."

Astrid smiled. It was always funny when someone called Neustatter *herr*.

"I heard you might be hiring."

"We are. Are you looking for work, *Herr* Pfeffer?"

"*Ja.*" He glanced downward and generally seemed uncomfortable with that answer. Very stiffly, as if he were resisting the urge to turn and point out his family, he added, "I have been taking day labor jobs in Grantville for two years now. I am looking for something steady."

Neustatter was nodding slowly. "What are your skills?"

"I can farm. Quite well." Pfeffer shrugged. "But I cannot buy a farm or buy into an arrangement inside the Ring of Fire. Outside the Ring . . . I have asked to join several *gemeinde*, but they choose people they know, and it is hard to fault them for that. I take day labor jobs with villages around the Ring as often as I can, to make myself known to them."

Neustatter was still nodding. Pfeffer was doing everything right. It just had not worked out for him.

"Have you tried the Army or the National Guard?" Neustatter asked.

"I looked into it," Pfeffer answered. "I have my wife and children and my parents. If I enlisted, all of my pay would not be enough to keep them in Grantville. I want my children in school, and my parents near Leahy."

That was . . . a really good reason, Astrid thought.

"Ever been in a fight?"

"*Ja*, a few."

"I will not say *ja* or *nein* today." Neustatter handed him a business card. "Our office is on Route 250, out past the high school. Come see me tomorrow."

"*Danke, Herr* Neustatter."

Pfeffer excused himself and collected his family.

Neustatter raised an eyebrow as Wolfram and Anna joined him and Astrid.

"I like Agathe," Anna pronounced.

Johann darted up before anyone could say more.

"There's a fight!" he blurted out. "Well, there will be. Ditmar's team."

"Take us there," Neustatter directed.

Johann sped off down the road, across the bridge, and toward the post office. A crowd had gathered, leaving open space in the middle. Ditmar, Stefan, and Lukas were facing off against half a dozen men.

Neustatter pocketed his *halstuch* and motioned for Wolfram and Astrid to do the same.

"I said you're a coward!" one of the men roared at Ditmar.

Ditmar eyed the man's non-descript clothing, boots, buff coat, and hat. He saw no indication of rank or unit anywhere. "You talk a lot," he told the man.

"We are going show you who the toughest mercenaries are!"

"Six of you. Three of us. Does that make you tough?" Ditmar asked.

"I am going to . . ."

Neustatter eased out of the crowd behind the men and stepped up between two of them. He threw his arms around the shoulders of both and put all his weight on them.

"Looks like a fight." His tone was cheerful.

One of the men tried to shove him away. Neustatter clung to him all the harder. Then the pushing and shoving started.

Wolfram pushed out of the crowd and stepped up to another of the men confronting Ditmar's team.

"Three and three," Ditmar told their leader. "Now you look a lot tougher."

They did not appear to want a fair fight. But then a couple more showed up.

"What is going on here?" the first demanded. He shoved a couple observers out of his way. "This is . . ."

"As far as you are going." Astrid stepped in front of him and put her hands on her hips. She did not draw. Yet.

He was a lot bigger than she, but he paused long enough to consider that. His partner, a thin, wiry man, did not. A small bludgeon appeared in his hand, and he gave Astrid a wide berth as he bore down on Neustatter.

He did not see the man who tripped him. He sprawled on the pavement, and the new arrival grabbed one of the men wrestling with Neustatter by the back of the collar. Astrid was exchanging glares with the man she had stopped and did not have time to look. But she heard someone hit the ground.

"I am going to take that gun away from you," her opponent told her. He drew a knife.

Voices in the crowd contributed helpful advice about taking knives to gunfights.

"Break it up! Break it up!" came an authoritative voice.

"*Polizei*." Neustatter's voice carried over the crowd. "NESS, collapse into formation."

Astrid knew what Neustatter meant, so she backed up a few steps. Her opponent's knife disappeared as if by magic.

MISSIONS OF SECURITY

Officer Estes Frost wanted to arrest everyone, but the crowd was giving him an earful. Astrid was standing between Neustatter and Wolfram, back-to-back with Ditmar, Stefan, and Lukas. Then she realized there was someone else on the other side of Wolfram. She caught a glimpse of workman's clothes and thought it was probably Phillip Pfeffer.

"Does everyone have eyes on your families?" Neustatter asked. He was not looking for them. He had locked eyes with the nearest opponent and was very deliberately tying his *halstuch* around his neck.

Astrid realized what he intended and started doing the same.

"*Ja*," came Stefan's voice.

"*Ja*," Wolfram said.

"*Ja*." That was definitely Phillip Pfeffer's voice.

One of the men who had been confronting Ditmar's team was quick-witted. He followed Phillip's gaze and quickly spotted his family.

"It would be a shame if anything happened to your fam—"

Officer Frost was right there. Or rather, his nightstick was. He deftly placed it alongside the man's jaw and turned the man's head to face him. Astrid noticed a scar just above the nightstick and wondered if the man had been hit with one before.

"I do not like threats. There had better not *be* threats. You do not know what anyone's family looks like or where they live or work. Is that understood?"

The man swallowed, considered his options, and muttered agreement.

Estes Frost turned toward NESS. "You, too."

"No idea who they were or where they were going next, Officer," Neustatter belted out.

The way he said it told Astrid that Neustatter knew exactly who these men were—and that made them mercenaries from Schlinck's Company, of course. She did not know if Officer Frost realized that.

"Everybody, clear out."

Officer Frost sent them off in separate directions. NESS ended up on Buffalo Street, headed in the general direction of Spring Branch and Murphyhausen.

"Is everyone okay?"

When they had assured Neustatter they were all fine, he asked, "What would everyone like to see in Grantville today?"

Everyone exchanged glances.

"I am sure there must be something at the fairgrounds."

Astrid watched Anna and Phillip Pfeffer's wife Agathe walking along, already deep in conversation. Johann had just as obviously already introduced himself to the Pfeffers' son, who looked about his age. Astrid had to look around for Neustatter. He was trailing along behind everyone else, talking with Ditmar and Lukas in low tones. The two of them broke away and crossed the Marshall Street bridge.

Asking Neustatter what he had sent them to do would just call attention to them. Besides, Astrid was pretty sure what the answer was: find Hjalmar's team. She was a little worried for her brother, but not much. After all, Ditmar and his team had been holding their own, and she was certain that Officer Frost would have radioed Mimi Rowland. All the *polizei* would be watching for trouble.

Neustatter sought her out next. "You already know they were Schlinck's men."

"*Ja.* If you were not sure of that, you would have said more to Officer Frost."

"*Ja.* Describe each of the men you saw," Neustatter directed.

Astrid did so.

"Write it down when we get home. I will send the men to describe the ones they saw."

"You want me to build files," Astrid said.

Neustatter gave her a sharp, quick nod. Then he changed the subject.

"What do you think of Pfeffer?"

"I think you should hire him. Anna and Johann obviously think so, too."

"I will give everyone a chance to object, but I think that is what I will do." Neustatter was quiet for a minute. "Schlinck may have helped us today. Others saw the confrontation. You did well. All of us did."

"I do not know about that, Neustatter," Astrid told him. "The big man was within twenty-one feet. If he lunged, I was going to have to try to shoot him."

Neustatter nodded. "True. But, Miss Schäubin, why do you suppose a man twice your size felt he needed to pull a knife on you?"

Huh.

❉ ❉ ❉

Something was certainly happening in Hough Park. Long rows of tables and other displays stretched across the playing field between the community center and the fairgrounds.

They wandered over.

"Cool!" Johann and the Pfeffer boy exclaimed together.

The tables displayed mechanical devices. Some were obviously kitchen appliances, and some others placed next to them probably were as well. Astrid saw what she thought was a radio. At least it looked like a larger version of what *polizei* officers had on their shoulders. Another was a *record player*. She had seen those before. She had no idea what some of the other items were, but as she looked more closely, Astrid realized that often a single up-time item was paired with newly made . . . not copies, exactly . . . versions that could be made now.

"Where are the guards?" Neustatter muttered.

They looked around.

"*Polizei* over near the *parking lot*." Stefan said it without pointing or staring.

"Looks like he has just broken something up," Neustatter remarked. "Wolfram, Miss Schäubin, wander over. Be useful if the officer needs help."

As Wolfram and Astrid strode away toward the community center and parking lot, Astrid heard Neustatter giving the kids directions. "Look for anyone taking something that does not belong to them."

They were almost to the *polizei* officer when they heard shouting behind them. Astrid turned just in time to see Neustatter lay a man out with a right to the jaw.

"Officer! Officer!" she called. "Over there!"

"We have these two!" Wolfram shouted.

The officer glanced back and forth and then hurried toward disturbance at the technology displays. One of the two men he had separated immediately bolted.

"Mine!" Wolfram accelerated after him.

Wolfram was not as big as Karl, but he was not a small man, either. Astrid heard the impact. But she was looking at the other man, hands on her hips again.

She tapped the butt of her pistol. "Sit. Down."

He did.

Wolfram herded the other man back.

"What is this all about?" Wolfram demanded.

"He shoved me!"

"*Nicht.*" *Did not.*

Both men glanced across at whatever was going on at the technology display tables. They should not have. From watching Johann and his friends, Astrid knew the correct response was *Auch gemacht. Did too.* It certainly was not to get distracted.

"How much did he pay you to be the distraction?" Astrid asked.

Two mouths dropped open.

"Guilty consciences?" Wolfram asked. "Let us go for a walk."

Astrid and Wolfram took the two of them over to the *polizei* officer. He had just finished handcuffing the man Neustatter had punched.

"I think that was just a fight," the officer told them. "I wasn't going to book them."

"We think you should search them. See if they each have an equal amount of money," Astrid said.

"Ooohhhhh . . . Well, men?"

At the officer's prompt, both of them emptied their purses. Each had a handful of various change, a couple crumpled bucks, and a crisp USE twenty-dollar bill.

"Where did you get those?" the officer asked.

Two sets of eyes cut toward the handcuffed man.

"Guess I'll check your purse, too."

The officer found $160 in new twenty-dollar bills.

"Half up front, half on delivery, right?" Neustatter asked.

The prisoner started. He did not *say* anything, but they all saw it was so.

The officer spoke into the radio on his shoulder. "Dispatch, patrol eight. Three to transport. And, uh, call Schmidt."

* * *

The *polizei* took statements. By the time they were done, Ditmar, Lukas, and Hjalmar's team showed up.

"It sounds like we missed all the excitement," Hjalmar commented.

"We will bring you *up to speed*," Neustatter promised. "First, though, dinner."

They split up and bought food from any number of booths set up in Hough Park and in the fairgrounds. By the time they had eaten and exchanged stories, it was almost time for the fireworks.

Light blossomed in the sky, and a loud explosion rolled across the fairgrounds. The next one threw colored bits of light—embers, perhaps?— out in a circle. The next one was a different color. Some of them even tried to scatter the lights in patterns.

According to the up-timers, these were fairly primitive compared to what they remembered. Astrid considered what a sight up-time fireworks displays must have been. So much gunpowder and so many chemicals, just for fun. Maybe that was why only one town was permitted to come to their time.

The fireworks were thoroughly enjoyable. Astrid was not thinking about NESS business at all as they walked home. They dropped the Pfeffers off at their apartment and went back to our own. Neustatter took a couple of the men to check on the office. But everything was fine.

Then Astrid discovered Neustatter's other reason for checking the office. He had brought paper and ink. Astrid started writing down everyone's recollections of Schlinck's men.

Wednesday, July 5, 1634

NESS was very busy the next day. Astrid worked on a file for each of Schlinck's men. Ditmar and Karl went to the livery stable to make sure NESS's timeshare horses were still available for the upcoming mission to Schleusingen. Neustatter, Stefan, and Johann were talking about baseball.

MISSIONS OF SECURITY

That actually *was* business, because Astrid had convinced Neustatter that one of the best ways to advertise NESS would be to sponsor a baseball team. Instead of a few weeks of classified ads, little kids would be running around in team jerseys with the team name "NESS Agents."

The phone kept ringing, and it still startled Astrid every time. Most of the calls were men looking for work. A couple were businesses looking for a security service.

Phillip Pfeffer arrived for his interview. Neustatter kicked out everyone except Ditmar, Hjalmar, and Astrid. They all took chairs near the Franklin stove. It was not lit in July, of course, but it got them away from the desks.

"I was going to start out by explaining what you would be getting into," Neustatter began. "But I think yesterday you found that out. That is, what, our fifth fight in a year and two months." He stopped and thought a moment. "*Ja*, fifth. Three of them have been with Schlinck's men. But that does not mean that the next mission cannot turn into a firefight. You handled yourself well in the brawl. How are you with firearms?"

"I have brought down small game."

"I would spend quite a bit of time on the range with you," Neustatter assured him.

Phillip nodded. Astrid thought he looked relieved.

"All of us currently at NESS came from the same village," Neustatter explained. "We live together. Well, in two adjacent apartments—although I suspect that may need to change soon. So far, we set aside money for NESS's expenses, then we have bought food and other things we need, and given everyone a relatively small amount of spending money. I do not mind adding more partners to the current arrangement, nor do I object to switching to individual shares. Or some of each. What are your thoughts on this?"

Phillip was sitting very straight in his chair. "My main concern is for my family to be able to live in the Grantville area, close to the schools and Leahy Medical Center. I have to be able to pay for that."

Neustatter nodded. "As long as NESS is making money, I would give you your share, however we work that out.

"We are often away on missions. Usually these are a few days to a couple weeks, but we have one coming up that will be about a month. Is that something you can do?"

"*Ja.*"

"All right. I will talk it over with the rest of NESS and contact you tomorrow," Neustatter told him.

After dinner that evening, Neustatter asked for everyone's attention.

"We have been running NESS a certain way, sharing the profits," he began. "It is time to hire more agents, and they may not want to be part of that arrangement. We could include them in the food and common supplies and pay them a share of what is left. Or if they do not want to be included in that, pay them a larger share."

"If we are hiring," Stefan ventured, "I say we start with Pfeffer. He is a good man in a brawl."

"*Ja,*" Karl agreed.

Neustatter checked with each of them, and they voted unanimously for Phillip Pfeffer.

"Phillip has a wife, two children, and two parents," Neustatter stated. "He obviously wants to provide for them."

Heads nodded right away. None of them could really explain economic theory, but anyone who grew up in a German village could explain reality. Nine of them were NESS agents. Ursula and Anna's cooking, cleaning, and sewing enabled the rest of them to do what they did. Johann was the only one who did not have a job.

If they added Pfeffer, then they had to provide for five more people, too. They did not want to not add them, but there was a limit to how many times they could do this.

"Neustatter," Anna asked, "are you still planning to hire four men?"

"*Ja.*"

"Two of us run the apartments for nine of you," she pointed out. "If there will be thirteen of you, we need one more, too. Especially since Ursula and I are expecting. Hire Agathe, too. That gives the Pfeffers two shares."

"I like it," Neustatter pronounced.

So did everyone else.

Thursday, July 6, 1634

In the morning, Neustatter and Astrid went to the Pfeffers' apartment. It was south of Route 250, between the Church of Christ and Buffalo Creek, more or less across from the Grantville cemetery.

"Come in, *bitte*," Agathe urged.

They were introduced to Phillip's parents.

"*Herr* Pfeffer. *Frau* Pfeffer," Neustatter greeted them.

Phillip's elderly father shook hands firmly. He was a little stooped but appeared to be in good health.

"I cannot get used to being called *herr*," he said. "I am not sure what to think of it."

Phillip's mother was a short, grandmotherly type. With a twinkle in her eye, she said, "If everyone is a *herr* or a *frau*, how does anything get done? It seems to me that if everyone is noble, then no one is."

"Ah, but it is easier to give it to everyone than to take it away from the few who already were," her husband said.

Astrid smiled politely, then took a moment and realized it was true. She hadn't heard it said quite that bluntly before. Phillip might be concerned about his parents' physical health, but clearly there was nothing wrong with their minds.

Then she realized the Pfeffers were waiting expectantly.

"Phillip, I would like to offer you a job as a NESS agent," Neustatter told him. "And Agathe, I know you have your own home to take care of, but we would like to offer you a job, too, helping Ursula and Anna. Unless, of course, you would like to be an agent," he added quickly.

"*Ja* to the first, *nein* to the second." Agathe spoke just as quickly. "*Und* I cannot neglect our own household."

"We are perfectly capable to looking after ourselves for a few hours, dear," *Frau* Pfeffer declared.

After they left the Pfeffers, Neustatter told Astrid, "You are going to have to work out those finances."

"I know. At some point, Neustatter, you are going to need a second secretary."

"At some point," he agreed. "Right now, though, we should go find Jakob Bracht and Gottlieb Seidelman."

※ ※ ※

Gottlieb Seidelman lived in one of the many boardinghouses in Grantville. This one was right on Buffalo Street, one of the houses that Astrid had mistaken for *schlösser* the day they arrived in Grantville. It had a recent addition on what had been a side yard which was equal in size to the front part of the house. The builder had matched the overlaid boards on the exterior of the building.

MISSIONS OF SECURITY

Seidelman directed them to a parlor in the old part of the house. The couches and chairs were completely different from what Astrid had seen in the Hauns' home and appeared to be old and somewhat worn. She supposed they might have originated only two hundred sixty years in the future rather than three hundred sixty-some. But they seemed sturdy enough.

Seidelman politely listened to Neustatter.

"I wish I could, Neustatter, but I cannot. I am enrolling at the tech school. I have to take a job that will work with my class schedule."

"What program?" Neustatter asked.

"Applied Law. My family thinks I should try to be a lawyer, but I might apply to the *polizei*."

"You would be good at it," Neustatter told him.

Seidelman sighed. "Neustatter, I am going to take a job with Schlinck's Company. It is not personal. He can give me steady work on the *graveyard shift* at the tannery."

Neustatter simply nodded. "So they got the contract guarding prisoners?"

"*Ja.*"

"That will give you some good experience with what the up-timers call *the criminal justice system.*"

"It certainly will," Seidelman agreed. "I do not know what to think about sending common criminals to prison and then putting them on work crews."

"It is a technique," Neustatter allowed.

When they left a short time later, Astrid asked Neustatter, "What is this about Schlinck's Company guarding a tannery?"

Neustatter shrugged. "Grantville does not have enough prison space. Jail space, *ja*, for drunks and brawlers. But for men sentenced for a number of months or years . . . there simply is not space. At the same time,

Grantville needs a huge amount of leather. Think of how much we use. Only the most hard-up refugees will accept a job at a tannery, so someone realized that prisoners—prisoners of law rather than prisoners of war—could do the work. Prison was an attractive option for desperate men—"*three hots and a cot*," they called it. Now that they have to work in the tannery, there is no incentive to get arrested. There are road crews, too, for men sent to prison for lesser crimes."

"And Schlinck's Company?"

"The prison is right at the tannery. Someone has to guard it. Schlinck put in a bid and won."

"Why did you not put in a bid?" Astrid asked.

"I found out the requirements from the *polizei*. They wanted at least a dozen men on duty in each of three shifts, plus guards for the road crews. We would have had to make a joint bid."

"That would be nothing but trouble," Astrid stated. "Unless it was with Bretagne's Company."

"Captain Bretagne was not interested."

"You did not tell me this."

Neustatter thought. "I should have. I had decided not to bid on it and did not think about it again. But you are correct. I should tell you about jobs I turn down so that you can keep track of them."

"I should start a file on Seidelman."

Neustatter thought about that. "Hm. *Ja*. He is someone we could contact when there are tensions between NESS and Schlinck's Company. But do not leave that file in the office at night."

"Oh?"

"In how many mysteries does the detective's office get broken into?" Neustatter asked.

"A lot of them," Astrid answered. She thought it through. "We need a *briefcase*, because it would be just as bad to be seen carrying a file."

MISSIONS OF SECURITY

* * *

Jakob Bracht was much more amenable. Neustatter had tracked him down on a day labor job moving construction supplies. Bracht looked more than happy to take a few minutes to talk to them. He waved a hand, fingers spread, at the foreman. That man frowned but nodded. Astrid interpreted the conversation as "I need five minutes" and "Only five."

"I accept." He had not even bothered to find some place to sit down. Neustatter described how NESS worked.

"That is fine. I need the work."

"Do you have family?" Neustatter asked.

"Not here." Bracht's forthright manner seemed to vanish.

Neustatter remained quiet, and eventually Bracht said more. "I am unmarried, but I have family at home. I will send money to them."

"Naturally."

Neustatter waited a moment and then said, "Jakob, during Basic, it seemed to me that you might have been in some hard places in life."

Bracht stared out across the worksite. "True enough."

"Security consultants need to stay on the right side of the law. Mostly. The trick is knowing when."

"I would like to stay on the right side of the law," Bracht agreed.

"Have you seen any up-time detective movies?" Neustatter asked. "Or television shows. Either will do for this."

"*Nein.*"

Neustatter smiled. "Jakob, we need to watch some movies. Come see me after work Friday. NESS is on the left, past the high school."

* * *

Neustatter and Astrid, and sometimes Ditmar or Hjalmar, met with a couple dozen men over the next week. Most were responding to the help wanted classified ad. A few had seen the baseball team's jerseys. Johann, Willi Pfeffer, Josef Forster, and their teammates were certainly doing everything they could to publicize NESS.

Some applicants they could rule out right away. Others seemed promising. Neustatter asked them for references and sent Ditmar and Hjalmar to check those out. A few he followed up himself.

In the midst of this they found out that the mission to Frankfurt had been delayed. Friction had arisen among some of the businesses in Frankfurt and between them and the machine shops in Grantville. Some of the machine tools had already gone to the next buyers in line. Assuming they could work out their differences, the Frankfurt group would get the next available tools—which would push the mission into September.

A replacement mission showed up almost at once. Astrid heard a knock at the door, and Pastor Al Green entered.

"*Guten Morgen*, Miss Schäubin," he greeted her. "Doctor Gerhard has finished negotiations with the University of Erfurt, and the theology faculty has invited the *Bibelgesellschaft* to meet with them. In August."

Astrid blinked. "In August?" she repeated.

"Yes. The students were praying that NESS would be available."

"We had an August mission reschedule for September two days ago."

"Huh."

Astrid was not sure what to think about that. On the other hand, guarding the *Bibelgesellschaft* was a good mission. "I will talk to Neustatter, but I anticipate NESS will be able to take your mission. Will you be taking a wagon again?"

"I expect so," Green answered.

"Do you have specific dates? We can reserve horses."

MISSIONS OF SECURITY

* * *

Neustatter always asked Astrid's opinion after meeting with someone applying to be a NESS agent. After Reinhold Grötzinger left, Neustatter shut the door and resumed his seat in the semi-circle of chairs around the Franklin stove. He and Hjalmar both looked at Astrid.

"*Nein*," she said at once.

"Why?" Neustatter asked.

"He spent half the time asking about promotion and the other half looking at me."

"Eh. More like a quarter each," Neustatter allowed.

"The new men will give you the opportunity for a third team," Astrid pointed out. "But you are not going to put them all together and make one the team leader, are you?"

"Who do you think I should make the team leader?" Neustatter sounded genuinely interested.

"Otto could do it if he decided to. Wolfram is a specialist. Karl is, too, really. Stefan would not want to. Lukas should not." She knew Neustatter and Hjalmar would appreciate blunt honesty.

They exchanged glances.

"Not too surprising that my sister has the same thoughts I do," Hjalmar remarked.

"Some of the same thoughts," Neustatter clarified. "You both read our men the same way, and I agree with you on all of them. But what did you think of Grötzinger, Hjalmar?"

"He sounded like he knows how to guard someone or something. He *is* ambitious, although I do not know if that would be a problem. *Und* I agree he kept looking over at Astrid. It is not *that* he looks. It is *how* he looks."

"I trust all you men," Astrid said. "None of you look at me like that. Not even Lukas, because all of us from the village are family. If I were a tavern maid somewhere, I might *not* trust Lukas." She stopped short. "I am sorry. I spoke out of turn."

"You never need to apologize for accuracy," Neustatter responded. He stood and began pacing back and forth across the office. "We do need a third team, and I think I will lead it myself, at least at first. Miss Schäubin, I think you will be on my team."

Both Hjalmar and Astrid looked at Neustatter in surprise.

"Hjalmar, I need you to run your team in a fight, not protect your sister. Especially since I am going to give you one of the new men to train." He paced some more. "That is not criticism, Hjalmar. If I had a sister who was an agent, I would not leave her on my own team after her initial training." More pacing. "I think I will take Karl and put Wolfram on your team."

Astrid worked it out. Neustatter would want a couple men from the village on his team, men who could handle themselves which he ran all of NESS. He would put at least one of the new men on each team. If Neustatter had two men from the village and her and a new agent, that meant he was putting Wolfram on Hjalmar's team because Ditmar was getting two of the new agents.

"Who are you pulling from Ditmar's team?" Astrid saw Hjalmar smiling in approval at her question, but it was not that hard to work out. Neustatter's new team had five agents to the other teams' four because in a sense both he and Astrid would be *part-time* on that team.

"Lukas. *Und* Grötzinger is a *no-go*," Neustatter continued. He returned to his chair.

"We will see him again, working for one of the other companies," Hjalmar predicted.

"If he fits somewhere else, then he fits somewhere else. We have many options. Who do you recommend, Hjalmar?"

Hjalmar's brow furrowed, and he thought about it for some time. "Deibert."

"Why?"

"He told us what he knew and what he did not. Well, he tried. He was mistaken about a couple things, but he was honest with us. He had experience in his town militia, and he has actually been in a couple battles. Including Grantville."

"That is a good point," Astrid agreed. "NESS would benefit from having a veteran of the Croat Raid."

"Okay. Who else?"

"Ditmar would tell you Richart Stroh," Hjalmar answered. "He is a harder man than, say, Phillip Pfeffer. Not mean. Just unyielding. I think he would keep Bracht in line if Jakob started to stray. I have no problem with that. I think you are going to have to teach him when to step back."

Astrid could see that. For all that Ditmar and Hjalmar looked enough alike to be brothers, they were not the same. Her brother was more *easygoing*, as the up-timers put it.

"Miss Schäubin?"

"I think Stroh would fit right in on Ditmar's team."

"I agree. What if I put both Stroh and Deibert on Team One? Hjalmar, you get Jakob Bracht."

"Not Pfeffer?"

"*Nein.* You do not need two of Otto."

Hjalmar frowned and looked at Astrid. She shrugged.

"Ottos are useful," Neustatter went on. "You cannot have both of them. Besides, you will be a good influence on Jakob."

The three of them were still seated around the stove when Ditmar came in a little later and told Neustatter he had found something. When asked about the applicants, he indeed recommended Stroh.

"Ask Anna if she and Agathe would be willing to buy enough cloth for four more *halstücher, bitte*," Neustatter requested.

"I can go with them," Astrid offered. She started to rise.

"*Nein*. Ditmar can ask them. I need you here, Miss Schäubin, because what Ditmar found is a weapon for sale. How much can we afford to spend on weapons?"

She frowned. "Not a lot. But cheap weapons are . . ."

"Usually garbage," Neustatter finished with her.

"How much is the weapon?"

Neustatter told her, and Astrid winced.

"What is it?"

"An up-time shotgun. 16 gauge. Not as powerful as a 12 gauge, but easier to handle. And it is an over/under."

"Sixteen is less powerful than twelve?" Astrid wanted to be sure she understood.

"Gauge is how many lead balls of that size weigh one pound."

Astrid shook her head. "That is the silliest up-time measurement I have ever heard! Why cannot shotguns have caliber?"

"The .410 does," Neustatter told her. "The rest use gauge."

"You are sure this is not just up-timers *messing with us*?"

"Check the library."

"*Nein dank*." She rose and retrieved the ledger from her desk. She took a deep breath and extended it to her boss. "Neustatter, we have this much money."

"Oh, we have less than that," he assured her. "We are going to have to pay the new men ourselves for the Schleusingen to Erfurt mission. We cannot charge the Strategic Resources Board for agents who are still in training."

"You are right, of course." Astrid sighed because she had done the math. Four weapons like that shotgun, plus paying the new men, and NESS would be nearly out of cash.

"Pistols cost less," Neustatter pointed out. "Pistols in Suhl, Schleusingen, and Schmalkalden cost less than the same pistols in Grantville."

"How much less?"

They went over the numbers and arrived at an almost-reasonable solution. They could have done it less expensively, but Neustatter did not want .32s or .36s.

"*Nein*, if we have to buy cap-and-ball revolvers, I want something that is going to hit hard enough to put the target down. .40s. I would rather have .44s."

"We cannot afford that. We have to leave money set aside for Ursula and Anna's medical expenses."

"We do," Neustatter agreed.

On Friday, July 14, Neustatter and Ditmar told Deibert and Stroh they were hired—and that they would start training on Monday with their first mission later that week.

Anna and Agathe bought cloth, and by Monday they had made four new *halstücher*. Anna had requested enough money to include cloth for a flag, too, and began work on it.

Monday, July 17. 1634

On Monday, all nine agents from the village had assembled out front of the NESS office by the time the new men arrived at eight in the morning.

"Atten*tion*!" Neustatter ordered. "Present *arms*!"

All nine agents saluted crisply.

Jakob Bracht returned the salute with equal polish. Phillip Pfeffer was a moment behind him and made all the same mistakes Astrid had made yesterday when Hjalmar and Neustatter had taught her how to salute. Richart Stroh and Johann Deibert were slower but realized what they were supposed to do.

"Welcome to Neustatter's European Security Services. *I bin* Edgar Neustatter. At ease. This is not the USE Army or the SoTF National Guard. I have no need to keep you mentally off-balance and occupied with busywork every minute just so that you do not get into trouble. We leave Wednesday for a week-long mission, so there is more than enough legitimate work to do.

"Look, I do not disagree with how the up-timers set up basic training," Neustatter continued. "If you have a handful of drill sergeants, a couple hundred recruits, and limited time, you almost have to do it that way. But with nine of us and four of you, it makes no sense. We will adopt what is useful to us and leave the rest."

When heads nodded, he continued. "*Ja*, it should be just the leader of a formation who salutes. *Ja*, the lower-ranking should salute first, and that is you for now. I think that is the first time NESS has ever saluted. We do not do so on a mission, because that just shows everyone around who the leaders are. Just know how to do it if we end up at some formal occasion someday.

"Now, something more important. Ditmar Schaub"—Neustatter pointed—"leads Team One. That will be Stefan, Hans, and Richart. Hjalmar Schaub leads Team Two. Otto, Jakob, and Wolfram. I lead Team Three. Karl, Lukas, Astrid, and Phillip.

"We will start with two teams protecting their principals. Those are our clients. Phillip and Astrid, that is you. Teams One and Two have the bodyguard assignment. Take a couple minutes and get set up. Karl, Lukas, and I will be the attackers." Neustatter grinned. "No weapons."

Ditmar put his team around Phillip and Astrid in a diamond formation. Otto was drifting off to one side, Hjalmar and Jakob were out ahead, and Wolfram was trailing behind the others. They moved slowly across the gravel lot in front the NESS office. Hjalmar and Jakob had passed the end of the building, and the central group was in front of the writing supply store next to NESS when Karl stepped out from behind the western edge of the building. Hjalmar and Jakob moved to intercept him, but soon had their hands full. Neustatter and Lukas appeared next, moving straight for Phillip and Astrid. Stefan and Hans moved to block Lukas, while Ditmar and Richart tried to stop Neustatter.

Lukas quickly stiff-armed Hans Deibert aside, and then Stefan reached for him. The two grappled, but Lukas was a decade younger. He forced Stefan back.

Ditmar prepared to intercept Neustatter. Richart was on his left and was bigger than Neustatter. But Neustatter dove right, surprising Richart. Neustatter came up out of the shoulder roll. Richart spun after him, getting in Ditmar's way. Neustatter dashed over to Phillip and Astrid, tapping each in a shoulder with a closed fist. Then Ditmar tackled him.

Neustatter gave a sharp whistle and got to his feet. "Bring it in!"

Once everyone was gathered, he let each of them comment.

"We should probably move off the gravel," Astrid suggested.

"Not a bad idea," Neustatter agreed. "Now, how should you stop me next time . . . ?"

They ran through three more scenarios before Johann showed up. He watched wide-eyed. That time, Neustatter's five defenders successfully held off seven attackers. When he asked for comments, Johann's hand shot up.

"It's adult Cowboys and Croats!" the eight-year-old proclaimed.

"Also not a bad idea," Neustatter said. "Teams Two and Three, let us go get the horses."

By afternoon, NESS was running drills with the four timeshare houses and a carriage drawn by another pair. They were using weapons now, but shouting Bang! Gunfire tended to alarm both horses and neighbors.

Astrid was not the only one who noticed that they had skipped lunch. Since on missions Neustatter made sure they ate and slept, she knew he was making them train through lunch for a reason—guarding clients or a shipment under adverse conditions. Hopefully he would quit before dark, and Astrid was reasonably sure Neustatter could not cause bad weather.

By dinner, they were exhausted. Neustatter called a halt and sent them all to the apartment where dinner was waiting. They lingered over dinner. Astrid realized this was part of the plan, too—team bonding.

Neustatter announced there would not be night training. The men were leaving on Wednesday for Schleusingen and eventually Erfurt. He wanted them alert, so they needed to sleep the next two nights.

Tuesday, July 18, 1634

Astrid was tired enough that she slept straight through the night. They were back at the office by eight in the morning. Well, they were back at the office by the time the second train from Grantville to Schwarza Station passed by, which was supposed to happen a few minutes before eight o'clock. The railroad was nothing if not punctual, so she assumed that train was on time.

"Circle up," Neustatter directed. "Tomorrow we leave on a mission. I am planning on ten days: two to Schleusingen, one to Suhl, one to Schmalkalden, two to Eisenach, two to Erfurt, and two back here to Grantville. We are guarding a shipment of goods, so you know that could turn into twelve or even fourteen days if we break wheels or axles. We are taking our horses. Plan on four men on the horses, four on the wagons, and four walking. Miss Schäubin will be staying here, because someone needs to keep the office open.

"After this mission, some of us will be escorting the *Bibelgesellschaft* to a meeting at the University of Erfurt. Then those of us in the National Guard will be helping with the next *Adler Pfeffer* exercise. We have another long-range mission coming up in September. This one is to Frankfurt. It will take three weeks, minimum. Wolfram and Stefan will be staying here with their wives. Miss Schäubin will be running the office, and I may leave one other agent here since the contract is for nine.

"Today, however, is range day."

The *polizei* had an indoor pistol range, but they certainly could not shoot rifles and the shotgun there. Instead they went to an outdoor range off Murphy's Run. Their eye and ear protection were probably not up to up-time standards, but Neustatter insisted that they be as safe as possible.

NESS started on the pistol range. Neustatter loaded his .45 with black powder rounds. Grantville still had up-time rounds, perhaps millions of them. But they were carefully conserved.

An older up-timer was waiting for them. He wore an up-time cap, a long-sleeved shirt, a vest with numerous pouches, work pants, and boots. A whistle dangled from a cord around his neck, and his gunbelt held what Astrid recognized as a semi-automatic pistol, although she did not know what kind.

"Hi, folks. I'm Thomas Jessup. The first time I shot a gun I was seven years old, and this is my seventieth year shooting. My job is to make sure y'all are safe and respect what you're doin'. I'm gonna go over the rules . . ."

Once they were all where they were supposed to be, Jessup carefully checked the range. "Ready on the right! Ready on the left! Ready in the center! Fire!"

Neustatter drew and fired six rounds one after the other. As far as Astrid could tell, they all hit the target.

"Cease fire!"

At the safety officer's signal, they all went forward to check Neustatter's target. Neustatter circled the holes—they would be using the same targets until they were literally shot apart. Neustatter's shots were all in the man-shaped silhouette.

"These four would have killed a man outright." Jessup indicated those. "These two would have put almost anyone down and out of the fight. Thing you got to remember is that you can do everything right, and every once in a while, the other guy just doesn't go down. He just keeps shooting back at you. It's got nothing to with whether he's right or wrong. So there is no shooting to wound. None of you are the Lone Ranger, not even Neustatter here."

Astrid did not know who that was and made a mental note to find out later.

"One other thing. Neustatter, I know why you're using brass reloaded with black powder in that .45. But it's not safe. You are using smokeless rounds from up-time when you're out on a job, right?"

"*Ja.*"

"Use black powder reloads as little as possible in a semi-automatic."

After six years, the men from the village knew how to shoot. Ditmar and Otto were particularly good with pistols.

"Miss Schäubin, you are next."

Astrid put a pair of shooting glasses on. She tried to remember everything she had been told about how to shoot, decided that was too much, and concentrated on her sight picture and breathing.

"Fire!"

MISSIONS OF SECURITY

She breathed out and squeezed the trigger slowly. The .22 fired. Astrid followed through, cocked it, fired again. She methodically emptied the revolver, then flipped the cylinder out.

"Cease fire!"

As they walked downrange, she hoped she'd done well. She was pretty sure the first two were in the middle of the silhouette. After that . . . She had probably scattered shots all over.

Neustatter studied her target and handed her the pen. "Not bad, Miss Schäubin, not bad at all."

Astrid circled her shots. Four were close to the center, inside the line that defined them as kill shots. Three more would have been the sort of wound that ought to be incapacitating, except when it wasn't.

"The head shot was just chance," she admitted.

Thomas Jessup shrugged. "Do enough things right, and you make your own luck." He pointed to the last two. "These two in the leg, though . . . Well, he definitely would not be running anywhere, but just those two shots would not necessarily prevent a man from returning fire.

"Phillip, you are next," Neustatter announced.

Pfeffer, Bracht, and Stroh were beginners with pistols. Astrid could see they were about where she had been a few months ago. Deibert, on the other hand, was a natural. He was better than Stefan or Lukas and almost as good as Karl.

Then they switched to the U.S. Waffenfabrik rifled muskets. Those were completely different. Astrid thought she was terrible with a rifle. All the loading steps kept her from concentrating on shooting, and whenever she paused to try to clear her head, she realized how heavy the ten-pound weapon was.

Most of the men shot better with a rifle than they did with a pistol. Ditmar was almost scary, especially when he switched to the .22 rifle. Otto and Deibert were the exceptions, shooting significantly better with a pistol.

Finally, they all fired the shotgun. That was so much easier to handle than a black powder rifle, but it kicked a lot more.

After that, Jessup declared the range cold, and they passed around the cleaning supplies. Astrid was not a fan of this. She understood why it was important to clean a weapon. She also understood Neustatter was teaching field cleaning, and they would be doing a more thorough cleaning when they got home. They did not have the near-magical up-time products they'd heard about, like Break-Free and WD-40, but they knew how to clean. Once they were finally done, Neustatter stood and got everyone's attention.

"Good shoot today. The only surprises were good ones. We will keep coming to the range and get better. I did not see anything that makes me want to change what weapons our experienced agents carry. New men, you will be starting out unarmed. That is not because I do not trust you. It is simply that we plan to buy most of the weapons you will be assigned once we get there."

"One of them can carry the .22," Astrid offered.

"*Nein*. That stays with you. Wear it to the office. Use the shoulder rig. It is fine to wear a gunbelt when a group of us are in town, but a lone person seen carrying would be anyone's first target."

Wednesday, July 19, 1634

The men set out bright and early. Hjalmar's team lead the way, followed by Neustatter's new Team Three atop the wagons carrying their loads of machine tools. Ditmar's team brought up the rear on horseback. NESS looked impressive. Marching through Grantville might mean more inquiries at the office, so as soon as they were out of sight, Astrid hurried back to the office.

MISSIONS OF SECURITY

Those left in Grantville quickly settled into a routine. Agathe Pfeffer would come over to the apartments at some point during the day. Someone—usually Agathe, Astrid, or both—would take Johann Heidenfelder and Willi Pfeffer to their baseball practices and games. Sometimes Willi's little sister Elisabetha would tag along, but more often she 'helped' with dinner. Astrid went to class in the evening. A couple times, Anna went with her to the high school. She spent the time talking to a researcher in the library but did not tell Astrid what it was about.

A few people made inquiries at the office, although Astrid talked to just as many while watching the kids play baseball. During quiet stretches in the office, Astrid wrote another letter to Pastor Claussen and sent it off.

The Volley Gun Regiment, which had played a key role in winning the Battle of Ahrensbök, passed by Grantville on its way south. The Ram Rebellion appeared to be settling into a standoff, and Mary Simpson, Veronica Dreeson, and Duchess Maria Anna were missing. None of the newspapers were quite sure which situation the Volley Gun Regiment was being sent to. Every couple days another regiment passed through Schwarza Junction, five in all. One of them was the Red Lion Regiment.

On the evening of July 26, a messenger brought a telegram to one of the apartments. Astrid was the only one there, and the messenger was startled when she answered the door pistol in hand. She paid him and quickly read the message. It was from Neustatter. The men had reached Erfurt on schedule and delivered the shipment. The new men were doing well. The message contained three dollar amounts with no explanation. That was okay. The amounts were about what they had expected to pay for pistols and holsters. So, the new agents were now armed.

The men pushed hard and arrived home late Friday night. They slept late on Saturday, but by afternoon, Astrid was updating Neustatter on new inquiries. He updated her on Erfurt.

Monday, July 31, 1634

On Monday, Neustatter started assigning two men to each baseball practice and game. Both Ursula and Anna were approaching their delivery dates. Agathe was a tremendous help, but the Pfeffers had their own apartment, so Hjalmar and Ditmar started doing a lot of the cooking. Astrid helped out when she could, but Neustatter wanted her in the office.

NESS had a number of short missions. Ditmar's team were bodyguards for a businessman who had to settle a particular contract in coin rather than with a letter of credit. Hjalmar's team guarded an abnormally large payroll. One day Neustatter took his team and Ditmar's to Saalfeld. A couple business owners and their employees split the cost for NESS to keep the peace during a meeting that ran late into the night as they worked out a contract between the businesses and the union.

As busy as they were, Neustatter still found time for the dinner and a movie group. He came home one evening with very good things to say about *The Heroes of Telemark*.

CHAPTER 5: BLOOD IN ERFURT

Monday, August 7, 1634

On the following Monday, the *Bibelgesellschaft* again assembled at NESS's office. Neustatter had assigned Team Three to this mission. He, Karl, Lukas, and Astrid were mounted while Phillip would join the *Bibelgesellschaft* in the wagon. For the *Bibelgesellschaft*, the mission was led by Doctor Johann Gerhard and included most of the same students as before, plus Johannes Musaeus. That made sense; he had graduated from the University of Erfurt and joined the *Bibelgesellschaft* at the University of Jena where he was starting a second master of arts degree.

"*Guten Tag*, Katharina, Barbara."

"*Gut tag*, Astrid."

Astrid smiled at the Amideutsch. "How are you?"

"Excited," Katharina declared. "If a second university joins the *Bibelgesellschaft* . . ."

Astrid tried to follow along. Barbara shot her an amused look, which Astrid thought was safe to return.

They pushed hard to reach Erfurt in two days. By now, Neustatter had very definite opinions at which inn they should stay.

Thursday, August 10, 1634

The University of Erfurt theology faculty and the *Bibelgesellschaft* dove right into meetings the morning after they arrived. NESS stood watch outside most of the time. Just like at the University of Jena in June, there was a fancy dinner that night. Or maybe it was a banquet. NESS had not been to enough of either to know where the dividing line was.

On Thursday morning, they returned to business.

Astrid Schäubin was standing guard duty outside the University of Erfurt, out front with Neustatter. *Freedom of religion is a good thing. But guaranteeing it is a little more exciting than civics class suggested it ought to be.* She was thinking of the riot at the *revival service* that had taken place here in Erfurt in June.

"More students." Neustatter identified the two young men approaching.

"An honor to meet you, *Fräulein*. I am Matthias von Spitzer. And this is my fellow student, Friedrich von Alvensleben."

"Miss Astrid Schäubin of Neustatter's European Security Services."

"What is a security service?"

"We are private guards."

Both von Spitzer and von Alvensleben frowned. "Why is your company guarding the university?" von Spitzer asked.

"We're guarding the *Bibelgesellschaft*," Astrid explained. "Erfurt is a little tense right now."

Von Spitzer nodded. "The townspeople were celebrating the Congress of Copenhagen's recognition that both the city and the hinterland are formally independent of the archbishop of Mainz. The city has been a Stadt since '32, of course, but it is nice that the captain-general made it official." He laughed harshly. "But there are unanticipated consequences."

"Oh?" Astrid asked, even though she already knew what they were.

"The Catholics quickly realized that freedom of religion means no religious tests for public office. They lost no time nominating the archbishop's former bailiff for the city council. A lot of the townspeople are not at all happy about that."

"What do you think about it?" Astrid asked. She took a couple steps to her left, away from the door. The two students moved with her.

Von Spitzer didn't miss a beat. "I think if we all get behind one experienced candidate, we could elect a good Lutheran. But the Committee of Correspondence insisted on running their own."

"Who did you find who is willing to take on that challenge?" Astrid asked. She tried to project a very concerned tone.

"Actually, Friedrich's uncle is willing to run."

"Really? That is very civic-minded of him." Astrid was sure there a large dose of self-interest there, too, but did not see any reason to bring it up.

"He is going to make sure that the Catholics do not take over again," von Alvensleben began.

Before he could say more, von Spitzer cut in. "There has been some pushing and shoving, of course, but nothing we cannot handle. Say, this *Bibelgesellschaft*, you will be backing von Alvensleben, of course?"

"None of them are from Erfurt," Astrid answered. "Neither are any of us from Neustatter's European Security Services."

"Excuse me, gentlemen," she requested several questions later. "I need to get back to work."

"*Ja*, she does."

Von Spitzer turned and appeared to notice Neustatter for the first time. "Who are you?"

"*Ich heisse* Neustatter."

"*Dank*," Astrid told Neustatter once the two students were out of earshot.

Neustatter nodded once. "What did you learn about them?"

"*Niederadel*. Probably in the arts curriculum. Not serious political players in Thuringia. Just here in Erfurt."

"Explain," Neustatter directed.

"If they were *Hochadel*, we would have recognized their names. The theology students are mostly inside with the *Bibelgesellschaft*. Law students probably would have asked at least one question about security consultants, and they would have asked you. And law students probably wouldn't have made so many assumptions about the uncle's chances in the election. So they were probably arts. And they did not ask anything about Grantville or Thuringian politics. Their world revolves around their town."

Neustatter nodded again. "Remember that your conclusions are only likely, not certain, and did not rule out medical students. But I agree with you. Anything else?"

"I think you had a good idea convincing the BGS to send Dr. Gerhard instead of Father Kircher or Brother Green."

"I have heard about those scuffles von Spitzer mentioned. They sound more serious to me than he seems to think. Having Kircher around in clerical robes would just set Lutherans off. And Green would get in an argument."

Without pointing, he said, "There is Phillip across the street. Let's check the guards, Miss Schäubin." Neustatter stretched, which Astrid knew was a signal to Phillip to stick around for a few minutes.

They left Phillip out loitering out front and generally blending in with the rest of Erfurt.

Karl Recker was supposed to be watching one of the building's other entrances, and that's exactly what he was doing. Karl carried a U.S. Waffenfabrik flintlock rifle, and it was at order arms—butt on the ground, right hand grasping the barrel just below the muzzle. Karl's right arm was fully extended, holding the barrel at an angle pointed away from himself, and his left fist was on his hip. Most of the time, NESS was not into spit and polish, but Neustatter made an exception for standing static guard duty. Karl's stance was flashy but not impractical. His rifle could be at port arms diagonally in front of him in two movements and aimed with only one more. And because nobody in Erfurt had gotten around to forbidding it, he had a bayonet fixed.

"Carry on, *Herr* Recker," Neustatter said formally.

Neustatter and Astrid rounded the building to where Lukas Heidenfelder was supposed to be. Lukas was not guarding the back door. Astrid suspected that Neustatter wouldn't have lost it if Lukas had merely been slouched against the building with weapon in hand, but he wasn't even watching his area of responsibility. In fact, he was kissing a woman. He had one arm around her—the one holding his U.S. Waffenfabrik rifle.

Neustatter closed in at a lope and threw a right cross into the back of Heidenfelder's neck. Lukas's head bounced off the woman's, somebody's tongue got bitten, and Lukas whirled around. Neustatter grabbed his rifle with one hand and threw a couple quick jabs with the other.

The woman started screaming and flailing at Neustatter. Astrid darted past him with her left arm up to protect her head and her right hand firmly covering her holster. She shouldered the woman away.

Neustatter hauled Heidenfelder to his feet. "Lukas!" he roared. "What do you think you are doing? A passing student could have killed you with a penknife!"

Heidenfelder babbled.

Astrid glared at the woman. "Who are you?"

"Trudi Groenewold. You are in so much trouble when my pimp . . . "

Neustatter's laughter cut her off. Still holding Lukas up with one hand, he fished a card out of a shirt pocket with the other. "A pimp who has not been run out of town by the Committees? Really? Do you seriously expect me to believe that? Here, give him my card. Since we are telling lies, his second can use it to contact me."

"So he is not . . . " The woman closed her mouth, clambered to her feet, and started to run off.

"Look, I know you and Lukas have been seeing each other. Just stay away when he is on duty." Neustatter turned to Astrid. "Miss Schäubin," he directed in a perfectly calm voice, "make sure no one got past Heidenfelder. Then take the front and send Phillip back here."

"*Ja*, sir."

Astrid checked the inside of the building. The *Bibelgesellschaft* meeting was still going strong, and she could hear them discussing Jewish scholars. Apparently, they'd moved on to the Old Testament. She kept going. She encountered three students, two of whom tried to *chat her up*. She stepped outside, spotted Phillip, and jerked a thumb over her shoulder. He sauntered across the street and around the building.

Neustatter came around the other side of the building about fifteen minutes later.

"All clear, Miss Schäubin?"

"All clear, Neustatter."

"Lukas is at the same door as Karl."

Astrid nodded. In a guard position that was both flashy and uncomfortable, she suspected.

"I considered firing him. He considered quitting. He still may. He considered fighting me. That will not happen."

Astrid sucked in her breath. "Neustatter, Lukas is angry much of the time. He might decide not to fight fair."

"Of course he would not fight fair. First of all, I train all of you not to. Second, Lukas knows he wouldn't win a fair fight with me. What he's trying to decide right now is whether he can sneak up on me."

Astrid didn't think so, but she felt she had to warn her boss. "Neustatter, he does have a rifle. What if he just decides to take a shot at you?"

Neustatter grunted. "I have had to discipline Heidenfelder before. In Wallenstein's army, a lot of men did things. The men from our village knew there were certain things they couldn't do. Heidenfelder tested the limits a couple times."

"What happened?"

"I disciplined him. The captain disciplined me. I blew the captain's brains out at Alte Veste."

"*Herr* Neustatter, you scare people."

"*Fräulein* Schäubin, that way there are fewer I have to shoot."

✳ ✳ ✳

Astrid spent the next hour or so fairly angry with Lukas for complicating the assignment. Neustatter had circled the building a couple times, leaving her alone out front. Being the sole guard out front took some getting used to. Neustatter was back soon enough, though.

He had just returned from his second circuit when they both heard raised voices down the street.

"Stand ready," Neustatter directed. "Our men are all in place, and the BGS meeting is still going."

Whatever was going on down there seemed to have a crowd forming. After a few minutes, the crowd started moving their way.

"Miss Schäubin, send Phillip, Karl, and Lukas out here. Then you take position right outside the room where the BGS meeting is. You will have to watch your back."

Astrid ran for Karl and Lukas's door. After she'd sent all three of the others to Neustatter out front, she took position outside the lecture hall.

Not ten minutes later, the front door was wrenched open. Astrid could hear a ruckus outside. One man strode in, questioned a student near the door, and made straight for the lecture hall.

Astrid drew her pistol but kept it pointed down. "Who goes there?"

"Town watch. We are here to question the heretics."

"Why?"

"For murder!"

Astrid swiftly considered and rejected several options. Neustatter would not want her to shoot the town watch. Besides, he was carrying only a cudgel and a short sword. Instead she stepped back.

"Sir, if you are referring to the *Bibelgesellschaft*, they're inside. They have been inside all day. I am sure Dr. Gerhard and the Erfurt professors will confirm that, and I will stay right here."

The watchman looked her way. "*Fräulein*, you and your pistol may stay between the heretics and me, but I cannot have you armed and behind me."

"That is reasonable," Astrid agreed and preceded him into the lecture hall.

"Doctors, please?" the watchman requested. "I am Watchman Meinhard, investigating a murder."

The professors, the *Bibelgesellschaft*, and the Erfurt theology students all poured out of the room. Astrid fell in beside Katharina Meisnerin and Barbara Kellarmännin.

"What is happening?" Katharina asked.

"I do not know," Astrid answered. She was concerned that the watchman had gotten past Neustatter. But once they stepped outside she almost laughed in relief.

MISSIONS OF SECURITY

The watchman had left his partner outside, uncomfortably parked between the mob on one hand and Neustatter, Karl Recker, and Lukas Heidenfelder on the other. As the theology faculty, students, and BGS crowded through the door, one of the good citizens of Erfurt took the opportunity to swing his quarterstaff at Neustatter's head. Neustatter ducked the staff and delivered a side kick to the man's midsection. As he doubled up, Neustatter quickly relieved him of the quarterstaff. A second Erfurter jumped in. Neustatter faked a swing at his head and used the other end of the quarterstaff to sweep his legs and dump him unceremoniously in the street.

Neustatter spun the quarterstaff with practiced ease as Karl and Lukas's rifle butts came up. The good citizens of Erfurt backed off.

"What is going on here?" Watchman Meinhard demanded.

A dozen people started talking at once.

"Silence!"

That must be Johann Gerhard's dean voice, Astrid surmised. It certainly worked.

"Watchman Meinhard?" the theology dean invited in a normal tone.

"These citizens found blood a couple alleys from here. They believe someone has been murdered by the heretics."

"When did this murder take place?"

"Within a few hours," a deep voice called from the crowd. "I walked through there this morning, and there was not any blood there then."

"The *Bibelgesellschaft* has been inside since eight o'clock this morning," Neustatter stated. "We have been watching the doors."

"Clearly you and your men were in on it!"

"Nonsense," Neustatter stated. "Who was killed, anyway?"

"You know! You did it!"

Neustatter planted one end of the quarterstaff in the dirt and spoke very slowly. "No, I do not know who was killed. If I did, I would not have asked. And I have not hurt anyone except these two fools in the dirt who decided it would be a good idea to attack a security consultant without being sure of the facts. Perhaps the town watch could identify the body before we move on to such minor considerations as motive."

"There is no body," a voice called out.

"Yeah, the heretics took it!" a nasal tone added.

"So, ah, what makes you think there has actually been a murder?" Neustatter asked as condescendingly as possible.

"There is blood all over the alley!" Several other people shouted contributions, too, but that was the gist of it.

Neustatter looked at the town watchmen. "Have you seen the alley?"

"Ah . . . just a glance. But we left Jost there."

"*Ja*, take the heretics back to the scene of the crime." That nasal voice from the crowd was getting really annoying.

"The heretics have been inside the classroom with us all day," one of the Erfurt professors said. Astrid thought and finally dredged up a name—Niclas Zapf. Nicolaus Zapfius when he was writing.

"Yes, they have."

"And who are you?" the watchman asked.

"I am Dr. Johann Gerhard, dean of the theology faculty at the University of Jena. And who, good sir, are you?"

"Uh, Watchman Heinkel."

The crowd quieted down quite nicely, Astrid observed.

"It probably would be a good idea to view the scene," Meinhard stated loudly enough for everyone to hear him. "Let's go."

"One moment, please," Neustatter requested. He reached out a hand to one of the men he dropped. "Are you willing to let the watchmen sort this out?"

"As long as they make the right decision." He accepted a hand up.

The other man didn't. "I want your name!"

MISSIONS OF SECURITY

"Edgar Neustatter. Neustatter's European Security Services. You are with the Committees, aren't you?" When the man did not answer, Neustatter sighed loudly. "A quarterstaff is your weapon of choice. You jumped in ahead of the watch. Tell Dieter Strauss hello from me."

"You know Strauss?"

"Of course I know the head of the Erfurt Committee of Correspondence. What kind of a security consultant would I be if I did not know the important people in cities I operate in? If I give you your quarterstaff back, do you think you could refrain from taking a swing at me?"

"He had better," Meinhard warned.

The Committeeman nodded sullenly.

* * *

The townspeople and a good chunk of the university congregated at the mouth of the alley. "Jost, we brought everybody," Meinhard told the watchman who had remained there.

"That is a lot of blood," Dr. Zapfius acknowledged.

Astrid could not see any of it. She, Karl, and Lukas were sticking to Katharina and Barbara who were in the center of the group of BGS students staying on the edge of the crowd. Phillip was mingled into the crowd.

"It was that one!" a woman shrilled.

Astrid snapped around to see a woman pointing at Neustatter.

"I saw him! He was sneaking off!"

"When was this?" Neustatter shouted over the hubbub.

"Yesterday."

The watchman who had stayed at the scene—Jost—poked at Neustatter with his cudgel "Where were you going?"

"Martial arts lesson," Neustatter replied with a grin. "Do that again. I will demonstrate. It will be fun."

Watchman Meinhard stepped in. "Knock it off, Jost. I am not sure what a *martial arts* is"—he repeated the English term—"but I saw him take Huber's staff away from him and trip up Goren with it."

"Why have you not arrested him?" Jost demanded.

"Because it was self-defense on Neustatter's part and stupidity in the first degree on Huber's part," Meinhard answered. Huber glared at him.

Neustatter laughed. "You got that one from Dan Frost, didn't you?"

"I did. You know *Herr* Frost?"

"He helped me set up my security company."

Astrid noted that Neustatter seemed content to talk shop with the city watch in front of a hostile crowd.

"I see," Meinhard said. "And these *martial arts* lessons?"

"Fighting styles from Japan and China that a few up-timers know. Sometimes it is nice to have a surprise."

"So I see. Which up-timer teaches the lessons?"

"Gena Kroll."

Seeing Meinhard's blank look, Neustatter added, "Gordon Kroll's daughter. Dennis Stull's secretary. They all work for military procurement."

"Oh, right. I've met *Herr* Kroll. His daughter . . . is she not more or less betrothed to Sergeant Hudson?"

Neustatter was grinning again. "*Ja*."

"He and his friend Sergeant Allen do not like Germans. They call us Krauts when they have been drinking."

"Gena is dating one of the no-Kraut men?" Katharina asked.

Meinhard looked her way. "Why does that surprise you? And who are you?"

"Katharina Meisnerin of the *Bibelgesellschaft*. Most of us know Gena from Grantville High School. She defended us Anabaptists once."

Meinhard frowned. "Her betrothed may not let her do that anymore."

Neustatter laughed again. "It is clear you do not know Gena very well. Besides, you are underestimating Eric Hudson."

Meinhard blinked. "I never said his first name."

"No, you did not. But I know him. It is true that he says he dislikes us Germans. But he tends to forget that once he knows you. He likes movies—the up-time moving pictures."

Meinhard frowned. "Sergeant Hudson was transferred to Halle. He is courting Miss Krollin and watching movies in Grantville . . . "

"And drinking at the 250 Club," Neustatter added. "He is very efficient. There is a reason the Army put him in charge of train schedules."

Meinhard said, "We will need to verify all this, of course."

"Of course."

"Under close questioning," the nasal voice added.

"That is not going to happen," Neustatter answered. He didn't bother to turn around.

"This is Erfurt," another voice spat. "Not Grantville."

"They will be tried by our laws!" someone else in the crowd shouted.

"Thuringian law is the same in Erfurt and Grantville," Watchman Meinhard stated.

"They shot someone and carried him off!" came a shout from crowd. "They're working for the Catholics! They must be punished!" There was a general chorus of agreement from the rest of the crowd.

Neustatter shucked off his coat and let it drop to the ground. His holster was very visible as he turned around.

A few of the more perceptive citizens of Erfurt—and everyone who'd ever see one of the Western movies in Grantville—started moving away, thinking about such things as lines of fire.

"Calm down, all of you!" Meinhard ordered.

"We can take them!" one Erfurter insisted.

Karl and Lukas exchanged incredulous looks.

"Do something!" Astrid heard Katharina hiss at her brother Georg.

"What do you want me to do?" Georg asked.

"I don't know! Think of something!" Katharina was becoming frantic.

Georg started easing his way through the crowd toward the alley. He reached the empty space that had cleared when Neustatter dropped his coat.

Astrid decided that Katharina and Barbara would be safe enough for the moment. They were flanked by fellow students Horst Felke and Johannes Musaeus as well as having Karl and Lukas close by.

"Karl," Astrid said, "watch the others. I will cover Georg." She slipped through the crowd after him.

Meanwhile, Meinhard was telling his partner, "Heinkel, go to the base and ask if Sergeant Eric Hudson and *Fräulein* Gena Krollin would please accompany you back here. Be polite. Bring *Herr* Kroll and *Herr* Stull if they wish. The whole rest of the city is here—they may as well be."

* * *

Georg reached the intersection and stood there looking into the alley. The crowd was becoming increasingly aggravated. He knelt down. Astrid sighed. That would make him even harder to protect.

Suddenly Georg straightened and carefully walked a little way down the alley. "Whatever happened, no one was shot," he proclaimed.

Everyone in earshot turned to look at him.

"What?" Astrid demanded. "Of course someone was shot. There is blood everywhere."

"Not shot," Georg insisted. "Stabbed or cut. Perhaps bludgeoned. But not shot."

"Why do you say that?"

"The blood, it is not right," Georg said.

"Neustatter!" Astrid called. "There is something you will want to know." She waved Georg forward. "Explain."

"Whoever bled here, he or she was not shot," Georg said.

"Speak up!" someone hollered.

Neustatter motioned to the watchmen. "Gentlemen, we will not all fit. Perhaps the two professors and then you could pick out a couple dependable men?"

Meinhard nodded. He pointed at two men. "Rudolf Schwartz. Klaus Huber. You witness for the crowd. And for the Committees." Huber was the man with the quarterstaff.

Eight men crowding into an alley trying to avoid stepping in bloodstains was awkward at best. Once they were all at least close enough to hear, Neustatter said, "Say that again, Georg."

"This is not blood from shot," Georg said again. "This is blood from a blade." He pointed at a streak of blood on the wall, three or four yards from the end of the alley. "This is artery spray. It's about one American foot from the ground. Not head or chest level. And then whoever it was collapsed right there." He pointed at a section of wall where the pattern sloped down to the ground, ending in a pool of semi-dried blood. It was irregularly shaped, about three American feet by a foot and a half.

"Right," Meinhard said. "Then he picked up the body and left these footprints here." He pointed at a couple impressions that ended in a confused tangle with a smaller patch of blood at the edge of the alley where it met the street.

"What is the point of this?" Jost asked.

"Figuring out what happened," Meinhard told him. "Someone stepped in blood and walked to the edge of the street. There's no blood out in the street but there is this spot. As if someone who was bleeding stopped and stood here."

"It would have happened while they were loading the body," Jost said.

Georg pointed at it. "That is dripping. Uh, gravitational spatter, they call it. See how the drops here by the street are all round? And that—" He indicated a spray pattern. "is not gravitational. It's from a new wound." He squatted down to look closely. "There is also white stuff on the ground. I smell something, too." He sniffed the ground. "I think it is horseradish."

Jost opened his mouth to argue and then reconsidered. But Huber said it for him. "So the heretics stabbed him again and then put the body in a wagon."

"That is not what happened," Georg said. "Look at these blood drops."

Watchman Meinhard frowned. "There are two blood trails. We are standing in one of them! Everyone, step back against the wall." He pointed at the ground and traced the trail as everyone got out of the way. "One going into the alley and one coming back out?"

"Both blood trails are going in," Georg corrected.

"You could not possibly know that unless you saw it happen," Huber stated.

"It is very clear," Georg countered. "The footprints come out to the street. But both blood trails are going back in."

Meinhard took a close look. "Yes."

"You cannot tell that . . . " Jost began.

"Yes, you can. Blood drops from a moving person are not round. They are pointed, and they point in the direction of movement."

"I do not believe that," Huber said.

"Please, feel free to cut your finger and walk around," Georg challenged.

"Why, you!"

"That is enough, *Herr* Huber," Meinhard said without lifting his gaze from the ground. "Why do you know all this, Georg?"

"My sister Katharina keeps staying after school for *Bibelgesellschaft* work. I was bored waiting, so I took the forensics class."

"Forensics?" Meinhard stumbled over the word.

"Crime scene investigation."

"Ah. *Herr* Frost has told us a little about this. He said he will say more about it on his next circuit. I remember that he said the up-timers have a chemical that shows blood."

"*Ja*," Georg agreed. "Luminol. It is usually used to see where someone cleaned up blood. No need for it here." Then a thought struck him, and he laughed. "But it would not work here anyway, Watchman Meinhard. You can smell the horseradish, right?"

"*Ja*."

"Horseradish causes luminol to show a false positive," Georg said. "If we had any to spray around, I think this whole end of the alley would turn blue."

"Have you used this luminol before?"

"*Nein*. I have just seen pictures of it in a book. If there is any left at all, it is not enough to let students use it."

Meinhard was quiet for a few moments. "Could someone have put the horseradish there on purpose so that luminol could not be used?"

Georg thought about that. "I believe *Herr* Frost would say that forensic countermeasures suggest careful planning. Given the amount of blood everywhere, I do not think this was carefully planned. Certainly no one tried to clean up the scene. I think the horseradish is just an accident."

"Good point," Meinhard agreed. He turned his attention back to the scene. "Steps in the blood, tracks it to the street, spills blood there, two people come back this way," he mused. "Steps over here around the blood pool."

"I did not see that one," Georg admitted.

"It is just blood drops. There are no footprints."

Georg cocked his head to one side. "Why not? If there are footprints going out, there should be footprints coming back."

"This is hard ground," Meinhard pointed out. "We are not leaving footprints either."

Georg thought about that for a minute. Then he stamped on the ground. "Look—I can leave a footprint if I stomp. But why would anyone stomp after stepping in blood? I would scuff my shoes to scrape it off."

"He did not scuff," Meinhard observed. He pointed at a misshapen footprint. "Georg, he slipped!"

Georg understood at once. "He slipped in the blood and stumbled to the edge of the alley. Wait—then he stood around bleeding? Why was he bleeding?"

"He stabs the other guy . . . " Meinhard began. "No, the other guy stabs him. No, that is not right, because they walk off together."

"Do we know they left together?" Georg asked.

"There are the two blood trails," the watchman pointed out. "They never cross." He began again. "The first man walks through the alley and stabs someone. He slips in the blood. The victim injures him at the edge of the street. But the second man arrives. They kill the victim, and they load the body on a wagon, then walk back down the alley."

"Why would they not just ride away on the wagon?" Georg asked. "Especially since the first man was wounded?"

"So, there is a third man driving the wagon . . . " Meinhard shook his head. "No, that is far too complicated." He looked at Jost. "Do you have a theory?"

"Not anymore," Jost answered. "But yours has the big blood stain made before the one next to the street. But the one next to the street is dried, and the big one is still sticky. Does that not make the one by the street older?"

Astrid watched Georg and Meinhard exchange looks of consternation. Then they both practically dove at the blood stain by the street.

"Where did we go wrong?" Meinhard asked.

"I do not know," Georg muttered.

They kept staring at the blood stain. At length, Georg observed, "It is not just dried. It is *clotted*."

"Well, yes," Meinhard agreed. "Blood clots."

"The larger bloodstain is not clotted like this." Georg sounded excited. "It is not older. This one is two different blood types!"

"What?"

"The first man and the second man were both wounded at the edge of the street. This is blood from both of them. It clotted because they are different blood types," Georg pointed. "See the arterial spray there? It is not clotted because it is from only one of them."

"Two men were injured here?"

"Since they were both hurt and left walking side by side, I do not think they could have carried a body," Georg said slowly. "One of them is bleeding badly. He needs help, and soon."

Meinhard slapped his forehead. "That is why they went back into the alley. The clinic is this way."

Dr. Zapf spoke up. "The university medical faculty is the other way."

Meinhard shook his head. "We have been seeing more and more sick and injured people being taken to the clinic. It is just a couple of nurses. They are not really doctors. But a lot of people do not care.

"Jost, we are going to follow the blood trail. Go back and tell everyone else that if they come, they have to stay back and they have to use a different alley. Georg, let us go find these two men."

They followed the blood drops to the other end of the alley and out onto the next street.

"It is getting hard to see," Georg noted.

Meinhard grunted. "Less blood, too."

Halfway down the block they lost the trail.

"I do not see any more blood," Georg said.

"Me, either." Meinhard turned around. "Form a line."

He put Schwarz, Huber, Neustatter, Johann Gerhard, Niclas Zapf, and Jost in a line across the street, and they started slowly moving forward.

"Blood!" Dr. Gerhard called.

Several yards farther along Schwarz found another drop. After another twenty yards, they heard a hubbub as the crowd caught up to them.

Meinhard spoke up. "Jost, let us just check the clinic. If they are not there, we can come back with lanterns and look for the blood trail."

They were almost to the base when they met Watchman Heinkel coming the other way with three up-timers in tow, two men and a woman. The younger man was wearing SoTF blue. That probably made him Eric Hudson, although Astrid did not recognize any of them.

Katharina did, though. "*Guten Abend*, Gena," she called.

"Kat Meisnerin? Georg? Horst? What are you all doing here?"

"The *Bibelgesellschaft* came to Erfurt to meet with the university theology faculty. But people think that *Herr* Neustatter and his security service have killed someone."

Gena gave an unladylike snort. "That's ridiculous."

"Gena. Sergeant Hudson. *Herr* Kroll," Neustatter greeted them.

"What's this about, officer?" Gordon Kroll asked.

Meinhard gave him the short version.

"Wait, wait, wait," Sergeant Hudson drawled. "You think Neustatter and one of his men would attack someone in an alley? And then hide the body? Seriously?" He laughed.

"Why is this funny?" Watchman Jost asked.

Eric Hudson jerked a thumb at Neustatter. "The idea of John Wayne here using a partner to ambush a guy."

"But . . . why is it funny?" the watchman pressed.

"C'mon. Neustatter goes to the movies to watch John Wayne, Harrison Ford, and Arnold Schwarzenegger. He wouldn't knife someone in an alley. He'd rather have a shootout at high noon than a backstabbing."

Neustatter grinned.

"Plus, since you came and got us," Hudson continued, "you already know that Gena's been teaching him martial arts. Now if you had someone who'd been blown away on Main Street or had a broken neck, Neustatter'd be a suspect. But a stabbing? Uh-uh."

"That is . . . an interesting insight," Meinhard acknowledged. He glanced at Georg.

Georg shrugged. "Do not look at me. That is not forensics. I think they call that profiling."

"Let us go check the clinic before it gets completely dark," Meinhard directed.

✳ ✳ ✳

Lorrie Gorrell was finishing up with a couple sick kids while Maurine Kroll tried to keep the day's paperwork somewhat current. Someone banged on the door of the clinic. Maurine pushed back from the shelf pegged to the wall that served as a desk. Being on paperwork made her the receptionist, too. She opened the door to find her husband, daughter, and, well, probably not half of Erfurt standing there, but it seemed like it.

A quick glance didn't reveal anyone obviously in need of medical care. "What's going on, Gordon?" she asked. "Can I help you?"

"We hope so," said a man wearing the armband of the city watch. "There is a lot of blood in an alley near the university. We believe there were two men injured, and the blood trail led in this general direction. One of them would have been bleeding badly."

"Lorrie!"

The door to the examination room opened. Lorrie Gorrell ushered a woman and her two boys out. She was carrying the younger, who looked about six. The older was probably nine or ten.

"Keep giving them purified water and an aspirin morning, noon, and night," she directed, then asked, "What's going on, Maurine?"

"They're looking for a couple injured men, one bleeding heavily," Maureen told her. "They must mean Griesser and Unsinn."

Lorrie nodded. "Hans Griesser and Gerhard Unsinn came in this afternoon. Griesser had a deep laceration to his right arm, and Unsinn had a broken nose. I stitched up Griesser and did what I could for Unsinn's nose."

"Did they say what happened?" Meinhard asked.

To his surprise, Watchman Jost laughed softly. "I can guess. I know Unsinn, by reputation at least. He is a klutz."

"Yes," Lorrie confirmed. "Hurrying to bring a knife to his master."

Meinhard nodded. "I can see it. Not quite running, but moving fast. He slipped in the blood and stumbled forward just as . . . Griesser, you say? . . . came around the corner." He paused. "Where are they now?"

"They both lost a lot of blood," Lorrie said. "This isn't Leahy or Magdeburg Memorial. We don't give transfusions unless it's really life or death. I can't even give Sergeant Nagel's kids as much aspirin as I'd like to. I stitched them up and sent them to a tavern. At least they'll get some fluids back in their systems that way."

Maurine took a deep breath. "And I gave them some marijuana for the pain."

Gordon Kroll blinked a couple times. "You prescribed beer and pot?" he asked his wife.

"Yes. I told them to come back tomorrow. If they need it, we'll give them a pint of O negative and some chloram."

Kroll winced. "Let me talk to Dennis Stull and some others. We've got to see about getting you more medical supplies, especially if you're becoming the walk-in clinic for the city."

"Thanks, honey."

Meinhard cleared his throat. "Any idea which tavern they went to?"

"Probably *The End of the Woad*. It's closest."

"Thank you."

Maurine exchanged glances with Lorrie.

"Go with them," Lorrie said. "I'll close up here."

❋ ❋ ❋

Outside, Meinhard gave a quick summary that caused most of the remaining onlookers to disperse. Potential murder had been interesting; a clumsy journeyman was not. That left just three watchmen, Georg, the two professors, Neustatter, Astrid, Schwartz, Huber, Gordon and Maurine Kroll, Gena, and Eric Hudson. They filed into *The End of the Woad* and filled the place up.

"May I help you?" the waitress asked.

"City watch," Meinhard said. "Looking for Hans Griesser and Gerhard Unsinn."

"Right over there."

Griesser's arm was bandaged, as was Unsinn's nose. Both their shirts were bloodstained but they had cleaned themselves up.

Eric Hudson sniffed. "Must be our guys. That is definitely a doobie." Gena smacked him.

"*Herr* Griesser? *Herr* Unsinn?" Meinhard asked.

"*Ja.*"

Everyone crowded around them.

"I am Watchman Meinhard. Some citizens found a lot of blood in an alley, and they were afraid someone had been murdered."

"Ha! Not quite murdered, although Unsinn here stabbed me when he fell."

"Sorry," Unsinn muttered.

Griesser laughed. "He fell face-first into my tray of horseradish, too. Busted his nose and spilled the horseradish everywhere. Sorry, Unsinn, but I have had enough beer and *das weed* that it is funny now."

Unsinn had clearly had enough, too. He giggled. "I slipped in the blood."

Meinhard nodded. "We know. But where did the blood come from?"

The waitress came over with a platter of fowl and a pungent sauce.

"Some fool butchered some chickens in the alley. I saw some feathers."

Meinhard and Georg just looked at each other. Georg shook his head.

Neustatter clapped him on the shoulder. "This was good work, Georg. You could have a future in investigation." He turned. "And Huber? You would not be on the CoC sanitation committee, would you?"

"*Ja.* I have got work to do. *Fräulein* Krollin, I would like to speak with you about quarterstaff lessons."

She nodded.

"Neustatter, I will give you a decent fight next time." The Committeeman left.

"That explains everything," Meinhard said.

"Chicken with horseradish sauce?" Eric Hudson asked.

"Well, except that."

"That is easy," the waitress said over her shoulder as she passed by with a tray full of food. "The cook is determined to master the up-time turkey and dressing by the next *kirmess*. But he is not there yet."

※ ※ ※

They started back toward the university building, and Phillip quickly found them. Neustatter stepped aside to talk to him.

"Karl and Lukas have the all the members of the *Bibelgesellschaft* except for Doctor Gerhard and Georg Meisner outside the university building."

"We have Gerhard and Meisner," Neustatter murmured, "and a closed case. Rejoin them. We will catch up."

Doctors Zapf and Gerhard decided that the textual criticism discussions could resume in the morning. They proposed to discuss the incident over dinner. It sounded as though the students did, too. It quickly became apparent that this was going to involve a tavern.

Neustatter and Astrid exchanged glances. It was hard to see in the dark, but Astrid thought his glance meant, "*Ja*, there is going to be theologizing while intoxicated, but the *fräuleins* do have to eat." Astrid was not looking forward to it.

Katharina and Barbara ended up toward one end of a long table in a tavern that was a good bit larger than *The End of the Woad*. Astrid stationed herself against the wall behind the girls. Neustatter was doing the same toward the other end of the table, while Karl and Lukas were against the opposite wall. Phillip was sitting at another table, not wearing his *halstuch* and nursing a beer.

At first the conversation—the parts Astrid could hear, anyway— was largely Lutheran versus Catholic. She supposed it was not surprising that the Anabaptists were not speaking up more. But as the evening wore on, the Erfurt students started directing their questions to the two *Bibelgesellschaft* girls.

Katharina and Barbara proved adept at deflecting questions. Anything about Grantville or Calvert High School or the *Bibelgesellschaft* they answered readily enough, but they refused to get drawn into theological disputes. Once Astrid heard Katharina murmur to Barbara, "We really need Joseph and Marta for this part."

Astrid leaned forward and kept her voice low. "Who are Joseph and Marta?"

"Members of the *Bibelgesellschaft*," Katharina answered. "Brethren, like us." She seemed to study Astrid for a few seconds. "Not everyone was allowed to come."

She continued quickly and quietly. "Joseph and Marta's parents are the strictest. They are fine people, but before coming to Grantville, the Engelsbergs faced more persecution than my family did. Barbara's family faced the least amount. Georg and I had to persuade our parents to let us come, while Barbara simply asked."

Astrid nodded. That made sense to her. She tried to imagine what she would allow her children to do, if she were to have any.

"Nona and Alicia aren't allowed to come on these trips, either," Katharina added. "They are up-timers."

Astrid understood that, too. "Perhaps if there are more of these trips, Neustatter could speak with their parents."

Barbara, who had not said anything up until now, shook her head. She was blonde like Astrid, while Katharina was a brunette. Both of them wore head coverings which were similar to what many down-time women wore. Their style was more than a few years out-of-date, but it was not as though Astrid's own village had been *on the cutting edge of fashion*, as she had heard an up-time girl say at Calvert High School.

"That will not work."

"Oh?" Astrid's voice may have been a bit cool.

"They know Neustatter is an honorable man. They *know* that he got us to Jena in spite of what Pastor Holz wanted. Because we told them. But it does not *matter*." Barbara explained, "He is an *outsider*. Not Brethren. None of you are. The same is true for Nona."

"And the other? Alicia?"

"It will not work, but for a different reason. Alicia's brother just got out of the National Guard. Alicia's mother was really worried about him. Astrid, if Neustatter tells her he will protect Alicia, she will think Alicia would be in as much danger as Adam was."

Astrid was annoyed that that made sense, too.

Friday, August 11, 1634

When the Erfurt theology faculty met with the *Bibelgesellschaft* the next day, Neustatter stationed Astrid inside the lecture hall itself.

At first, she thought the whole incident would make the University of Erfurt theology faculty hesitant to have anything to do with the *Bibelgesellschaft*, but then she realized she had underestimated Doctor Gerhard. He began talking to Doctor Zapf about textual criticism in terms of forensics applied to documents.

Then Zapf turned to the students. "Is what you are proposing more of this forensics?"

Astrid saw the glances: Horst to Katharina, Katharina to Johannes, Johannes back to Horst. She read that as Horst was going to answer first.

"That is part of it." Horst's manner was very respectful. "Investigative forensics can look at the paper, ink, handwriting . . . perhaps we could call correlating events mentioned in secular histories a kind of forensics."

"And certainly, when we attempt to trace and classify variant readings, there are elements of forensics," Katharina continued smoothly. "Knowing linguistic peculiarities of different regions certainly helps. But for questions like, does Paul actually write like this, or was someone else the human author of Hebrews? I am not sure forensics is quite the right word, although the mindset is quite similar."

Doctor Zapf looked at Katharina with interest. "My understanding is that Anabap—Brethren tend to focus on the Gospels. It is interesting that you choose an epistle for your example."

"We usually save the ending of the Gospel of Mark and the *Pericope Adulterae* in John 7:53 through 8:11 for when there are not other people around." Katharina's tone could not have been more demure, but her face held the hint of a smile. "Sometimes it becomes . . . loud."

Doctor Zapf gave a great booming laugh. "We are inside. By all means, let us address those passages."

When they finally took a break and went out for a meal, Neustatter fell in beside Astrid. "It went that poorly, eh?"

Astrid shook her head. "*Nein*. Katharina warned it would get loud. But it is the loud of people cheering for a baseball team and arguing with the other fans, not the anger of the religious wars. Do not ask me about the details, though."

Neustatter smirked. "You could ask Miss Meisnerin about those on the ride home."

Whatever Katharina and the others said was effective, though. On the following day, the University of Erfurt theology faculty joined the *Bibelgesellschaft*.

Astrid did not ask Katharina about the details on the ride back to Grantville. Katharina was a nice girl, but enthusiastic about her interests. Instead Astrid talked with her brother Georg about forensics.

"Would reloaded brass have the ejector marks from all the weapons that have fired that casing?"

Georg looked puzzled. "Reloaded brass?"

"We have enough rounds with up-time smokeless gunpowder for a couple serious firefights," Astrid explained. "For practice, we fire rounds that have been reloaded with black powder."

"Bring one of these rounds—or better, an empty cartridge, *bitte*. We can probably use one of the microscopes at the high school to check the toolmarks."

"I will."

CHAPTER 6: BABIES

Ditmar and Hjalmar were in the office when the team arrived in Grantville. The *Bibelgesellschaft* thanked NESS and hurried off to tell Doctor Green and Father Kircher that the trip had been a success. Team Three took the horses to the livery stables. Ditmar came along while Hjalmar kept the office open.

Once they were brushing down the horses, Neustatter asked, "What news cannot wait, Ditmar?"

"The doctor told Ursula she is carrying twins. She wants Ursula to give birth at the hospital. Ursula has her own ideas about that, but Stefan put his foot down."

Astrid gave Ditmar a glance with a raised eyebrow before returning her attention to her horse.

"It was . . . exciting," Ditmar admitted. "Especially when Anna jumped in and asked Wolfram if he was going to make her have their baby at the hospital, too."

"What did he say?" Neustatter was genuinely curious enough to look up from brushing his horse.

"He said *ja*, if at all practical, first babies should be born at Leahy or the hospital in Jena because the first is a higher risk. If the first goes well, a midwife can handle the next as long as someone is available to summon an ambulance at need. Anna agreed that made a certain amount of sense."

"We listen to Karl when he tells us if a piece of metal can take the stress or not." Neustatter resumed brushing his horse as he spoke. "We should listen to the medic when he gives medical advice."

"*Ja*, that is more or less why Ursula and Anna eventually agreed," Ditmar told them.

"Speaking of you, Karl," Neustatter continued, "I think we will leave you here while we take that shipment to Frankfurt."

"Neustatter . . ." Karl began.

Neustatter set his cleaning gear on a shelf and turned to Karl. "I need someone with a cool head to help Miss Schäubin keep NESS open. Stefan and Wolfram are not going to get enough sleep with newborns in the apartment. I know that much."

"You will be on the road to Frankfurt without a medic or a blacksmith," Karl pointed out.

Neustatter shrugged. "It cannot be helped this time. But consider the new men. Is there one you could teach to be enough of a smith for what we often need on a mission?"

Karl thought about it. "Build is not everything for a smith, but—no offense, Phillip—I have a lot more weight to put behind a hammer than you do."

Phillip laughed. "None taken. It is true enough. *Und* Jakob is about my size."

"*Ja*. Richart, though . . . I will ask if he is interested." Karl looked over at Neustatter. "If he is not, build will not matter."

"True enough." Neustatter smiled. "Phillip, I have a different mentor in mind for you."

MISSIONS OF SECURITY

Wednesday, August 23, 1634

The eight original NESS agents had reported to Camp Saale for *Adler Pfeffer* a couple days ago, and Jakob Bracht had gotten his Reserve duty changed to align with them. A couple days later, when Astrid was in the office by herself, a knock sounded at the door. Leigh Ann and James Ennis came in.

"Good morning, *Frau* Ennis, *Herr* Ennis."

"*Gut tag*, Miss Schäubin." Leigh Ann's greeting indicated they were there on business.

"Please, sit down."

Leigh Ann began once they were all seated over by the Franklin stove. It wasn't lit, of course. Today was just about as hot as Astrid ever wanted it to be, although she noticed that neither of the Ennises seemed the slightest bit uncomfortable.

"James is home on leave, and we've finally had some time to talk about some things. James' mother is such a dear. She's been working at a day care in Grantville so that I can work from home and stay with the kids. With the restriction on using gasoline and the bad winter weather, Julia started staying in town during the week, you know. Comes home on weekends."

Astrid nodded. Leigh Ann had explained that before.

James took over. "They'll be lifting the gasoline restrictions soon. Not sure when, exactly, but it'll happen. Turenne's raid put us behind, but Wietze won't be our only source. That still leaves the winter weather. Pine Grove Road can be just plain dangerous when it's icy. My parents are in good health, but asking them to drive at night in bad conditions is a little much. None of us like the current situation. I want Leigh Ann's mom and dad both at their place, y'know?"

"Of course," Astrid said.

"So I've been thinking about that bridge. I still can't build something that would support a horse. But one that let Julia drive to NESS and then cross Buffalo Creek to the farm? That I can do. I'd like to have it finished in time for winter, but I'm going to need some help. There's no point in even doing it unless Julia can get across safely."

"You need one or two of us around when she crosses the bridge in the morning and afternoon," Astrid realized. "I will ask Neustatter, but I expect we can do that."

"Is Neustatter around?" James asked.

"*Nein*. Our original eight agents have Reserves this week. They are assigned to the Basic training class's *Adler Pfeffer* exercise. Jakob transferred Reserve units so that he could work with them." Astrid smiled. "Phillip, Hans, and Richart are on an assignment downtown today."

"So you're running the office," James observed.

"That's what she does," Leigh Ann said.

"If it's snowed when Julia needs to cross the bridge, we'll need you to clear a path." James sounded apologetic.

"Of course."

"If the snow or ice is too bad, Julia would still stay in town." James Ennis stared at the Franklin stove as though it were winter already.

Astrid nodded.

James sighed. "Never liked this arrangement, but couldn't figure out anything better. Last weekend, Julia hauled out all her Norwegian cooking gear—you know, making *krumkake* and *lefse* and so on."

Astrid had no idea what he was talking about.

"Huh. She was right. She said you wouldn't know, that just because your ancestors were Danish, and Denmark controls Norway right now, you wouldn't necessarily know what they eat."

"Herring?" Astrid ventured.

"What I'm talking about is way better. Anyway, Julia got this idea that somebody ought to introduce up-time Norwegian food to Norwegians. I wasn't sure if there were Norwegians in Grantville, but Denmark is an ally now . . ."

"And there are Norwegians in Danish service," Astrid finished. "I understand."

"Julia holds dinners, so she really needs to be able to get back and forth. And if she can do that, then we can make it so she can come home weeknights, too."

After everything the Hauns had done for NESS, Astrid felt an obligation to help. "I think we can make this work. It will be useful training for us."

Astrid was not sure exactly who made it happen—Leigh Ann knew a *lot* of people—but the permits for a bridge moved right along. It still took time; when the public hearing was held, Neustatter and most of the other men were over at Camp Saale for the next *Adler Pfeffer* exercise.

Thursday, August 24, 1634

Astrid woke with a start and sat up quickly. The bedroom was dark. Someone was shaking her. It was Anna.

"Ursula is in labor!"

"When did it start?"

"Just a few minutes ago."

Astrid dressed quickly and reached for her gunbelt. Since the men were away, she had moved in with Anna for the week. It was her job to run over to the livery stable and take Ursula to Leahy.

The summer night was warm, with just enough of a breeze. She had been told that up-timers considered even this cool, but it seemed perfect to her. Astrid did not even need a lantern; Kimberly Heights had enough lights that she could see her way as she ran over to the livery stable.

The night clerk was surprised to see anyone at this hour, but quickly brought out a litter carried between two horses. And a driver . . . conductor?

It took a little longer to get back to the apartment—the horse-drawn litter needed to follow the roads—and then she was helping Ursula and Anna into the litter.

"Is Mutti going to be okay?" Johann asked Astrid in a whisper.

"*Ja*, she is having a baby. Two babies. You can come with me."

"Where are you going?"

"To the NESS office. I am going to telephone Camp Saale and have your father brought to Leahy."

Astrid was not convinced it would work, but Neustatter had left her a *contingency plan*. So as soon as Ursula and Anna were on their way to the hospital, she and Johann hurried to the office. Astrid unlocked the door, turned on the lights, and reached for the telephone, taking all three for granted.

She spoke with *CQ*, who wrote down NESS's telephone number and told her an officer would call back shortly. From listening to the men talk about the National Guard, she suspected that this would be an instance of *hurry up and wait*, so she looked for something she and Johann could do.

Astrid rifled through first her desk, then Neustatter's. He had a deck of cards, more out of sense that security consultants ought to have cards than out of any desire to play.

"Oh! I know card games!" Johann exclaimed.

That did not fill Astrid with confidence. In short order, Johann proceeded to beat her at Go Fish and rummy.

"Do you know how to play poker, Miss Astrid?"

MISSIONS OF SECURITY

By the time the phone rang, she was convinced that Johann's up-time friends were a bunch of card sharps. She grabbed the receiver with a sense of relief.

"Neustatter's European Security Services. Miss Schäubin speaking."

"*Leutnant* Funcke, officer of the day at Camp Saale, Ma'am. Did you request that Private Stefan Kirchenbauer be released from drill?"

"*Ja, Herr Leutnant.* His wife is having a baby."

"When?"

"Right now. Horse-drawn litter just took her to Leahy Medical Center."

"All right. I will send someone to find him and deliver him to Leahy. It may take some time to find him."

"I assume he is with Edgar Neustatter in the *Adler Pfeffer* exercise."

"I know where they are *supposed* to be, Ma'am, but, ah . . ."

"Eagle Pepper," Astrid agreed. "Please have the driver telephone this number from Leahy." She recited it to him twice.

Part of the contingency plan had been to bring blankets with them. Johann was finally getting sleepy. Astrid lit a fire in the Franklin stove, and they rolled up in blankets near the stove.

She had no idea what time it was when the phone rang. She was sure it rang several times while she woke up, struggled free of the blanket, and stumbled to her desk.

"Hello. Neustatter's European Security Services. Miss Schäubin speaking."

"*Gut morgen. I bin* Sergeant Lutz. I have just delivered Private Stefan Kirchenbauer to Leahy Medical Center. The nurse at the desk says his wife is still in labor."

"*Danke.*"

"What's going on?" came Johann's voice.

"Your mother is still in labor, and your father just arrived at Leahy."

"Is she going to be okay?"

"*Ja.*"

They prayed for Ursula and the babies. Johann went back to sleep.

Astrid realized how hard the floor was. Eventually, she gave up and checked the clock. She got a little work done at the desk before awakening Johann. It was the first week of school, so she did not want him to miss class. They went back to the apartment just long enough for each of them to get ready for the day. Then Astrid put Johann on the bus to school and returned to the office before Phillip, Hans, and Richart arrived.

About eleven in the morning, the phone rang.

"Hello. Neustatter's European Security Services. Miss Schäubin speaking."

"Astrid! Stefan. They are here! Both of them! Margareta and Niklas. Ursula is very tired but happy."

Astrid did not think she had ever heard Stefan bubbling with happiness before.

"Congratulations, Stefan!"

"Bring Johann, *bitte*. After school, I suppose."

"All right. I can probably get a message to him now. He was worried."

"*Ja, ja*, if you would."

"I will take care of it."

After Astrid hung up, she turned to the new men. "Hans, you are with me. We are going to Johann at the elementary school and tell him that he has a new brother and sister, and they and his mother are just fine. Phillip, Richart, you have the office."

When they reached Blackshire Elementary School, Astrid figured it was good manners to introduce themselves to the security guard at the front door.

"*Gut tag. I bin* Astrid Schäubin of Neustatter's European Security Services. *Er ist* Hans Deibert. We are here to tell Johann Kirchenbauer that his mother had twins a little while ago, a girl and a boy, and they are all well."

The guard just looked at them. "Markus. My partner Christoph is inside."

Astrid nodded. "Hans, I am leaving you here under Markus's command."

Markus made no effort to block her way, and she spotted Christoph before she had taken three steps inside. He was positioned so that he saw the doors, but could not be seen from outside. Astrid nodded in approval and explained why she was at Blackshire. Then she did the same thing again in the office.

The secretary used the *intercom*—it did the same thing as a telephone but only within its own building—to call Johann's teacher.

"Do not just summon him. Tell him everything is fine, *bitte*," Astrid urged.

The secretary's eyes widened. *That may have sounded more like an order than I intended*, Astrid realized. But the secretary asked the teacher to send Johann Kirchenbauer to the office, and that everything was fine.

Johann arrived quickly. Astrid thought he had probably run. He was slightly flushed but not breathing hard. She wondered if he slowed down so that they would not know he had been running in the halls or because he had been steadying himself.

"Johann," Astrid said, "your mother had both babies a little while ago. She is fine. They are fine. Their names are Margareta and Niklas."

Johann's face lit up, and he threw his arms around her.

"You may see them after school."

"*Dank*, Miss Astrid."

"Your father is there, too. The National Guard brought him in from the field."

Johann looked up. "Will he get in trouble for missing training?"

"*Nein*. The officer of the day sent someone to pick him up and bring him to Leahy."

"Oh, good."

"Do you think you can go back to class now?" the secretary asked a couple minutes later.

Johann nodded. " 'Bye, Miss Astrid."

He was off like a shot. *Nein*, he had not stopped running because of the rules. He had been composing himself, just in case. Astrid shook her head. She hated that kids learned to do that. *She* had done that—she and Hjalmar and Ditmar—after their parents died. That is what the Ring of Fire meant, that with the knowledge from the future—a future—sometimes things did work out better. Best not to get overconfident about it, though. Many of the up-timers were nice people and well-meaning. But the Psalms said, "Put not your trust in princes." It was probably a good idea not to put her trust in up-timers, either.

Astrid shook her head again. Ursula had survived (which really was much more common than some of those up-timers seemed to think) and so had both babies. She had an office to run. She thanked the secretary and the security guards, and then she and Hans Deibert started back to the NESS office.

Neustatter was in the field, so Astrid figured it was her responsibility to ask. "Hans, tell me about their security. What do they do right and wrong?"

✷ ✷ ✷

Astrid took Johann to see Ursula and Margareta and Niklas after school. Greta and Claus were really cute babies. Then Astrid made sure Stefan and Johann and Anna got some dinner.

MISSIONS OF SECURITY

On the following day, she asked Agathe Pfeffer to walk her through how to make a full meal. Astrid could cook individual dishes just fine, although she was not on Ursula's level. Having everything ready at the same time was difficult. Back in the village, Anke had seen to that and given her and Gessel specific tasks. Here in Grantville, usually at least three people worked together to prepare NESS's meals. Astrid wrote down the times as Agathe guided her. She thought the results were . . . edible. Not offensive, but nothing to remark on, either.

She wanted to work on her cooking, but they had a mission in Grantville on Saturday. She, Phillip, Hans, and Richart spent most of the day standing around displays of the latest instruments. Then Astrid cooked. Her timing was better, although she thought the food was still bland. She thought she might not be using enough of the spices. In the evening, she started dividing the kitchen between the two apartments. Ursula and the babies would need some privacy.

Ursula and the babies came home on Sunday afternoon. The men got back from training Tuesday night.

Astrid hugged Hjalmar. "How are you?"

"Exhausted." He looked it. "Neustatter was right. Veterans from Ahrensbök helped run the training. Between them, the up-timers, and Neustatter being a cowboy, we did a lot of night attacks. Astrid, the up-timers have *optics* that can see at night. The few that they have are not the best that existed in their time, but by the end of the week we were good enough that they had to use technology to beat us."

"Did they?"

"*Ja*, until we stole some."

Ditmar was standing nearby and started laughing. "They thought they were lost and searched the fields. Picture hundreds of men standing fingertip to fingertip, sweeping back and forth as oxen plow a field."

"Oh!" Astrid could see this in her mind and giggled.

"We got in a lot of trouble after we ambushed the other side in the dark, and they realized we had *night sights*," Hjalmar resumed. "But they did tell us to seize every advantage. But do not think we were just *goofing off*. There was a lot more emphasis on protecting the civilians, working with them, and incorporating them into our force. Seems Neustatter gave people ideas."

Ditmar was looking around the apartment. "You moved the kitchen?"

"Part of it. We will need two. I think this will be our main cooking area for now, but Kirchenbauers and Kuntzes will need to be able to do some cooking, too. Much of the time, we can cook dinner here and take it next door to them."

"Good plan, Miss Schäubin. I like initiative." Neustatter had made his way across the apartment's central room to her.

"Good to see you, too, Neustatter," she told him.

"Is there anything I need to know right now?"

"Ursula is doing well. The babies are Greta and Claus. They are doing well, too. We had a couple inquiries I can explain tomorrow. *Und* the hearing for the bridge went well. The permits will be granted as long as it does not disrupt the river or navigation on the river."

Neustatter laughed. "Navigation? They have a canoe race once a year. Once or twice I saw people drift by on *inner tubes*."

Astrid shrugged. "James wants to get the bridge built before the ground freezes."

Neustatter was abruptly serious. "Whenever we are not out on a mission, we will help. Karl will be skilled labor. The rest of us can lift and carry. But we do the mission to Frankfurt in September."

Neustatter gave the men the next day off. He spent part of the morning in the office, going over the books with Astrid. Then in the afternoon, he and James Ennis walked the riverbank.

Thursday, August 31, 1634

On the last day of August, NESS reestablished its in-Grantville routine. They made breakfast, took some next door to Kirchenbauers and Kuntzes, opened the office, trained, and cooked dinner. In between, the men helped James prepare the bridge site, took Johann and Willi to their baseball game, and got to see Greta and Claus. After naptime, Astrid acquired Elisabetha Pfeffer as her 'helper.' She mostly played with the office supplies.

Astrid was preparing dinner when Neustatter came alongside her.

"Miss Schäubin, I do not expect you to do most of the cooking."

"Aw, you are just saying that because I cannot cook."

"I would never say that. Not unless I could cook better." Neustatter stopped joking around. "This is better than we ate in the village, *ja*?"

"*Ja*," Astrid agreed. "That is the ingredients, not my cooking. Ursula..."

"Ursula is a very good cook," Neustatter agreed. "You are a fairly good cook yourself, and if you want to get better..."

"Practice."

Neustatter's shrug conveyed "of course." "I think I will start assigning cooking duty, with the understanding that we should listen to any suggestions from Ursula or Agathe. Once most of us leave on the Frankfurt mission, the rest of you will have to make it work."

"Agathe started tonight's stew this morning. I am just following the directions she gave me."

"It smells good," Neustatter stated. "But if you would like an assignment, while we are gone, find out how someone could learn to cook in Grantville."

"Really?"

"We *should* practice investigations, even though most of what we do is guard duty."

If Neustatter wanted her to investigate, she would.

Friday, September 1, 1634

The next morning, Astrid was sitting at the desk in the office thinking about ways to find out about cooking. She had just added *Ask an up-timer* to the list, wondering if she dared bother Leigh Ann about this, when there was a knock at the door.

Two men entered. One was the short man who had asked Ditmar for a background check on a farmer and his wife. *Wesner.*

"*Guten Tag,*" he began. "I am Casimir Wesner, on behalf of the von Hessler family. This is Issachar Frankel."

Wesner shook hands with me, but Frankel gave a slight bow instead. Astrid returned it. Not everyone preferred to shake hands. Frankel was dressed . . . differently. Astrid had spotted a small . . . she was not sure what the correct name for the cap was.

"I am Jewish," he stated.

Oh. Astrid nodded.

"Is *Herr* Neustatter available?" Wesner asked. "I would like to hire NESS."

"Neustatter will be back shortly. Have seats, *bitte.*"

Wesner took one of the chairs by the stove, and Frankel tentatively followed suit. Astrid came out from behind the desk and sat down, too.

"Tell me what you need, *bitte.*"

Issachar Frankel looked startled, but Wesner nodded.

"Miss Schäubin, if you recall the background check on the farmer Heinz Kraft and his wife?"

She nodded. She was not going to forget a strange request like that.

"The same village, Kleinjena, has lost its butcher. The von Hessler family requested a butcher, kosher, and samples of a number of foods. So, I searched and learned there are many rules. Eventually I found Issachar, who is a *shochet* and willing to relocate."

Astrid wondered why he was willing to leave Grantville.

He seemed to know what she was thinking. "I shall be sorry to leave Grantville, Miss Schäubin, but *Herr* Wesner offers an opportunity to run my own shop. I have learned much here, but I am just one employee in the slaughterhouse by Stockyard Three. There . . ."

Astrid could see that, but she did have a question.

"Forgive me, *Herr* Frankel—"

"I am not a *Herr*."

Astrid gestured toward the nameplate on the desk. "Neustatter calls me Miss Schäubin because when he first came back to our village, I told him he should not call me *Fräulein*."

Frankel smiled for the first time. *Gut*. They had some common ground.

"I know little about this. Pardon me if I say something wrong, *bitte*. If you are Jewish and work in the slaughterhouse?" She certainly did not want to offend him.

"Stockyard Three and its slaughterhouse are all kosher," Frankel stated. "The meat is kosher when it leaves. Many of us Jews buy from there. Some of the rest of you do, too. A few people insist on meat from One or Two. The way almost all of you cook, it does not matter if you buy from One, Two, or Three."

That was interesting.

"But Kleinjena made a fair offer, for me to be the village butcher. They have some empty houses and offered two to my extended family. They agreed to fence in the cattle, which will also keep the pigs away."

"What can we do for you?" Astrid asked.

"My family and I will journey to Kleinjena in October, and we must take cattle with us. By then we will be able to afford some Hungarian grays and some up-time crossbreeds. We know how to raise cattle and how to butcher them. But moving them long distances? We need *cowboys*."

Astrid laughed. "Neustatter will love this mission."

Sunday, September 3, 1634

Stefan and Ursula had waited until the rest of the men were back from National Guard training to have Margareta and Nicholas baptized. They asked Wolfram and Anna to be godparents. Pastor Holz was away from Grantville, so Stefan approached Pastor Kastenmayer at St. Martin's. Astrid couldn't help feeling that a mother ought to be there for her children's baptism. Most of the men's expressions varied from smiling to impassive, but Otto's expression was tight. Astrid wondered if he were thinking the same thing she was. But it was a lovely service.

CHAPTER 7: THE BATTLE OF FLIEDEN

Monday, September 4, 1634

The up-timers had some strange holidays, but in Astrid's opinion, Labor Day was the strangest. They celebrated it by *not* working. However it originated, they really used it to mark the end of summer. Neustatter gathered everyone in NESS together and invited the Hauns. They attempted to cook up-time foods: sausages, burgers, sauerkraut, potato salad, dumplings and cabbage. Everyone found foods they liked, although not always the same ones. And then there were desserts: apple *kuchen*, cake, and *krapfen* doughnuts.

After they finished dinner, Anna stood and began unwrapping a bundle.

"NESS needs a flag," she said. "Two of them, I found out."

She held up the first one. Its thirteen red and white stripes were standard for an SoTF flag, but its five-pointed white stars were arranged into a big six-pointed star on the blue field.

"Very nice, Anna!"

"There are thirty stars. One for each county."

Then she held up the other flag. It had a red upper half and a white lower half with a triangle taken out of the side furthest from the pole. Yellow letters in the center spelled NESS.

"A cavalry guidon! *Danke*, Anna! We will carry these with us," Neustatter promised.

The next day, four wagons carrying tools and goods set out for Frankfurt with a teamster driving each, nine NESS agents guarding them, and a representative of the machine shops along to supervise delivery and installation. Neustatter and Ditmar's teams were riding horses—NESS's four time-shares and two rentals—and Hjalmar's team was on the wagons. The flag and guidon were lashed to the front corners of the lead wagon.

Neustatter planned to cover twenty miles a day—minus broken wheels or axles. They would travel four days, then give the horses a day off.

They were only two days out when the first wheel broke. This was a well-funded expedition, though, and had a couple spare wheels. They lost three hours putting the new wheel on, which was not bad at all.

Monday, September 11, 1634

Everyone had settled into a routine, and while they were short of Neustatter's ideal goal, they were not truly behind schedule. The expedition had passed Fulda the day before and heard that some of the up-time administrators were missing.

Neustatter was in the lead wagon, standing on a box of equipment in the wagon bed. Lukas was in the second wagon, and Karl was in the fourth. Ditmar's team led the way, while Hjalmar's team was the rear guard. The road descended a hill, and the teamsters slowed to increase the distance between wagons.

Neustatter frowned. That was unavoidable, but it left the wagons vulnerable to attack from the side. The woods that came up to the edge of the road on the right were dense enough to—

He spotted the glint of sunlight on metal coming around the edge of a tree.

"Gun!"

A deep whoom echoed over the wagons as whoever it was fired immediately.

Neustatter drew his Colt and returned fire. One of the horses pulling the wagon shied and then tried to bolt. Neustatter shifted his weight to keep his balance and pulled the M1911 back on target. But the man was now behind the thick tree.

Two men, shouting and brandishing blades, charged out of the trees at the second wagon.

A rifle cracked somewhere behind Neustatter as Lukas dropped one of the men. The other kept coming.

Neustatter jumped over the side and charged into the woods. The man who had initiated the ambush was reloading.

Neustatter's Colt swung to the right, fired. That man was down. Neustatter continued on.

Another man among the trees up ahead, out of position, but carrying a wheellock pistol. Neustatter fired twice. One shot hit the man, and he dropped the pistol. Neustatter expected him to fall, but instead the man tugged a sword from its scabbard. Neustatter waited for him to close. He crouched and fired a single shot at ten yards, hitting the mercenary in the neck.

"Neustatter!"

That was Ditmar, doubling back.

BLAM!

Shotgun. Then that was Ditmar *and* Richart. They would have left Hans holding the horses' reins. Neustatter cut to his right, away from them.

Other shots rang out from the back of the wagon train. Five, maybe six pistol shots, a mix of snaphance cavalry pistols and black powder revolvers, punctuated by a rifle shot. That meant Hjalmar, so the rear guard was engaged. The two bangs that ended of the engagement sounded different. That meant Otto had shot at someone with his up-time .38, and the lack of return fire suggested he'd hit his target.

Neustatter paralleled the road, working his way toward the back of the wagon train. He circled around the thickest undergrowth and ducked under low-hanging limbs, moving in a crouch, holding with the .45 in a two-handed grip.

He spotted movement and stepped behind a tree. Peering around the trunk, he saw one mercenary hurriedly reloading another of the large cavalry pistols. Neustatter drew back. He pulled a fresh magazine from his pack and switched out the one he'd been using. Then he carefully moved to the next tree. It gave him a different angle, and now he could see a second mercenary. He scanned the area, including behind him, and spotted no one else. Just these two, then, unless they had someone really far out on a flank. Pistols and swords suggested mounted troops, so there would be horse holders, of course, but they should be a good distance back.

Neustatter started easing forward again. He wanted to walk right up to the first one, but the man finished reloading and leaned around his own tree.

"Drop it!" Neustatter barked.

The man whirled around. Neustatter saw his arm coming up and pulled the trigger. The mercenary fell, his pistol unfired. The second one bolted east, the direction the wagons had come from.

MISSIONS OF SECURITY

Neustatter heard the man yelp, and a cavalry pistol fired. Silence settled over the forest. He started picking his way in that direction.

"Martin!"

The single word rang out, and Neustatter smiled.

"Katie!" he called back, completing the old challenge and countersign he and his men had used during the war.

Hjalmar hurried into view and reported. "Three down here. Two are alive. We lost a horse on the third wagon."

"I got three. I think Richart got one."

"We need to find Ditmar."

Neustatter and Hjalmar started to retrace Neustatter's steps. They had gone only a little way when they heard a soft call. "Martin!"

"Katie!"

They spotted Ditmar and Richart moments later, working their way through the trees toward them.

"Richart got one." Ditmar spoke quietly.

"That is seven." Neustatter also kept his voice low. "They will have horses. Hjalmar, go back to the wagon train. Standard post-ambush actions: secure prisoners, treat wounded, gather intel. I need the up-time weapons with me."

"*Ja*, sir." Hjalmar was gone in a flash.

"Spread out," Neustatter directed. "Twenty yards. We sweep forward. Do not fire if you can avoid it. I want their horses." He fished a round from the partially depleted magazine and topped off the current one. Then he recovered the shell casing from the round he had just fired.

The three crept forwards through the trees, which started thinning out considerably. Ditmar held up a hand first. He pointed, and Neustatter spotted four horses, all facing inward, with a horse-holder at the center.

Neustatter edged forward, scanning for the others. He spotted another group of four horses off to his right. He thought through the skirmish and wished he had asked Hjalmar if the two men who had charged toward Lukas's wagon were included in the three down he had reported. *Nein*, Neustatter decided. Hjalmar had been in a fight at the back of the column, not in the center. There were probably nine attackers, which meant a twelfth man should be somewhere nearby, holding four more horses.

Neustatter looked at Ditmar and motioned with two fingers toward his eyes, then tapped the top of his head as the drill sergeants had taught them.

Ditmar held up two fingers.

Neustatter turned to Richart and did the same. Richart was not in the military, but Neustatter had taught the new men (and Astrid) the up-time arm and hand signals. The Colloredo Regiment had had some signs, too, but Neustatter did not want NESS using two systems and mixing them up. Nine of them used the up-time system on National Guard duty already, so that was what NESS had adopted.

Richart showed two fingers, too.

Neustatter signaled. The three of them moved carefully forward. They advanced from tree to tree, covering about twenty yards of straight-line distance. Then Neustatter slowly raised a clenched fist. The next time Ditmar and Richart looked his way, they both stopped.

There was not a signal for water, but Neustatter pointed ahead and left, toward where the ground dropped away. Then he made a wavy motion with his hand and pantomimed scooping up and drinking water. He saw Richart nod; he understood there would be a stream at the bottom of that draw. Richart tapped himself on the chest.

Neustatter turned and communicated the same thing to Ditmar, who nodded. The third horse-holder had probably taken his animals to get a drink.

MISSIONS OF SECURITY

If Richart could get closer enough for an open shot with a shotgun slug, then he and Ditmar could take the other two . . . if Neustatter could get close enough for a pistol shot.

Neustatter pointed at Richart and made an over-the-hill motion with his hand. Then he extended his forefinger and thumb like a gun and jerked his hand up to simulate the recoil of firing. Then he motioned to himself and Ditmar and made gun signs with both hands.

Richart nodded and tapped his chest again. He would shoot first.

After Neustatter conveyed all that to Ditmar by sign, he started crawling forward. Silence was more important that speed. He eased a couple fallen limbs out of his way, pushed some leaves aside. He reached partial cover behind a tree. The two horse-holders he could see were just standing there, occasionally adjusting the reins they held in their hands. Neither was looking around. Neustatter settled in, took the Colt in a two-handed grip, and found his sight picture. Then he waited.

About ten minutes after Richart had started down the hill to the creek, a shotgun blast boomed through the woods. A couple of the horses shied, and one screened the horse-holder from view.

Ditmar's .22 rifle cracked. Neustatter glanced that way, saw that horse-holder stumble. He surged to his feet and sprinted toward the remaining one. The man's full attention was taken up by the horses. One of them was still jumpy.

Neustatter was fifteen yards away when the man's head jerked around.

"*Gib auf!*" Neustatter ordered. "Give up!"

The man fumbled for a weapon.

Neustatter ran up to the nearest horse and slapped its flank. It bolted, and the horse-holder got half-twisted around before wisely letting go of those reins. He lost another set at the same time. That horse took off, too.

Neustatter smacked the man upside the head with his .45. That knocked him cold.

Hjalmar and Phillip arrived as Ditmar was tying horses' reins to convenient trees.

"I could use some help here!" Ditmar called.

"Where's Neustatter?"

"On a horse, chasing down a couple others that bolted. One of you check over the hill. Make sure Richart is okay."

Two hours later, the teamsters were grumbling while they hitched one of the cavalry horses to the third wagon.

"*Ja*, in the end this is going to cost us a full day. Maybe two," Neustatter agreed. "And slow us down the whole trip. But equal shares in a dozen horses—Lorenz, Heinrich, is that not worth the extra trouble?"

"How are we going to share a horse? And why is this going to cost us a whole day?" The gray-haired Heinrich sounded understandably cautious.

"We need to drop the prisoners in the next village and send messengers back to Fulda to get the National Guard to come take them. And possibly defend the village in the meantime."

Heinrich grimaced, but Lorenz pointed out, "We are all unhurt. Not like the . . . what? Eight men we just buried."

"We will be ready to ride in a few minutes," Neustatter promised. "Let me tell you about shares in a horse . . ."

Flieden

"We cannot take this risk," the village *amtmann* insisted. He indicated several men at his side, standing across the road. "Men I trust have seen cavalry on the road the past two days. Dozens of them. We do not know who they are, but they are certainly not from the State of Thuringia-

MISSIONS OF SECURITY

Franconia." He was a wiry, tough-looking man, probably in his fifties. Neustatter suspected he owed his position to sheer hard work and determination.

"We will stay until State of Thuringia-Franconia forces arrive," Neustatter promised.

"Neustatter! Who knows how long that will take?" Tobias exclaimed. He was one of the other teamsters, not one with whom NESS had worked before. "We need to press on."

"You should go," the *amtmann* told Neustatter. "The cavalry who rode through said if there was any resistance, they would burn Flieden."

Flieden was bigger than Birkig, but smaller than their home village. Its two rows of houses thickened to a third row in the middle of the village. Right now, NESS and the wagons were just inside the eastern edge of the village.

"If we leave, they may attack anyway," Neustatter pointed out. "Women and children run for the hills, older boys try to move the animals up there. You men die trying to buy time." He gazed off at the hills. "Sometimes villages let the enemy occupy them, hoping they will limit themselves to stealing a few things. It becomes more and more things over time. Often women and girls are attacked."

Neustatter's eyes tightened as he focused on the *amtmann*. "Which one is your plan if this cavalry attacks?"

"Flee."

Neustatter nodded in understanding. "Then you should send the women and children off now."

The *amtmann* looked down.

Neustatter looked from the *amtmann* to the other Flieden men standing with him. He watched them realize that their plan probably would not work.

He was supposed to deliver machines to Frankfurt.

Neustatter gazed out at the rolling hills. "Where are the *adel*? What forces can you expect from them?"

"None. Many of them oppose the State of Thuringia-Franconia. The others have few forces."

"Neustatter, we have to go." Ernst Wunderlich, the machine shop representative, shaded his eyes against the setting afternoon sun with a worried expression.

Neustatter nodded and stepped back. Once he reached the wagons, he ordered, "NESS, circle up. Teamsters, *Herr* Wunderlich, you too."

"Thoughts?" he asked.

"We need to get out of here," Tobias stated. "Before more cavalry show up."

"They will be just like Wallenstein going through a village," Stefan stated.

"*Und* Flieden?"

"They are on their own," Wunderlich stated.

Jakob Bracht nodded, clearly unhappy. "They should flee now."

"They ought to, but will not," Johann Deibert stated. "People do not want to give up almost everything they have when the danger is not yet certain. Then when it is certain, it is too late."

Neustatter let the men talk while he listened. Flieden had two choices, both bad. Well, there was a third option—hope that the enemy cavalry suddenly had more pressing concerns. But the nearest force was the Fulda Barracks Regiment, and it was scattered, looking for missing up-timers.

Neustatter considered whether those two facts were connected. Strange things happened in war. But two strange things happening at the same time, having nothing to do with each other? Neustatter glanced over at the four wounded ambushers they had prisoner in the wagons. He could ask later, when one of them woke up.

MISSIONS OF SECURITY

But anything he learned from them would be just information. Useful to know, perhaps necessary to survive. But it was not the decision itself.

Most of Flieden was going to die because they were too stubborn. Should NESS risk themselves for people who did not want their help?

The wagons were lined up in the road, pointing west. Enemy cavalry lay ahead of them, but cavalry had to sleep, too. A tight column showing no light might make it through. But that would leave Flieden defenseless, so that option was out.

Too stubborn to evacuate . . . When you got right down to it, though, the villagers should not have to evacuate at all. Flieden was their home.

Herr Augustus had ordered Neustatter and his men away from their homes to war. When they had finally been able to return, they'd had to leave their own village immediately. They could not have held it, not even if most of the villagers had joined them, and all the reinforcements would have been on *Herr* Augustus's side. Then they'd had to leave their new home in Murphyhausen because it was indefensible. But Flieden . . .

Flieden was none of those things. Friendly reinforcements were not that far away, and the village could be held.

Besides, NESS wasn't just the men from the village anymore. They were citizens.

Neustatter wasn't going to run out on an SoTF village. This was the Fliedeners' home.

Flieden needed a better option.

Neustatter strode toward the lead wagon and began untying the guidon.

"What is he doing?" Wunderlich asked.

"Wagons with an armed escort might be left alone," Ditmar explained. "As long as they do not see those flags."

"Risky," Hjalmar warned.

Neustatter moved around the wagon and untied the flag. He started back to the group.

"Of course, that is not what he is going to do," Ditmar said.

Neustatter tossed him the guidon. Ditmar caught it.

Lukas Heidenfelder sighed. "Neustatter, are we really going to *Adler Pfeffer* this village?"

"Could be."

Stefan saw the teamsters exchange looks. "That means *ja*, we are going to do it," he told them.

The face of the machine shop representative reddened in outrage. Ernst Wunderlich babbled something about precision parts.

"NESS, faaaall . . . *in*!" Neustatter ordered.

The *amtmann* watched with increasing irritation as the very small formation—three ranks of three—marched up and halted at Neustatter's command.

"Neustatter, we have a contract!" Ernst Wunderlich roared. "I am ordering—"

"My men and I are trained in village defense. We can show you what to do. Tell me about the cavalry you have seen and heard about."

"Neustatter! I demand we leave at once!" Wunderlich began.

"We are not placing ourselves under your command!" The *amtmann* spoke right over Ernst's rant.

"My company will appeal to the government!"

"—demand you leave at once!"

"Enemy cavalry—"

"Are any of you in the National Guard?" Neustatter's voice cut across all the others. "I am activating all reservists in the area."

A chorus of *Nein!* answered him.

"Now I am activating the unorganized militia. That is all men eighteen to forty-five years old, along with any older or younger men and any women who want to join in."

One of the villagers standing with the *amtmann* bristled. "We will not—"

Neustatter spoke quietly. "Lukas."

Heidenfelder stepped clear of the formation. His right hand flashed to the stock of the U.S. Waffenfabrik rifle on his left shoulder, and he slammed it butt-first into the man's chest. The blow knocked him to the ground.

Men began to shout angrily.

Neustatter slammed the end of the flagstaff into the ground.

"*Silence!*" he thundered.

Everyone shut up.

"Flieden Militia Company, faaall . . . *in!* Two ranks, right here. *Amtmann*, your name?"

"Bernhardt Zeithoff."

"Fall in beside *Hauptmann* Zeithoff!" Neustatter lowered his voice and addressed Zeithoff. "Understand, Zeithoff, that while you are *hauptmann* of your village militia, and I am a corporal, I *will* be in command until the cavalry is beaten or we are relieved by the Fulda Barracks Regiment."

"Or you are dead," Zeithoff pointed out.

Neustatter gave him a thin smile. "Could be. But I do not fight fair."

"Neustatter, we have to get the machine parts to Frankfurt." Ernst Wunderlich was practically pleading now.

"*Nein*, because once I send three men to Fulda, we will not have a sufficient escort." Neustatter turned to one of his team leaders. "Hjalmar, take your team to Fulda and get help. Ride as long as you can see, find a village inn, and set out at dawn. Take the best three captured horses as remounts."

"Yes, sir." Hjalmar stepped back. "Otto! Jakob!"

"*Nein!*" Tobias protested.

"I would rather not," Neustatter agreed. "But with cavalry out there, even all nine of us would not be enough to deliver your shipment. How many of these machines would not survive being struck by pistol balls?"

Wunderlich's wince answered that.

Neustatter turned to the villagers, many of whom—including the man Lukas had struck— had arrayed themselves in two rows. Neustatter wouldn't call them ranks, not yet. *Build morale.*

"We *are* the State of Thuringia-Franconia," Neustatter stated. "So are you. Do you know about the Croat Raid on Grantville?"

"Of course. But they had all their guns . . ."

"Against over two thousand Croats," Neustatter added. "This force you have seen—how many? Maybe a couple hundred total?"

Zeithoff looked at him shrewdly. "Not even that many, I should think."

"Then we can hold," Neustatter stated. "If Hjalmar's team returns with the SoTF National Guard, we will drive the dragoons off. If they do not, we will do it anyway." *Don't confuse image with reality.* He heard that in Dan Frost's voice. "First, I need everything you know about this cavalry. That will tell us how to prepare. Then I need to know what weapons you have."

"Not likely!" Zeithoff exclaimed. "That would let *you* plunder the village."

"*Herr Amtmann*, we already could." Neustatter spoke in a matter-of-fact manner. "We simply do not want to. So, *Herr Hauptmann*, I need to know what weapons you have."

"Hmphh." Zeithoff clearly had his doubts.

"*Und* I cannot promise no casualties," Neustatter continued. "People die in battle. But we will do everything we can to make sure it is the other side that does the dying." He let that sink in for a moment. "Do any of you have clay bowls? I need one or two dozen, and I cannot promise they will not get broken."

"Clay bowls?" Zeithoff, Wunderlich, and the teamsters were all mystified.

Lukas chuckled. "You will like this part."

"Then I need the wagons to block the road."

"*Machines*, Neustatter," Ernst hissed.

"We will unload those and store them somewhere safe," Neustatter told him.

"Unload, reload," Tobias grumbled. "More delays."

Neustatter remembered something. "Get the wounded prisoners out of the wagons and into a house. Ditmar, post a guard. Now, how many cavalry are east of Flieden?"

"Just the one squad rode through," Zeithoff told him.

"*Gut*, for two reasons. That probably rules out a two-front attack, at least at first. It also means we can send men for help. I need six men who can ride. Married men. Send them in pairs to rally the three closest villages. They are to come back here, and those villages will send their own men on to three more. Now, if you were coming from the west, how would you get closer to Fulda without going through Flieden?"

Neustatter put everyone to work—NESS agents, teamsters, and villagers alike. By sundown, the road through the village was blocked by wagons. Clay bowls were partially buried in the road on both approaches, with a few more obvious in the fields nearby. A lit lantern was hung from a tree branch in a belt of trees sheltering the west side of the village. Two wagons were positioned across the road on both sides of the village, at the second pair of houses from either end. Next to the wagon barricade at the western end of Flieden stood one of the machines they'd been transporting to Frankfurt, with a pair of muskets fastened to it.

"What does that do?" one of the villagers asked Richart, who had rigged the thing.

"Absolutely nothing." Richart grinned. "But if you did not know that, had heard tales of the up-timers' *machine gun*, and caught a glimpse of it in the dark, might you not approach some other way?"

"And break an ankle in those holes we dug," the villager reasoned out. "Or trip on one of the ropes and bring cooking irons crashing down."

Ditmar nodded. "Right. Look, this is not as good as we could do in Birkig, but the National Guard pays that village to help with training. It is good, because the training destroys a lot of their crops. By now, the villagers there know how to rig all this—and more—themselves."

Neustatter sent Phillip out with five men from the village, and they found cover from which to spring an ambush—nowhere near the lantern in the woods. Hans Deibert took charge of five more men at the barricades.

"And where will you be?" the *amtmann* asked Neustatter.

"Questioning the prisoners. Assuming I find out what I want to know, after that I will be asleep in the inn until I take the second watch."

※ ※ ※

Neustatter knocked on the door of house where the wounded had been taken. The house was of half-timber construction and looked well-cared for. After a minute, the door swung open, revealing a stooped, older man.

"*Ich heisse* Corporal Edgar Neustatter. Are you a doctor?"

"*Nein*. Just Hermann Topf. I treat people if I can. Sometimes it works. I have set bones. But I am no doctor."

"How are the wounded?"

Topf stepped outside and pulled the door closed behind him. "One has died. Another might. The other two? As long as the blows did not damage their brains, they should recover."

"If we can get them to Fulda..."

"Why?"

"I have no reason to want them dead," Neustatter stated. "When they ambushed us, *ja*. But our drill sergeants gave us a list of reasons we should want them to survive."

Topf gave him a skeptical look.

Neustatter returned a lopsided grin. "All I can do is tell you what Drill Sergeant Huffman told us. I cannot promise it will work out that way.

"First, having some sort of law of war can help prevent savagery. If one side knows the other will try to keep prisoners alive, it may do the same for theirs. Second, someday some of yours may be captured, and you can exchange them. Third, they are of intelligence value. That means they can give us information. That is what brings me here tonight."

"To make them talk?"

"I simply want to know what unit they are and in whose service. If they tell me more, *gut*."

"How are you going to get them to tell you that?"

"I was thinking about giving them some food and small beer and talking with them." Neustatter held up a hand. "I know. It does not sound like it would work, but Drill Sergeant Huffman said that is what the most effective *interrogators* did up-time. If they are scared for their lives, they will lie. Then they confirm what you think you already know. That's bad intelligence. Bad intelligence gets your people dead."

Topf still looked skeptical.

"So, have they eaten?"

"I have not had time. I will go get something."

Two of the three surviving prisoners were still unconscious. One had been hit pretty badly in the leg. Neustatter had seen wounded men before and thought Topf was probably correct that this one could go either way. The other two had been knocked out. Hjalmar had buttstroked one of them with a clubbed musket, and he was still unconscious. The other was the young soldier whom Neustatter had pistol-whipped.

Neustatter sat down next to him. "I am Edgar Neustatter."

The man—more of a boy by age, but Neustatter figured anyone who marched or rode in the ranks was a man—looked at him very warily. Eventually he stated, "Hans."

"We had three Hanses in our unit. Young Hans got killed at Dessau Bridge. Old Hans died of sickness later on. Town Hans got killed . . . I guess it has been about three years now."

"Are you saying I am going to die?"

"I would prefer not to bury another Hans, if that is *okay* with you."

The young man snorted and then winced, raising one hand to his temple. "I am not ready to die yet."

Topf came back with a mug of beer and some food. Hans dug right in.

"Looks like Hermann Topf here has patched you up," Neustatter said. "I sent for reinforcements. They might have a medic. I do not know."

Hans paused between bites. "We have a regimental surgeon, but he is worthless. He would have cut John's leg off by now."

"What regiment? I will be sure to stay away from this doctor."

"What is yours?"

"SoTF National Guard Reserves, out of Grantville." Neustatter delivered that in English, because he'd heard an accent.

The wounded cavalryman swore.

"Irishmen," Neustatter observed.

"Aye," the young man blurted out. "*Ja*, they're Irish. Me, I am from Bavaria. Picked up some of the language from them."

Neustatter nodded. "Irish out of the Low Countries?"

"Nay. Maybe headed there. I do not know," the wounded man added quickly. "Came east from Bohemia last year. That is when I joined." He took a hefty swallow of the beer.

"Irish . . . Irish . . . Bohemia," Neustatter mused. "They would have left when Wallenstein took over. What were their names?" Somebody Irish was in that research paper about Wallenstein he'd bought and read to NESS on the bus to Erfurt. At length, he came up with a name. "Butler. Some Scots or Irish. A French name."

He saw from the man's expression that he was on the right track.

"They are the ones who killed Wallenstein up-time. I imagine your unit had to run for it. Which one of them are you with? Butler?"

The young man hemmed and hawed for a moment, then said, "I don't suppose it matters. MacDonald's dragoons."

Neustatter nodded, trying to convey that he'd expected that information. But—

"Dragoons, you say? Your squad was outfitted as cavalrymen."

"Nay. Just never enough muskets to go around."

"*Ja*, is that not the truth everywhere?" Neustatter saw no reason to point out that it was generally not true in the SoTF National Guard. Instead he shook his head. "Short on everything, probably. What were you doing *here*?"

The man shook his head. "I don't know. They don't tell us that."

"*Ja*, that happens everywhere, too."

Tuesday, September 12, 1634

The first watch was quiet, and Neustatter spent at least half of it asleep. Neustatter and Lukas led the second watch, and nothing happened. Ditmar was at the western barricade on the third watch when day dawned, and Richart had taken a fresh team into the woods.

The five villagers with Ditmar were tiring. A couple of them had their forearms on the side of one of the wagons. One of them picked his head up as it started to droop. Ditmar could sympathize. He thought the dawn watch was the hardest to stay awake through. He weighed the resentment he would create by telling them to be more alert compared to the risk of an actual attack. Ditmar hadn't reached a decision when another man's head suddenly came up.

"Horses!" he hissed.

Ditmar didn't question the man. He simply listened. *Ja*, that was horses. He touched two men on the shoulder. "Wake the village."

A pair of riders came into view. Their horses were at a walk, and the riders were scanning ahead and to both sides of the road.

Ditmar decided these were scouts. He had not heard just two horses.

He saw one of the scouts stiffen as he caught sight of the barricade. The man obviously said something to his partner, for both of them pulled up and studied the village. The second one looked around and then pointed, drawing the other scout's attention to the light in the woods. The two of them wheeled their horses around and rode back the way they had come.

Neustatter arrived at the barricade in just a couple minutes, and other men began streaming into position.

"Two mounted men," Ditmar summarized. "Scouts, I think. Unless I miss my guess, there is a company of mercenary cavalry on the way."

"Dragoons, according to one of the prisoners. Hopefully a short company." Neustatter raised his voice. "Cavalry detachment, mount up!"

In a few minutes, the riders reappeared. There were three of them this time. Ditmar saw that two of them were the original scouts and suspected the third was either a sergeant or an officer. A good way behind them came riders in a column of twos.

"*Ja*, a short company," Ditmar said. "About forty or fifty men."

The third man with the scouts was studying the barricades when Neustatter and Phillip led twenty mounted men—fully a third of Flieden's men of fighting age—out into a fallow field.

"So that is why we dug shallow pits out where they would do no good," muttered one of the men at the barricade.

"*Ja*," Ditmar confirmed. He waved theatrically, motioning half a dozen village boys into position at the wagon. Then he pointed at the two men standing behind Richart's contraption. One of them sketched a salute.

He knew that if those dragoons charged, a lot of villagers were going to die. On the other hand, a lot of mercenaries would, too. But Ditmar did not expect them to charge. The men at the barricade plus the defending cavalry should be able to break a charge . . . unless the mercenary dragoons figured out that only the six NESS agents had any idea what they were doing.

The two forces remained in their respective positions for some time, perhaps fifteen or twenty minutes. Then the man accompanying the scouts wheeled his horse and rode back to the main body. He spoke to the right-side rider in the front rank.

One is the officer. The other is the sergeant. My targets, Ditmar decided.

A few more minutes passed, and then the main body began to pull back.

One squad remained behind. *Keeping watch.*

Ditmar sighed. This had now become a straightforward tactical problem: how to extract Richart and the five villagers with him from the woods without touching off a battle. The short answer was that they were going to lose another day on the delivery of their cargo.

About nine in the morning, Neustatter led his "cavalry" back toward the village. They passed in front of the two wagons of the barricade and took up position south of the road.

The squad of mercenaries had remounted as soon as Neustatter's group began moving. Twenty minutes later, they began dismounting again, weighting their numbers on that flank.

That meant they could not see Lukas, who was standing on the north side of the third house north of the main road, counting from the western side of Flieden. He waved both arms over his head and then motioned toward himself with both hands.

A few minutes later, Ditmar saw a man at the edge of the woods. The man pointed north. Ditmar understood. Richart and his men were going to return via a big circle to the north. He posted a watch for them, and then began cycling villagers off-duty. There was no point in exhausting everyone. Rotating the men home would reassure their families.

Ditmar was just finished a hunk of bread about midday when one of the village boys dashed up.

"We see the men returning!" he blurted out.

"To arms!" Ditmar ordered. "Everyone on the line!"

He had two reasons for that. First, if the dragoons mounted up, they could still intercept Richart and his men. That would be true even if half their number stayed to oppose Neustatter's horsemen. Second, obvious activity ought to draw the mercenaries' attention to the barricade rather than to the men trying to return to the village.

It almost worked. The mercenaries remounted. So did Neustatter and his men. Then one of the mercenaries pointed north.

Richart and his men were a couple hundred yards from safety. They broke into a run.

A couple mercenaries nudged their horses and started in that direction.

Ditmar wrapped the sling of the .22 around his left hand and leveled the rifle. Two riders were crossing from left to right in front of him, and several other mercenaries were spurring their horses into motion.

He led his target, exhaled slowly, and squeezed. The .22 fired with a metallic snap. Ditmar saw the rider twitch and knew he had hit him. The man stayed in the saddle, keeping a grip on the reins. But he made no attempt to draw a weapon of his own.

I got him in the right arm or shoulder, Ditmar decided. He loaded another round.

Suddenly, the lead pair of riders turned away. They headed west, angling back toward the road. A couple of the others veered after them. Others continued on, and Ditmar led his next target.

Then all of them broke to the west. Ditmar pulled the rifle back to a port arms position.

"What are they doing?" one of the teamsters asked.

"They are withdrawing out of range," Ditmar answered. "Richart and his men will be here in a minute, so that part is good. But unless I miss my guess, they are going to dig that bullet out of their man's arm and decide they are up against up-time weapons."

"*Gut*. Then they will stay away."

"Or their commanding officer will launch an all-out assault to capture up-time weapons," Ditmar warned. "It could go either way."

Richart hurried up a few minutes later. "*Dank*, Ditmar. That *was* you, *ja?*"

Ditmar nodded.

Neustatter and his men rode in shortly after.

"Nice work," he told them both. "Let us cool the horses down and start rotating men off-duty again."

"Do you want to pursue them?" someone asked.

"*Nein*. Not unless something changes. There is too great a chance they could turn the tables on us. We will wait for Hjalmar's team to return, hopefully with SoTF troops."

Over the course of the day, the villagers tired of the novelty of the sort-of-siege. Neustatter took a mounted patrol west in the mid-afternoon, spotted the mercenary squad about a quarter mile down the road, and quickly returned to the village.

"We definitely wait," he said. "They are competent. We would lose men trying to force our way through, and there is no reason to. Besides, the rest of their company cannot be too far away."

At dusk, shouts went up from the barricade on the eastern side of Flieden.

"Horsemen!"

"Cavalry, mouuunt . . . *up!*" Neustatter ordered. "Ditmar, reinforce that barricade with twenty infantry!"

But as Flieden's "cavalry" massed near the eastern barricade, Neustatter studied the seven approaching shapes and then called out, "Martin!"

A faint "Katie!" came back from the approaching horsemen.

"Our men," Neustatter stated loudly. "You can see the tan uniforms now. That's Hjalmar's patrol."

Three of the shapes resolved into Hjalmar, Otto, and Jakob. The other four were clad in orange-pink uniforms.

"At ease," Neustatter ordered. He heard Ditmar repeating the order.

Hjalmar and one of the men in the orange-pink uniforms rode up to Neustatter. Hjalmar saluted.

"Team Two reporting, Corporal Neustatter!"

Neustatter saw chevrons and saluted, and the third man returned it.

"*Ich heisse* Sergeant Dietrich Sperzel, Fulda Barracks Regiment," he said. He looked a few years older than Neustatter and wore his hair long.

"Corporal Edgar Neustatter, SoTF Reserves. My men and I are Neustatter's European Security Services. We were ambushed by a squad of mercenary dragoons while escorting machine parts to Frankfurt."

"Your men showed me the spot," Sergeant Sperzel said. "Good work fighting your way through."

"*Dank*. Do you have more men on the way?"

"Half a company, but they are on foot and should arrive about midday tomorrow," the sergeant answered.

Sperzel, Neustatter, and Hjalmar all dismounted. Two men approached them.

"Sergeant Sperzel, Ditmar Schaub is my Team One leader. Bernhardt Zeithoff is the *amtmann* of Flieden. I called up Flieden's unorganized militia with him as *hauptmann*."

Captain Zeithoff had a couple questions about the watch.

Sperzel let Neustatter do the talking.

Neustatter concluded. "*Amtmann* Zeithoff, you should evacuate the women and children from Flieden. You can give them a sufficient escort."

Zeithoff shook his head. "We do not want to leave." He sighed. "Some believe we would be ridden down on the road. Others that their goods would be stolen."

"I would not divide my forces," Sperzel stated. "Except to get the women and children out of here, I might."

"The majority would stay."

Sperzel and Neustatter exchanged looks. "If some leave and some do not, there will be trouble in the village in the future," Neustatter pointed out. "Worse if one of the two groups suffers casualties."

"I understand," Sperzel replied. "I do not *approve*, but I understand."

Once Zeithoff moved off with his answers, Sergeant Sperzel spoke again. "However you were planning it, there is no reason for me to second guess your deployments. In fact, Neustatter, I will speak bluntly since there are no villagers in earshot just now. My men and I are part of the Fulda Barracks Regiment, and we are not universally beloved by the citizens of Buchenland. As long as Zeithoff and the rest of the villagers will follow your orders, keep giving them. How did you establish your authority?"

Neustatter explained, with a few interjections from Ditmar and Hjalmar.

"And you even have some men from neighboring villages. These dragoons, they should go someplace else. I do not know why they are staying here."

"I talked to one of the prisoners last night," Neustatter said, "but he says he does not know anything. I think I believe him."

"Tell me about the casualties."

"For us, so far just one of the draft horses in the initial ambush. We defeated the ambush—killed eight and captured the other four. One of them since died of wounds. A company of about forty or fifty approached Flieden this morning. We are prepared . . ."

Sergeant Sperzel blinked several times during Neustatter's summary of events.

"Show me the defenses, *bitte*," he requested.

Zeithoff and Neustatter gave Sperzel a complete tour. When they returned to the western barricade, Neustatter directed, "Hjalmar, you and your team get some dinner and some sleep. My team will take the first watch."

"I do not see a lot of weapons." Sergeant Sperzel spoke quietly.

"Flieden has about forty matchlocks and arquebuses. The cavalry has ten, there are five at each barricade, and the infantry force has twenty. The pair hooked up to that machine do not work. Men have started arriving from other villages. Not many—perhaps forty. They have maybe a dozen arquebuses and matchlocks between them. Two crossbows. The rest have axes or scythes."

"You have twenty cavalry," Sperzel noted. "What is the other half armed with?"

"Farming implements. I tried to keep them in back. Whoever commands those dragoons is skilled. He may have figured it out by now."

Neustatter and Sergeant Sperzel conversed and planned throughout the first watch. They did not station any men in the woods. Ditmar's team took the second watch. It was quiet, as was the third watch for Hjalmar's team.

Wednesday, September 13, 1634

Neustatter had left orders that he was to be awakened early. He immediately checked the watch.

"All quiet," Hjalmar reported.

The pre-dawn was cool and humid. Hjalmar's team were all wearing their blue NESS coats. The complete absence of wind was the only thing that prevented the morning from feeling absolutely raw.

"I did not get a chance to talk to you last night, Hjalmar," Neustatter said. "Good job."

"*Dank.* We ran into Sergeant Sperzel's patrol, and they rode into Fulda with us. This Fulda Barracks Regiment is . . . different. They do not have the same technology that the National Guard troops at Camp Saale do. But their camp is well-run. It is called Barracktown, outside Fulda. Young officers, good sergeants. The commander is an up-timer, Major Derek Utt. We did not meet him personally, but everyone says he is solid."

Neustatter nodded.

"I think they are used to making do. You saw that Sperzel studied things like the clay bowls carefully."

Neustatter nodded and looked out over the barricade. "How was the ride?"

"Long. We switched horses and switched back. The up-time saddles are so much better, but we could not take time to change the tack." Hjalmar waved his hand at the defenses. "This looks like a complicated plan. Much more so than that village north of Prague."

"I could not have made this plan back then," Neustatter agreed. "And Sperzel?"

"He seems a good man." Hjalmar shrugged. "He did not give us any trouble about keeping our weapons when we entered Barracktown. Asked good questions. Got us right to an officer."

"*Gut.* Send one of your guys to wake him and another to Zeithoff." Neustatter's words were suddenly clipped. "We have visitors."

Hjalmar took one look at the squad or so of riders coming into view and sent two men racing to rouse Sperzel, Zeithoff, and the rest of the village.

Neustatter studied the approaching dragoons carefully. He figured there were plenty of ways the enemy could lose this battle but most of those involved either cockiness or foolishness or both. Yesterday's action—or lack of it, really—suggested a sober professional was in command. For just a moment, Neustatter wondered about the ambush NESS had foiled. It had been less professional, launched before all their men were in position. Sloppy. Not like the captain over there now.

Neustatter decided that if he were attacking, he would either rush the barricades at dawn or tie up the defending force with a distraction.

That squad of dragoons was advancing at a walk.

"Ditmar!" Neustatter shouted.

MISSIONS OF SECURITY

"On the way!" The Team One leader and several residents of Flieden were thirty yards away, hurrying toward the barricade.

"Take your team and ten infantry south." Neustatter pointed. "The way those horses are taking their time tells me someone's got dismounted dragoons closing in, so watch yourself."

Ditmar started giving orders.

"What is happening?" Sergeant Sperzel did not waste time with a greeting.

Neustatter sketched the situation.

"My men and I will reinforce the center."

"*Ja*, Sergeant." That was exactly where Neustatter wanted them.

He turned, spotted Captain Zeithoff, and pointed north. "*Hauptmann*, get five men with matchlocks up on roofs, *bitte*. The south or east side of the roofs, watching off to the northwest."

"You think they will attack on both flanks?" Sergeant Sperzel asked.

"Not sure. They might just move up dismounted dragoons behind that mounted squad. But I would not want a long exchange of fire at the barricade. The mounted men can ride around it if there are only a handful of men there. Easier to make us thin our lines."

Black powder weapons thundered to the south.

"Still close to nighttime, no wind," Neustatter noted. "Sound carries. That is not as big a *firefight* as it sounds. But, *Hauptmann*, send someone to make sure Hermann Topf is ready to treat any wounded. Is there anyone who assists him?"

"*Nein.*"

A matchlock thundered from a nearby roof.

"Hallo the roof!" Neustatter called through cupped hands. "What do you see?"

The man was busy reloading while trying to maintain his balance. He leaned into the slope of the roof—shingled, not thatched—and braced the butt of his matchlock against one foot.

"Men coming through the meadow!" he called down.

"How many?"

"Hard to say!"

Neustatter heard the first shot. It was not quite light enough to spot the gunpowder smoke yet, but a return shot from a rooftop suggested that someone had probably spotted the muzzle blast itself. Gunshots peppered the air to the northwest. A few more replied from rooftops.

"*Hauptmann* Zeithoff, send a team to get all the women and children out of the outermost houses. Move them east," Neustatter ordered. "Hjalmar, get your team and five more men over to the right, and let me know if those dismounted dragoons start closing in."

That left the five Fliedeners at the barricade, Sperzel's four, Neustatter's own three, and ten men from neighboring villages. Plus thirty men with farm tools. If the dragoons Neustatter could see charged, they'd take casualties. But if even ten of them made it past the barricade, they'd scatter the defenders.

Neustatter turned to the men gathered at the barricade and spoke as though he were giving directions for what they would be doing in the fields today. "If they charge down the road, I want the lead horses dead. I want them thinking about the clay bowls and the pits."

"Any horse can step over those!" one of the men from Flieden shouted.

"Sure could," Neustatter agreed. "Almost any horse I ever met could do it. But when the horse in front just took a musketball in the head? And there are loud noises everywhere around? Horses panic just like people do. They make mistakes. I want to see a lot of mistakes."

MISSIONS OF SECURITY

"Someone once told me that I was more likely to get into a high noon shootout than a backstabbing. I think it is time for that. We have the range advantage."

"But only seven rifles with that advantage," Sergeant Sperzel pointed out. "And limited ammunition."

A few minutes later, a man dashed over from the south side of Flieden (which wasn't all that far from the north side of Flieden). He ran up to Neustatter and Sperzel but addressed Zeithoff.

"Bernhardt! Claus is hit! Johann and Franz are bringing him in!"

"Take Claus to Hermann Topf's house." Neustatter spoke calmly. "Two of the men with farm tools take over from Johann and Franz."

"Johann and Claus are brothers," Zeithoff told him.

"Very well. Two men take their weapons and get back on the line. Phillip!"

Phillip Pfeffer ran over.

"Find Ditmar. Bring me a report," Neustatter ordered.

"*Ja*, sir."

Sergeant Sperzel gestured with his chin, and Neustatter obligingly stepped aside so that the two of them could talk privately.

"Neustatter, we need to hold until the half-company gets here. If the dismounted dragoons rush both flanks and the mounted men charge . . . I do not think the villagers will stand and fight."

"I agree. I think the horsemen are going to advance. I would like to take our cavalry and fight that part of the battle behind the barricade."

"Not in front of it?"

"Sergeant, when the National Guard trains recruits near Grantville, basic training ends with an exercise called *Adler Pfeffer*. The recruits attack a village, then they defend it. The villagers are paid by the National Guard. My men and I have gone back to help with this exercise."

"That is not something we have in Barracktown." Sperzel shook his head. "You are right. Sooner or later, they are going to send mounted dragoons right up the road. It just depends on how patient their *hauptmann* is. But what does that have to do with fighting on this side of the barricade?"

"Two reasons, Sergeant. First, it means the dismounted dragoons on the flanks will not be able to shoot our cavalry. Second, the militia will be defending their homes. The dragoons are going to have to pass left or right of the wagons. If several of our men can meet each of theirs as he emerges, our chances are much better. And I want to pull my men with revolvers to the center. Six shots each."

"Is that what you are carrying?"

Neustatter drew his weapon. "*Nein*, sergeant. Colt 1911 semi-automatic, seven-shot magazine. Johan, Jakob, and Phillip have the new revolvers—and Otto has an up-time .38. *Und* I have been holding out. The dozen snaphance pistols we took from the squad that ambushed us are in these wagons."

"What were you saving them for?" Sergeant Sperzel demanded. He sounded genuinely angry.

"The decisive moment." Neustatter was unflustered. "I think three men in each wagon, lying low until you give the signal. Once the mounted dragoons are bunched up trying to go around the wagons. There will not be time to reload."

"If we lose, they will massacre the village."

Neustatter remembered the conversation he'd had with Ditmar after their defense of Birkig in basic training: "Next time, we probably ought to get farmers and the unit out . . . One of several errors."

The civilians didn't want to leave, and it was probably too late to get away, anyway. Militarily, the best course of action was to abandon the village. But Neustatter could understand why people didn't want to leave their homes. They'd just have to hold until relieved.

"What time is it?" he called out.

"Who knows?" someone called back. "Seven o'clock, maybe."

"Six hours," Neustatter declared. "We need to hold for six hours."

Lukas heard him. "That is twice as long as Birkig."

Neustatter was grateful Heidenfelder hadn't added the rest: ". . . and we never lasted the full three hours in that mission." On the other hand, that was against three companies of SoTF veterans with a couple cannons. Here in Flieden, they were facing only about fifty dragoons.

But they had only four men from the Fulda Barracks Regiment, six NESS agents who were Reservists, and three other NESS agents. And about a hundred militia, only half of them with firearms.

"On the other hand," Neustatter said aloud, "our messengers have already reached the nearest base. Reinforcements are coming. We just need to hold the fort." He smiled. "That is a lot better than Birkig, where we were losing to buy Sara Carroll time to warn Camp Saale."

Phillip raced toward them. "Neustatter! Two men down! The dragoons are closing in!"

Neustatter turned to the men from nearby villagers and counted off ten of them. "Go get the wounded. Recover their weapons if possible." He addressed the ten with arquebuses. "You are under Philip's command. Five of you fire at a time. Give Ditmar's men time to withdraw. Go.

"*Hauptmann* Zeithoff! I needed these houses opened up. If there are any tables inside, put them on their sides outside. Build a wall. Lukas will show you what I mean. Take as many of the unarmed men as you need."

Neustatter had already set eight men aside. The two with crossbows were behind the wagons along with five men with matchlocks who were the guard force there.

"You men all said you have fired a pistol before," he said to the other six. Heads nodded. "Up in the wagons. There is a box under the seat of each. There are six pistols in each. Do not raise them into view, but check them over. When the mounted dragoons charge, stay down. Once they bunch up trying to pass left and right of the wagons, fire one pistol and then the other. Aim. And fire. Point blank range."

"Sounds dangerous. Where are you going to be?" one man challenged.

"Right here. I am going to create the cavalry pile-up you are going to fire into. I want the men down, not the horses." Neustatter had a thought. "I do not really know what the National Guard rules are, Sergeant Sperzel. Who keeps the horses we are going to capture? I think the villagers should get some of them."

"That is above my pay grade," Sperzel answered.

Men came running up from the fields south of Flieden.

"There are too many of them!"

"Run! Run!"

"Halt!" Neustatter ordered. "Get behind these tables. Take a knee. Give the rest of your men some cover fire."

One man threw away his weapon and ran. Neustatter tackled him, stripped the powder horn and bag of musketballs off him, and let him go. The men scrambled to his feet and raced off, making it to the eastern edge of Flieden before the laughter of Flieden's "cavalry" brought him up short.

Neustatter had already recovered the man's matchlock. He stepped behind one of the tables. It was part of an intermittent row from the second house south of the road to the third and on to the fourth.

"I have not used one of these since basic training." His words were loud but casual as he loaded the matchlock. "Five, six," he counted as two more men ran back into the village. He held the slow match next to another man's, succeeding in relighting it.

MISSIONS OF SECURITY

Ditmar was next. He and another man were carrying one of the casualties. Two more men were right behind him with the other casualty. Then Phillip's squad began falling back.

About a dozen dismounted dragoons approached in a skirmish line. Neustatter let them close inside seventy yards.

"Take a knee, men," he ordered. "They will fire soon."

The oncoming line halted.

"Quiet!" Neustatter ordered.

Some of the defenders actually heard the order to the dismounted dragoons to make ready.

"Pick your targets." Neustatter spoke more quietly. He selected the man he thought was probably in command of this detachment.

"Fire!" Neustatter gave the order first.

His target slumped, although Neustatter didn't know if he'd actually been the one who hit him. Nor did he know whether the man was badly injured or not. He ducked behind the table rather than trying to find out. One militiaman was hit.

"Charge!"

Neustatter popped back up. He saw nine dismounted dragoons charging.

"Phillip! Johan! Richart! Aim!" Neustatter dropped the matchlock and drew the .45. He held the Colt in a two-handed grip. At thirty yards, he exhaled, squeezed the trigger, and the semi-automatic fired. He brought the sights back on target and fired again. The man was reeling from the first shot. Neustatter thought the second had been a wasted shot and moved to the next target.

He fired twice, and the man stumbled. Neustatter heard the distinctive blast of Richart's shotgun and the reports of black powder revolvers. He turned back to his left and found a third target.

Neustatter fired once and missed. But the man suddenly turned and fled. Neustatter looked further left and saw no attackers. He spun back to his right and saw a dragoon going down. The noise of gunfire died away, and the battle appeared to be over on the southern edge of Flieden. An eerie silence was punctuated by scattered shots on the north side.

"Lukas! Richart! Prisoner teams!" Neustatter ordered. "Hans! Phillip! Step inside a house to reload! I don't want the dragoons getting a good look! *Hauptmann* Zeithoff, have men take the wounded to Topf!"

Neustatter crouched behind the table and turned to his left. He ejected the magazine from his pistol and slammed a fresh one home. Then he holstered the Colt and dug out five rounds to bring the mostly depleted magazine back up to seven. A moment later, he was on his feet, striding toward the two-wagon barricade in the road.

"Report," Sergeant Sperzel ordered.

"Dragoons to the south forced our men back into town. We just broke their charge." Neustatter was not even looking at Sperzel. His gaze was fixed on the mounted dragoons.

"Sorry, Sergeant." But he still watched the dragoons. "They are a lot closer than they were."

"They stopped when all hell broke loose on the left," Sperzel told him.

"Have you sent a runner to our right?" Neustatter asked.

"*Nein.*"

Neustatter looked around for the teamsters and beckoned the two he saw forward. "Where are the other two teamsters?"

Lorenz shrugged. "They disappeared."

Neustatter snorted. "Like Jimmy Hoffa."

Lorenz and Heinrich both laughed.

"We are not much good to you in a battle, Neustatter," Lorenz pointed out.

"You are about to be. Lorenz, run over to those houses on the south side of Flieden. I want Hans and Phillip here at the barricade. *Und* I want a report from Ditmar." Even as Lorenz hurried off, Neustatter was speaking to Heinrich. "Heinrich, I need a report from Hjalmar on the north side. I do not know what roof he is on. Be careful, but tell me how close the dismounted dragoons are."

It took longer than Neustatter wanted, but he forced himself not to fidget. Phillip and Hans showed up first.

"How is the left?" Neustatter asked them.

"Quiet," Hans told him. "I think we had a half a dozen men hit. A handful of dragoons fled."

Ditmar showed up a couple minutes later. "Neustatter, Sergeant Sperzel, the left is secure for now."

"*Dank*, Ditmar."

"Rescue teams and prisoner teams are working."

"Good work," Neustatter told him. "Send teams for any weapons the dragoons had."

"Already on it. With your permission, I will get back there."

"Go," Sperzel agreed.

"*Und* with permission, I will check the right," Neustatter said.

He had a feeling the right was in trouble. He'd heard intermittent fire, but it had died away.

Before Neustatter was even fully away from the barricade, he encountered Heinrich. The teamster was at a dead run.

"They are overrunning the houses!" the man gasped out. He kept going.

Neustatter pivoted to his right and sprinted toward the horses. "Cavalry, mount up! Mouuunt . . . *up!*" *Now* it was just like Adler Pfeffer.

He mounted one of NESS's horses, and within a minute, twenty mounted men were cantering across an open area where the three rows of houses in Flieden narrowed down to two, aiming north between the second and third houses from the western end of the village.

Neustatter spotted a dismounted dragoon coming around the corner of the third house. The man brought up his matchlock. Neustatter fired first, second, and fourth. The first two shots were enough to throw off the dragoon's aim. The last one hit him in the side.

Neustatter pulled on the reins, directing his horse around the same corner. A second dismounted dragoon was caught by surprise. He did not get his matchlock leveled in time, and Neustatter kicked at it. It spun away. Neustatter heard an impact. At least one of the cavalry following him had thudded into the man.

Neustatter rode east. Three dragoons had already gained the roof of the next house. Neustatter dimly recognized the roof shingles were brown, not faded to an almost-gray like the roofs of most of the other houses. At ground level, two more dragoons were helping another up toward the roof.

None of the dragoons were taking fire, so at least a couple of Flieden's defense were down or had been run off. Neustatter reined in, leveled the Colt, and shot one man off the roof.

The other two spun around. One lost his footing and slid. Neustatter fired two rounds at the other. Some of the cavalry fired, too. One round hit. The man swayed, regained his balance. Somewhere a rifle fired, and the man pitched to the ground.

Neustatter fired his last round into one of the men boosting his buddy up. He'd rushed it and was fairly certain the man was not seriously wounded. But it certainly caused him to lose his grip, and the man halfway onto the roof crashed down onto him. Neustatter nudged his horse with his knees while ejecting the magazine. He slammed a fresh one in.

Only then did he glance back. Enough of the "cavalry" had followed him to overrun the half dozen dragoons, four of whom were already wounded. He saw a couple cavalry bypass that action. *Gut*, he would have backup.

Neustatter rode past the fifth house (with another nearly gray roof and some fancier external trim) without seeing another dragoon. Well, there was one down in the field north of Flieden. He cornered around to the east side of the house and slowed the horse to a walk. The flank had been overrun, but the dragoons hadn't cleared all his men from the roofs. So where were the rest of them? At least there did not seem to be noncombatants in the area. He wondered who had gotten them out of the line of fire.

Two dragoons suddenly burst out the front door of the house. Before Neustatter could even spur his horse, one went down in a hail of gunfire. The other dove back inside.

Up-time weapon. Six shots. Revolver. Otto.

"Martin!" Neustatter shouted.

A shot rang out. Aimed at him. *Badly* aimed at him. Neustatter had no idea where the shot had come from.

He edged his horse around the next corner, back onto the road. Neustatter aimed the Colt at the door as he rode past.

He turned north, getting between the fourth and fifth houses. That cut down most of the firing angles, except for the window on the west side, unusually close to the front of the building. Neustatter aimed at it, expecting the man inside to poke a musket or pistol barrel out any time now.

The dragoon proved to be cannier than that.

Neustatter didn't have time for this. He swung back around to the road. The two riders following him were approaching the house.

"Halt!" Neustatter ordered. "Dismount! One of you cover the window. The other cover the door. Just keep him there."

Neustatter saw one man dismount, so evidently, they were going to follow orders. Or at least try to. Neustatter touched the reins and headed back the way he had come. A confused melee was still going on behind the house next door. None of the dragoons were still on the roof. At least half his cavalry was involved, including some of those with farm implements.

Neustatter rode past them, gathering up a few riders on the fringe. He had to check the first house in the row, the northwesternmost house in Flieden.

A shot spooked his horse, kicking up dirt about a yard left of its front hoof. Neustatter managed to hold on. He wasn't sure if the horse's antics caused the second shot to miss, or if it would have missed anyway. But it seemed he'd found the rest of the dismounted dragoons.

Neustatter wanted to charge. But he couldn't account for about half a dozen of the enemy. They could all be in there. So he wheeled left, between the second and third houses.

The four mounted men following him pulled up in confusion.

"Ride with me!" he shouted. He nudged the horse to a canter across the open ground in the middle of Flieden.

It was risky. There were dragoons inside two houses that he knew of, and they could be looking his way. And there could be one or two more just about anywhere.

But he had to get back to the western barricade before the dragoons in the first house figured out that if they took the second house, they could enfilade the entire barricade. If they did that, the mounted dragoons could charge virtually unopposed.

Neustatter's horse didn't have time to reach a gallop before he reached the barricade. A man from the Fulda Barracks Regiment was already kneeling at the corner of the right-hand wagon, firing back at the house.

Then he drew back to reload, and Hans Deibert peppered the house with his revolver.

A whole lot of people were scrambling for cover.

Then Sperzel, another of his men, and Lukas fired into the house. Ditmar opened up a steady fire, a shot every five seconds or so with the .22 rifle.

Neustatter tossed his reins to one of the other riders and slid off his horse.

"Get those tables!" he ordered.

Sperzel stole a look down the road. "No time, Neustatter! Here they come!'"

Neustatter couldn't see over the wagons from where he was. But he kept running to the front left corner of two-wagon barricade. He spotted an unarmed man and grabbed him.

"I am the lookout!" the man proclaimed. "They are coming!"

"I know, I know!" Neustatter pointed south. "Run over and get my men. I want everyone over there right here, right now."

He popped up over the side of wagon on the left. "You three ready?" he asked the men lying in the bed of the wagon.

"*Ja,* we are ready."

"When I shout, pop up, AIM, and fire. One pistol at a time!" Neustatter warned.

"Rifles front!" Sergeant Sperzel ordered.

"Pistols, reload!" Neustatter added. "Do not fire until I give the order!"

Neustatter had a couple seconds to glance around. The defense was disorganized. A solid push by the dragoons, and . . .

Sergeant Sperzel shot the lead rider in the head.

The charge disintegrated and men peeled off in both directions. It would have been a caracole, but they didn't even fire.

Neustatter took careful aim, but the range was long, and he did not think his three shots hit anyone.

Sperzel swore.

Neustatter satisfied himself that the dragoons were not going to suddenly wheel about, then took a few steps over to the sergeant.

"*Exzellent* shot, Sergeant."

"I did not mean to break the charge," Sperzel said ruefully. "I know you wanted them closer in for pistol work."

Neustatter spoke quietly. "That was my plan, but I honestly do not know if we could have stopped fifteen mounted men. I did not get an exact count. There may have been twenty, and we would have been hard-pressed. Better that you broke them early, I think."

Some of the villagers at the barricade were taunting the enemy. The four men from the Fulda Barracks Regiment were not.

"That is a good officer over there, Sergeant," one of them stated, "*und* a disciplined company to pull back on command."

Another said, "Look! They are dismounting."

"Aw, crap," Neustatter said. "He *is* good. They are going to try to close in again. They are good skirmishers. We have taken casualties, too."

"Rally the flanks," Sperzel commanded.

Most of the men from the left flank were running toward the barricade. "Ditmar, take charge of them," Neustatter directed. "Hold the houses but stay out of the fields."

Neustatter grabbed Richart and assigned him to suppressing fire on the northwesternmost house. Once there, it took several minutes to get the "cavalry" under control. A couple men and a couple horses had been injured.

"You four"—Neustatter poked each of them in the chest—"get these two to Topf. You four, dismount and *sneak* up to the second house. One at a time, fire at the first house and *don't get shot!*"

"You and you, cover these dragoons. Just because they look dead does not mean they are. Now you two, check them. If any of them are alive, get them to Topf."

"We could take care of that . . ."

"You will do it my way," Neustatter snapped.

That took care of all the cavalry at this house. He turned and beckoned to the four who had been following him around.

"Dismount. Which of you can hold five sets of reins?"

"I can," a thick-set man volunteered.

"The other three of you come with me," Neustatter directed. "Are your slow matches still burning?"

One man's had gone out, but he quickly got it relit.

"We should have thirteen men over here," Neustatter told them. "I left two of our cavalry watching the house behind us. There was a dragoon in there."

One of the men grimaced. "That is Friedrich's house. The enemy has probably stolen everything." Then a thoughtful expression crossed his face. "Friedrich always says he cannot see what goes on in the back corner of the field. I bet I can sneak right up to the window."

Neustatter nodded. "Do it. I will cover the window."

The man crept up and carefully peered in. Then he came back.

"I do not see anyone," he reported.

Neustatter made his way past the window to the front corner of the house. The two cavalrymen he'd stationed here were nowhere in sight.

Then he heard someone call, "Martin!"

"Katie!" Neustatter shouted back.

Otto Brenner stood and waved from between the two westernmost houses in the middle row—without exposing himself to fire from that last house in the northwest. He pointed.

Neustatter looked in that direction and spotted Hjalmar on the next roof. That explained who had shot the one dragoon off the roof. Hjalmar would have line of sight on the house the dragoons held, although it would probably be a difficult shot.

Neustatter drew back so that no one to the east or west would see him. He pointed at Hjalmar, then at Otto. Finally, he held three fingers before stretching both hands out to each side, palms up, and tilting his head. He hoped they understood: Where is your third man?

Otto pointed to the house where Neustatter had expected to find a trapped dragoon guarded by two cavalrymen. He held his hand with two fingers down and waggled them to indicate a man running. Then he used both hands in a bounding motion. The gait was all wrong, but Neustatter knew he meant a mounted man. Otto continued the pantomime, and Neustatter quickly understood that Jakob and some of the other men he'd sent to this flank had flushed the dragoon out of the house and carried him off. That meant that somewhere, someone had established a prisoner collection point.

Next Otto told him that four villagers had been shot in this area.

Crap. This *was* just like *Adler Pfeffer*.

It took longer than he wanted, but Neustatter got the right flank under control. He reported back to Sergeant Sperzel.

"Sergeant, the enemy holds the last house in the northwest. Probably about four of them in there. We had several men killed or wounded on the right. But we have contained the attack."

Sperzel sighed. "Casualties are piling up." He glanced down the road. "About a dozen of them have dismounted and are spread out like skirmishers. They have been coming closer."

Neustatter followed Sperzel's gaze and frowned. "A dozen? I see a dozen mounted. How can they have that many left?"

Smoke blossomed in front of one of the skirmishers, then another.

"Long-range battle?" Neustatter wondered. "They have to know their fire will not accurate from that far away."

"They are fixing us in place," Sergeant Sperzel pointed out.

"No need," Neustatter countered. "They could leave any time they want. Unless . . ."

"A few of them approach to recover any wounded?" Sperzel wondered.

"Maybe, but I have a bad feeling about this, Sergeant."

Neustatter started doing math. "Fifteen south, fifteen north, fifteen mounted in the center, *ja*?"

Sperzel shrugged. "About that. More than twelve but less than twenty in each group."

"I saw nine men charge on the left. That means six or so were down. Or maybe did not charge." Neustatter paused and recalled what he had seen on the right. "I know what happened to eleven dragoons on the right, and we are reasonably sure there are four men in that house. So, if they have two dozen in the center now . . ."

"Reinforcements, you think?" Sperzel asked.

"What time is it, Sergeant?"

"Certainly not nine o'clock yet."

"Then let them besiege us, Sergeant. That takes time. We need to hold for at least four more hours."

Sergeant Sperzel reorganized the men at the western barricade while Neustatter and Zeithoff reorganized the rest of Flieden.

"Four dead, eight wounded." Zeithoff was beyond angry. "If you had ridden away from Flieden night before last like I asked . . ."

"We would have run into these dragoons not very far down the road. We would have shot up the first squad we ran into but then we would have had to retreat back this way. Flieden would have a lot less time to prepare, so those dragoons might have come charging right down the road. Our casualties—yours *und* mine—would have been higher." The edge disappeared from Neustatter's voice. "I am truly sorry we lost anyone."

Hermann Topf's house was crowded with wounded. Flieden's pastor and several women were now assisting Topf. Neustatter wished he'd brought Wolfram. And he hoped that the promised half-company of the Fulda Barracks Regiment had a medic.

Next, Neustatter checked on the prisoners.

"*Nein!*" he shouted. "We are not locking them all in a house together." He pointed at two men from Flieden. "You and you, bring back ten men armed with farm tools."

As soon as they arrived, Neustatter opened the door of the house with his left hand. He leveled the Colt with his right.

"Walk out here one at a time," he ordered. "I am not going to do anything to you except inconvenience you."

A single file of five prisoners shuffled outside. They were the ones well enough to walk.

Every time Neustatter passed a tree, he ordered one prisoner to kneel, cross his ankles, and hug the tree.

"Now, two of you stand guard. The other eight of you, drop those scythes and get the wounded prisoners still in that house over to Hermann Topf. He has a bunch already." Neustatter took the two sentries aside and spoke quietly. "After ten minutes, these prisoners will not be able to stand without assistance. They will be fine. Lay them down for a few minutes every hour or so. We do not want to hurt them."

"*Ja*, we do," one of the sentries argued.

"*Nein*. Straight up attack on a defended position. Their *hauptmann* is smart, too. I have not seen a single attack against women or children. *Nein*, our issue is with whoever sent them."

"I have been thinking about that," Zeithoff declared. "This attack does not make sense."

"You noticed that, too," Neustatter observed. "The only reason to attack Flieden is that we made a stand here."

"Maybe they want you and your men dead."

"Why?" Neustatter countered. "They do not know we wiped out their other squad. They probably suspect it by now, but they had no reason to suspect it when they committed to attack Flieden."

"They are invading," one of the Flieden militia declared.

"A cavalry company with no support? What kind of invasion leaves dragoons besieging a village for two days? They ought to be scouting, or General Brahe in Frankfurt will catch them between his army and the Fulda Barracks Regiment. *Nein*, they are on a mission they cannot abandon. Have to be. They could have drawn back and ridden two miles around Flieden and been on their way yesterday afternoon."

He took that observation back to Sergeant Sperzel.

"Sounds like you broke up a rendezvous, Neustatter," Sperzel told him.

"Could be," Neustatter agreed. "Probably is. Reckon I better divide the militia into ten-man squads and resupply ammunition. With your permission, Sergeant?"

"Do it," Sperzel told him.

"*Hauptmann* Zeithoff, whom do you recommend as sergeants?" Neustatter asked.

He started on the left and noticed that the dismounted dragoons had advanced a few steps.

"They are going to keep that up until they are in range," Neustatter told the men on the left. "Make them be careful. No need for all of you to blaze away at them, but if one of 'em stands up to dash forward, somebody shoot him for me."

"*Ja*, Corporal Neustatter."

Neustatter had to follow a circuitous route back to the north side of Flieden. He took several men with him. Once there, he pulled some of the non-cavalrymen back so that he could brief all ten at once.

"Johann, *Hauptmann* Zeithoff says you are the sergeant," Neustatter began. "Your job is to guard this flank. There are only two things to do. First, keep the dragoons in the last house from spreading out. We do not care if they stay there. But we do not want them to get reinforced. So if more of 'em start sneaking through the fields, shoot them. But—second thing—keep your heads down."

Then he started pulling Flieden's "cavalrymen" back to locate their horses. Naturally, some of the horses had run off. But Neustatter was able to place eleven mounted men in the middle of Flieden, out of the line of fire. They were all armed with pistols taken from the Irish dragoons.

He left *Hauptmann* Zeithoff there, too, in command of fifteen men with matchlocks.

"You are the reserves," Neustatter told him. "We are going to be firing back and forth all morning. At some point, you may be the last men with gunpowder. I will send a runner if we need you. But if you see the dragoons attack the barricade, come running."

Once he returned to the barricade—taking the long way around a few houses to stay in cover—Neustatter took a knee next to where Sergeant Sperzel was crouched down.

"*Gut.* Your NESS men are here."

"*Exzellent.* I lost track of Jakob."

"Tough-looking man, carries one of the new revolvers?" Sperzel asked. "Came by dripping blood. Stop, Neustatter! I sent him to Topf. It is not bad. Go bring Zeithoff's reserve up to where the three rows of houses narrow down to two rows."

Neustatter understood at once. "Ready to fall on a force that flanks the barricade from either the north or the south?"

"*Ja.*"

"Economy of force, the up-timers call it."

"What's that?"

"The minimum force necessary to accomplish something. What we have on the flanks. That allows us to achieve another principle, mass. Overwhelming force at the critical point here in the center."

"I am not sure another fifteen militia with matchlocks is overwhelming."

"It is not ideal," Neustatter admitted. He looked at Sergeant Sperzel's expression and began to suspect that the up-time terminology was not part of the Fulda Barracks Regiment's training. No matter. Sperzel obviously had enough combat experience to intuit the principles of war. He just didn't have the up-timer names.

Neustatter peered under the wagon at the dismounted dragoons. They had dared another five yards or so.

No time like the present . . . "The up-timers have nine principles of warfare. They got them from a German." At Sperzel's raised eyebrows, Neustatter continued. "The first is objective. Ours is to hold Flieden. Theirs . . . we will come back to that. . . ."

Neustatter had reached 'unity of command' when the dismounted dragoons opened fire.

"There is a rare mistake," Neustatter observed. "All firing together, I mean." He paused to count the smoke puffs. "Twenty-one, I think."

"*Und* I still see plenty of mounted men." Sperzel's tone was sour.

"You are right. They have been reinforced by a second company."

"The second company's *hauptmann* is senior. He is calling the shots—literally. The *hauptmann* we have been facing for two days now would not make this mistake," Neustatter stated.

"That is guesswork, but I tend to agree," Sperzel replied. He raised his voice. "Hold your fire, men."

The second volley was ragged. A few men on the south side of Flieden returned fire, but not all. Neustatter nodded to Ditmar, who dashed over to remind them not to match shot for shot. They did not have enough ammunition to keep that up indefinitely.

The dismounted dragoons hadn't hit anyone so far. That didn't change with their third volley.

"Interesting," Sperzel said. "Do you see where their *hauptmann* is?"

"South of the road, about the sixth man in?" Neustatter ventured.

"Exactly. *Und* his sergeant is in about the same place north of the road."

"How do you know that?" one of the men from Flieden asked.

"Watch," Sperzel told him. "They are almost reloaded. Count six men south of the road."

"I see the sixth man."

The fourth volley rippled out.

"Oh!"

"Exactly. He fires first. The men to either side of him are firing when they see or hear him fire. The sergeant north of the road is doing the same, and his men follow him," Sperzel explained.

"Sergeant, would you like him targeted?" Neustatter asked.

"Absolutely." Sperzel did not hesitate. "Not that I do not respect him . . . in fact, because I *do* respect him."

Neustatter hurried off to locate Ditmar. He found him in the house furthest west. It was not only beyond the wagon barricade but set about twenty yards back from the road, just far enough they the defenders inside couldn't coordinate effectively with the men at the barricade.

"Neustatter, did you just run through a volley?" Ditmar asked.

"I do not know that 'through' is the right word. There may have been some rounds in my general direction. Speaking of which, have you seen their pattern?"

"That the man in the center of the line fires first? *Ja*." Ditmar looked back out the window. "Probably a sergeant."

"Sergeant Sperzel and I were wondering if that is the *hauptmann* of the company we have been facing, sent out by the *hauptmann* of the newly arrived company. Can you hit him?"

"Interesting thought. Maybe." Ditmar looked back to Neustatter. "But if I do, that squad may charge this house."

Neustatter held up his M1911 Colt.

"All right," Ditmar said. "Before or after the next volley?"

"After. We do not need some competent dragoon hanging back during the charge and covering his buddies."

Ditmar eased his .22 rifle into position, resting the last couple inches of the barrel on the windowsill. He waited for the man to level his weapon, then exhaled and began squeezing the trigger. As soon as he saw smoke, he fired.

The volley rippled down the line.

"No idea," Ditmar announced before anyone could ask. He waited for the smoke to drift clear.

"Must have missed." Ditmar aimed again. He fired. Fired again. Fired again.

Neustatter saw the man go down. A couple other dragoons rushed to his side. The other dragoons spattered a few shots at the house while the first two carried the officer to safety.

"Too far for a moving target," Ditmar grumbled. "I hit him, but not badly. They have his arms over their shoulders. He is moving mostly under his own power."

"This house is going to get shot to pieces now," one of the men from Flieden predicted. "Hans will be angry about it—and rightly so."

He was right. Musketballs began thudding into the house at regular intervals, making different noises depending on which part of the half-timber construction they hit. The thunks into the wood were a lot more disturbing than the louder impact of lead balls against stone.

"Get away from the window," Neustatter ordered. "You are right. We are going to have to abandon this house." He counted off three men. "You three and Ditmar, run back one house after their next volley. We four will cover you. Find positions to cover us."

The door of the house faced north. Ditmar cautiously looked out to the west.

"They are advancing!"

"My team, fire from the window!" Neustatter ordered. "Ditmar, coming through!"

Neustatter ran out the door and dropped to one knee. He brought the Colt up, fired two shots at the nearest dragoon, and began moving down the line. "Run, run, run!"

Ditmar and his three men took off. A couple Flieden men in the next house gave them additional cover fire.

Neustatter ejected the empty magazine. Thirty yards. He slammed in the next one. Twenty-five. Brought the pistol up. Twenty.

He fired twice, and the dragoon stumbled and fell. Neustatter tracked left and fired two shots that both missed. But that dragoon hit the ground. Neustatter spun back to his right in time to see a dragoon go down. Then the rest broke and fled.

"Cover me!" Neustatter leapt to his feet and ran to the men who had been shot. The first was dead. The second was not. He lifted the man in a fireman's carry and ran back.

"Neustatter!" Ditmar shouted. "What are you doing?"

Neustatter spilled the man to the ground behind the second house. "Pressure on the wound," he ordered one of Ditmar's men. He'd hit the dragoon in the side. The injury did not look immediately fatal.

After Ditmar studied the battle for a moment, he asked again, "What *are* you doing, Neustatter?"

"Gathering intel." The dragoon had red hair. Neustatter played the odds and addressed him in English. "Soldier, can you hear me?"

The man moaned.

"You with MacDonald's regiment?"

The dragoon moaned in pain. Somewhere in there was a "yes."

"Your officer—captain, yes?—was he pushed aside by the new captain?"

Ditmar shook his head. "That may have been another yes, Neustatter. But maybe that is just what we want to hear."

Neustatter allowed himself a thin smile. One of the many reasons Ditmar and Hjalmar were his team leaders was their ability to step back and assess new information. Stefan was cynical enough to disbelieve all of it, and Lukas tended to get caught up in the possibilities and believe too much of it. He needed team leaders like the Schaub cousins.

For a moment, he was distracted by the thought that he had a third Schaub. A Schäubin, actually. Once Astrid had some more experience, he ought to make her the Team 3 leader so that he wasn't trying to run a team and the overall mission at the same time.

Neustatter snapped back to his immediate concern.

"The captain commanding you skirmishers just now, is he the one who was in command yesterday?"

The man gasped in pain. "You . . . shot . . . him," he got out.

"Had to," Neustatter stated. "He is too good. But I saw two men help him to the rear under his own power."

"Oh . . . good. Only . . . good captain . . . MacDonald's . . ." The man gave up trying to say more.

"I will have two men take you to the medic." Neustatter looked up at a couple of the Flieden men. "You heard? That is intelligence. I will tell

Sergeant Sperzel we may take greater liberties with the other *hauptmann*. See to it that this man gets to *Herr* Topf."

"Topf is not a *herr*."

Neustatter sighed. "Flieden is fighting in its own defense. Have the *adel* or the *lehen*holders come to the defense of your homes?"

"*Nein*."

"Who are the real *herren*, then?" Neustatter stood. "Now let's reoccupy the first house. It is Hans's home, *ja*?"

About ten minutes later, Neustatter made a cautious dash back to the barricade.

"Report," Sergeant Sperzel ordered.

"Wounded the officer and drove off the advance on the left, Sergeant," Neustatter said.

"Good work, Neustatter." Sperzel pointed at matchlocks propped against the two wagons. "I thought about arming ten more men, but there is not room for them here. There is not much gunpowder left, either. So they are loaded and waiting. If the mounted dragoons, charge, we will fire our weapons, then grab these."

Neustatter nodded in understanding. "They ought to charge soon."

"Ought to. I do not know if they will," Sperzel returned.

"Is the other half of the dragoons' skirmish line still lying in the field about seventy yards out?"

"Most of them. A couple fell back with the other half of the line."

Minutes passed.

More minutes passed.

Neustatter checked with Sperzel and started cautiously putting men back up on rooftops. They drew some fire, none of it accurate.

Hjalmar nimbly dropped to the ground from his own roof and made his way to Neustatter.

"Neustatter, most of the skirmish line north of the road is still there, but someone just ran up to them. He was zigzagging. I could not get a decent shot."

"Orders," Neustatter surmised.

"They are thinning the line!" one of Sperzel's men called. He was peering over the wagons. "Every other man just dropped back ten yards!"

"Leaving? Or a new plan?" Sergeant Sperzel mused.

"Hjalmar." Neustatter delivered his instructions calmly. "Take Lukas. Get up on a couple roofs that can cover the barricade. Ditmar, anyone who looks like he is in charge is your target. Hans, Jakob, you are with me on the left of the wagons. Otto and Phillip, you are on the right of the wagons, but do not step out until Richart puts a few shotgun blasts into that house to keep those dragoons' heads down."

Sperzel looked at Neustatter. "You figure they are going to charge." It was more of a statement than a question.

"*Ja*. The first *hauptmann* would not have. Not now. This second one . . . how many cavalry officers have you met who would not roll the dice on a charge?"

Sperzel snorted. "None." He raised his voice. "You men in the wagons! The dragoons might be getting ready! Stay down but sound off!"

They did.

"That is all six," Sperzel told Neustatter.

"We are as ready as we can be," Neustatter told him.

Nothing happened.

"We have got to get a telescope or binoculars," Neustatter stated several minutes later.

"Astrid is not here to write that down," Ditmar reminded him.

"I think I will leave my ink and quill right where they are in my pack," Neustatter returned.

"I suppose you could throw it at them."

Throw it! Neustatter looked at Ditmar. "Explosives. We need explosives."

"Not enough gunpowder left to burn up on grenades," Ditmar pointed out.

Neustatter certainly didn't want the militia thinking about doing that. Quickly, he asked, "What have we seen in *Adler Pfeffer?*"

"Alcohol."

Neustatter spun around. "*Hauptmann* Zeithoff! Are there bottles of liquor in Flieden?"

Zeithoff looked suspicious. "Why?"

"Grenades." *Ja*, technically he meant Molotov cocktails. He didn't have time to explain the difference.

Five minutes later, they had two bottles of genever.

"Light a little bit of that," Neustatter directed.

They tried and failed repeatedly.

"Ditmar?"

Ditmar laughed. "Remind you when this is over to write yourself a note to find out when alcohol will burn?"

Lukas spoke up unexpectedly. "I know. Not enough alcohol. Too much water. You have to get some of the water out, but you cannot, because the alcohol will boil off first."

Neustatter, Ditmar, Zeithoff, and Sperzel exchanged glances.

"Sounds right to me," Neustatter declared. "We need another plan. What else burns?"

"Straw." Zeithoff's answer came instantly. "I am surprised the battle has not set any on fire yet. If Flieden catches fire . . ."

"Straw in the dirt, though . . ." Neustatter mused. "Either side of the wagons, where they would have to come through . . ."

"A man with a torch on each side . . ." Sperzel added. "I like this. Sure, there is a fire in the road for a couple minutes . . ."

"That could spread," Zeithoff worried.

"You still have unarmed men. Have them bring the fire buckets forward, then scatter some straw."

Neustatter expected the dragoons to put two and two together and charge before Flieden's defenders were ready. How hard was it to connect water buckets and straw and realize there was going to be a fire? But maybe their plan was not to come straight down the road.

"What if they split in half and hit both flanks—further back where we have no defenses set up?" Neustatter asked.

Zeithoff paled, but Sergeant Sperzel shook his head. "We shift forces when we see them move. But we need barriers to cut down their choices."

"More tables and furniture," Neustatter told Zeithoff. "A solid line between houses. They will ride for unobstructed gaps between houses. That is where we will defend."

He didn't point out how deadly that could be. Then he realized something.

"Better idea," Neustatter corrected himself. "We will station ourselves behind the passages that *have* tables. Spread straw across the ones we do not have enough barriers for. Once they see one burn, they will stay away from all straw."

That was . . . flimsy. But the new *hauptmann* of dragoons was no *rocket surgeon*.

Some minutes later, they were crouched behind the wagons, as ready as they were likely to get. Ditmar muttered, "I cannot believe they are giving us more time to prepare. We should have done this the first night."

"You are right," Neustatter admitted. "I did not think of it until now."

"Neither did the rest of us," Ditmar pointed out.

"The first *hauptmann*'s plan seemed to be to scout us and then strike the flanks in hopes of thinning the center."

"And then charge the center," Ditmar finished. "It might have worked. But this new man . . ."

"He has surrendered the initiative to us," Neustatter stated, "but we dare not take the offensive. They would defeat us in the open field." He dropped his voice to just above a whisper. "*Und* we do not have enough ammunition for a drawn-out, long-range duel."

"What if they chased our cavalry?" Ditmar asked.

"Ambush?" Neustatter asked. He thought it over. "Suppose we empty twenty saddles."

Ditmar grimaced. "That is optimistic, *und* it still leaves them about fifty. We do not want all seventy galloping at us right now."

"Once the Fulda Barracks Regiment half-company arrives," Neustatter stated. "They can be the ambush."

"Fifty SoTF troops? That would do it."

"You snipe leaders," Neustatter directed. "I fire. The rest of the pistols wait for the counterattack. I can load a new magazine by then."

"Neustatter, do you remember when the firing rates of the U.S. Waffenfabrik rifles and SRGs were impressive?"

"Still are, in large battles," Neustatter pointed out. "But with revolvers, a semi-automatic, and a shotgun . . ." He gave Ditmar a thin smile. "Miss Schäubin is going to frown at me, ever so politely, when I give her the replacement ammunition expenses."

Ditmar got a look in his eye. "Neustatter, I still think you and Astrid . . ."

"*Nein.* We are a lot alike. Maybe too much."

"Neustatter, you are an officer in all but name. Astrid is . . . a secretary."

"*Und* a NESS agent, Ditmar. Think where she will be in six years. Further along than we were when we first came to Grantville." Neustatter stood and stared over the wagons at the dragoons.

Ditmar switched directions. "So you are compatible."

"There is nothing wrong with your cousin, Ditmar. She is a fine young woman." Neustatter shrugged. "I just do not think of her like that. *Und* I do not think she thinks of me like that."

Ditmar sighed. Neustatter took that as confirmation that he had had this conversation with Astrid, and that it had ended along similar lines. What was taking those dragoons so long?

"Astrid reads many books," Ditmar observed. "I think she is expecting an up-time romance. Are you as well?"

"Only if I were to court an up-timer," Neustatter answered. "But neither do I expect a cold contract."

"That is reasonable," Ditmar agreed. "Astrid says our little *gemeinde* is family, and that one ought not marry close family."

"Something to that," Neustatter stated. He got a sly look in his eye. "What about you?"

Ditmar looked confused. "What about me?"

"Astrid."

"*Nein.* Hjalmar and Astrid may as well be my brother and sister rather than cousins. We grew up together after our parents died." Ditmar shook his head as if to clear it. "Same reason as you, only stronger."

"I think we have discovered just how much time these dragoons are wasting," Neustatter declared.

"They could leave," Ditmar pointed out.

"Unless we were correct before, and we are in the way of their rendezvous," Neustatter reminded him. "If so, they can keep wasting time, right up past noon. Why they have not sent half their men on a wide circle around Flieden, I do not know."

"Maybe they have."

"That is a disturbing thought. First thing I would do is try to ambush our reinforcements."

"Why leave anyone here at all? Who could they be meeting who cannot ride cross the fields?"

Neustatter looked at him. "Someone with a wagon."

Sometime later, a shout went up from the east barricade and carried throughout Flieden.

"*Hauptmann* Zeithoff, let us find out what that is," Neustatter suggested.

They found a group of men at the barricade. Zeithoff quickly ascertained they were from a nearby village.

"Twelve more men," he reported to Neustatter. "All armed."

"That is good," Neustatter said. "Men, *Amtmann* Zeithoff here is the *hauptmann* of militia. I am Corporal Neustatter, from the SoTF National Guard Reserves, and Sergeant Sperzel of the Fulda Barracks Regiment is at the western barricade. *Hauptmann* Zeithoff will get you settled in. *Danke.*"

Neustatter let Zeithoff take care of that while he talked to the five men stationed at the eastern barricade.

"I appreciate reinforcements as much as you do, but if you see any soldiers from the Fulda Barracks Regiment, do not shout, *bitte*. It is essential that we surprise the enemy. Send someone to the western barricade to tell us, and we will come talk to their officers."

The men agree to do so.

"We heard the battle is over," one of them ventured.

"We have beaten off two or three attacks," Neustatter told them.

"We heard many are dead."

"A few," Neustatter corrected. "More of the enemy. We are going to win. The enemy is simply deciding if they have one more attack in them or not."

He waited a moment before giving orders. "One of you look toward the west so that you see any battle that starts. Two of you watch the north and south, because a smart enemy would split up and come from both directions. The other two of you look east, because the Fulda Barracks Regiment is coming."

They muttered assent, and Neustatter returned to the western barricade.

"What time is it?" Lukas muttered a while later.

Neustatter pointed to a shadow. "Not noon yet."

Lukas started watching the shadows. Neustatter did not. The infantry would get to Flieden when they got to Flieden—assuming they had not been ambushed.

Neustatter snorted. This second *hauptmann* was not going to do something like that. So far, he seemed the sort to make threats and bull his way through.

Neustatter realized something. "Sergeant Sperzel? In their place, would you not have sent a sergeant forward with a flag of truce to demand our surrender?"

"I would have done so before the sun set last night," Sperzel agreed. "They would have to expect it would be rejected, but it would have kept our sentries anxious all night."

Eventually Neustatter spoke, but quietly enough that only Sergeant Sperzel and Ditmar heard him. "I can think of only two reasons not to talk to us. The first is that their larger plan depends on them not being identified. The second is that they plan to wipe us out."

"Or both," Sperzel pointed out. "You have been careful to take prisoners. If they mean to remain unknown, then they must regain their men *und* kill all of us *und* Flieden."

"They have to know they would miss at least a few of our mounted men," Ditmar pointed out.

"Perhaps they have a larger force coming up behind them," Sperzel suggested.

"Then they are courting a battle with General Brahe as well as the National Guard," Neustatter pointed out.

"Why not ride to the Spanish Netherlands?" Sperzel suggested.

"Perhaps they are lost?"

"All the more reason to bypass Flieden or send a truce flag."

Neustatter looked around and saw the defenders were growing increasingly impatient.

"Maybe that is it." He indicated the other men behind the wagons with a quick shake of his head. "Tempt us into attacking them? Or at least letting down our guard?"

One of those men shuffled his feet and loudly told his squad, "We cannot keep this up forever."

Neustatter took a couple steps in that direction. "*Ja*, we can—but they cannot. How much food can they have? Tonight, our unarmed men will eat first, then replace half of you at a time."

"Are they going to attack?"

"Could be. If they do, we are ready." Neustatter made that statement confidently.

Presently, Lukas spoke up. "Neustatter, I think the shadows are starting to lengthen again."

Neustatter hoped the Fulda Barracks Regiment was on schedule. He studied the dragoons. A number of them were dismounted and appeared to be checking their horses' tack.

"Sergeant Sperzel."

Sperzel was standing next to Neustatter in an instant. "They are about to do something."

Neustatter laughed. "At high noon, no less."

"They are pulling the dismounted men back," Sperzel observed, "*und* leading horses forward."

"They are either going to charge or they are going to leave," Neustatter stated. "Men in the wagons, stay down a little longer. Same plan if they charge, except now we have straw on the ground to each side. We will light that with torches. When I give the word, fire one shot at a time. Aimed. Point-blank."

Neustatter found Zeithoff. "*Hauptmann,* bring up the reserve." Then he detailed unarmed men to run to either flank with instructions.

Jakob appeared at his side. "This is it, is it not, Neustatter?"

"Could be, Jakob. How are you, really?"

Jakob made a noncommittal noise. "Eh, they winged me in that first rush on the right but I will be okay."

Neustatter studied him.

"Topf bound it. I am not bleeding. I can shoot a pistol and reload, Neustatter."

Neustatter considered. "All right. I want to take a look at it before night."

Another man raced up, drawing a shot from the occupied house. Neustatter recognized him as one of the men from the eastern barricade.

"Men coming down the road from Fulda in a hurry," he reported. He pointed to Sergeant Sperzel and his men. "Dressed like them."

Neustatter exchanged glances with Sperzel and suspected he had the same nasty grin that the sergeant did.

"Run back. Wave them in. Bring them up to that last house in the middle," Neustatter directed. "Quick and quiet as you can."

The man dashed off.

"This is going to be close," Sperzel warned. "Neustatter, watch the dragoons. I will watch for *Leutnant* Mehler."

Within a few minutes, shots peppered the house that a few dragoons were still holed up in. A man wearing the pink-orange uniform of the Fulda Barracks Regiment ran up to the barricade.

Sergeant Sperzel greeted him. "Salute, sir. I do not want to show those dragoons over there who you are."

Neustatter turned and saw a young man, unusually tall for a down-timer, almost six feet. He had unruly dark hair and looked untried.

Neustatter copied Sperzel's lead. "Salute, sir. Corporal Edgar Neustatter, SoTF National Guard Reserves."

"*Leutnant* Johann Mehler. What is the situation, Sergeant Sperzel?"

Sperzel gave a quick summary. Mehler shot Neustatter a look.

"I agree with Sergeant Sperzel, sir." Keeping his arm below the level of the wagon, Neustatter motioned toward the dragoons. "They are either going to attack or leave."

Mehler studied them briefly. "They are about to charge," he stated. "I see a man testing how his sword draws from the scabbard. No one does that to ride away."

Sperzel had already smacked one of his men on the shoulder. He dashed off to bring up Mehler's half-company.

"The dragoons will pass the wagons left and right," Mehler stated. "Neustatter, your men and the villagers need to stay behind the wagons and leave those passages clear for us to shoot through. My men will be further back and fire as the dragoons pass the wagons."

"That is sneaky, sir. I like it," Neustatter told him. "We intend to set the straw on fire."

"Not until the lead riders reach it," Mehler ordered.

"There are men with pistols in the wagons. My men have four revolvers and a shotgun. I—"

Multiple cries sounded at once.

"Here they come!"

"They are charging!"

"Ready!" Neustatter ordered. He heard that echoed on the left flank.

"I will be with my men," Lieutenant Mehler stated. "Hold your positions, and we will get through this."

"Ditmar."

Ditmar Schaub leveled his .22 rifle and tracked one of the men leading the charge. He squeezed the trigger. The weapon fired with a metallic snap. He chambered the next round and fired again.

Neustatter saw a horse pull up short and immediately get buffeted by other horses thundering by on both sides.

The ground seemed to shake as seventy dragoons galloped toward them. They stayed pressed together in a narrow column to avoid the clay pots along the edges of the road.

"Take aim!" Neustatter ordered. "Torches!"

Sperzel bellowed, "Fire!"

The first four horses and their riders went down in a hail of gunfire. Before the echoing whoom of the muskets died away, individual pistol shots rang out as Neustatter, Otto, Phillip, Jakob, and Hans Deibert fired methodically. Some of the riders returned fire with their own pistols.

The torch bearer on the right had already panicked and thrown his torch into the straw. It caught with a whuff. The oncoming dragoons split once they passed the half-buried clay bowls, and those aiming to the right of the wagons veered away from the sudden flames. Richart fired into them with a distinctive pattern: two shotgun blasts, pause to reload, two more blasts. Their path put them broadside to the Flieden men on the right. From his housetop, Hjalmar led one horse and pulled the trigger. The horse stumbled and fell. Another horse crashed into it, and a small pileup began.

The dragoons riding for the left of the wagons rode straight into an ambush. Neustatter leapt up on the left wagon. "Pistols!"

Six men popped up and blasted the column with a dozen shots. Neustatter used the confusion to carefully empty a magazine into the front of the column. Men and horses went down, but the column was still coming.

The designated man on the left had thrown his torch. The straw caught as the first few riders pounded past the wagons. A couple of them whirled their horses around to attack the defenders from behind. Others veered off in front the wagons, trying to get at the men within. One fired a pistol shot and hit one of the Flieden pistoliers in the head. He dropped without a sound. Another dragoon leaned out of the saddle, slashing with his blade. Neustatter twisted mostly out the way. He took some sort of blow to the ribs and calmly shot the man out of the saddle as he rode off.

Then he took a quick look around and ordered, "Down! Down!"

Lieutenant Mehler's volley emptied half a dozen saddles.

"Fire!"

Sperzel's men and the Flieden militia alike had grabbed the matchlocks taken from the dragoons' casualties. The volley crashed out across the wagon and shattered any hope the dragoons had of closing with the wagons.

Neustatter heard Mehler bellow, "Second rank, fire!"

He *felt* the pressure as the musketballs passed overhead.

Then he popped up with a fresh magazine in his Colt .45.

The dragoons who had ridden off to the right—the north—wrapped around the first house and rode straight into the heart of Flieden . . .

. . . straight into a volley from Mehler's *other* platoon.

"Charge bayonets!" the Fulda Barracks Regiment lieutenant ordered. "Cavalry, charge! Second rank, fire!"

Three more saddles emptied. Eleven mounted Fliedeners started forward. Their formation was ragged, their gaits were confused. Neither one mattered. The dragoons wheeled and fled, peppered with fire from villagers defending the right flank.

MISSIONS OF SECURITY

The Fulda Barracks Regiment platoon on the left moved steadily forward, one rank passing through the other and then firing. A couple dragoons who had made it past the wagons and were still in their saddles whirled their horses around and galloped back the way they had come.

The larger number milling around beyond the wagons, already teetering on the edge, saw them coming and broke.

"NESS! Mount up!" Neustatter ordered.

"Mount up!" Sperzel told his men.

"Go!" Lieutenant Mehler ordered. "Do *not* get ambushed!"

Most of their horses were where they were supposed to be. Not everyone got the word, but Neustatter and Sperzel set off in pursuit with a total of six NESS agents and four Fulda Barracks Regiment soldiers.

Neustatter had himself, Ditmar, and his four pistoliers. Hjalmar was still up on a roof. Richart was more useful on the ground with that over/under shotgun, and Lukas had been busy capturing dragoons in the immediate vicinity of the wagons. Sperzel and his men had muskets. They would not be firing while mounted, certainly not while in motion.

The two columns of dragoons had merged together into a single retreating stream by the time the pursuit was underway. A few stragglers were still in sight.

Neustatter watched carefully as the pursuit approached the place the dragoons had used as their staging area. He saw a couple casualties, and a lone dragoon standing over them, sword in one hand, pistol in the other. He seemed less than completely steady.

Neustatter reined in. "*Hauptmann?*"

"Leave my men alone," the dragoon rasped.

"SoTF National Guard," Neustatter stated in English. "Lay down your weapons. My men will take you to the medic."

The man hesitated. Neustatter could see the bloodstain on his side now.

"It was a fair battle. Up-time rules of war. They captured me at Alte Veste."

The man seemed to sag. Whether in pain or relief, Neustatter couldn't tell, but his sword and pistol dropped to the ground.

"Otto. Jakob. Talk to the *Leutnant*, but recommend the usual. We will be right back."

Neustatter, Sperzel, and six others pressed on for about an up-time mile. They overtook a few men, each time ordering them to dismount and leaving a guard behind. Finally, Neustatter, Sperzel, and Phillip reined in.

"Any further and we would be asking to be ambushed," Neustatter declared.

"Agreed," Sperzel said. He wheeled his horse around. "Let us collect everyone and establish order in Flieden."

Thursday, September 14, 1634

"Pretty sure I said you men did not need to pull sentry duty," Lieutenant Mehler greeted Neustatter before dawn.

"Pretty sure you have a sergeant or a corporal who could handle this shift," Neustatter returned.

Mehler nodded. He still looked ridiculously young and untried, and after the battle and late night, his hair was even more of a mess. On the other hand, yesterday he'd simultaneously handled two platoons engaged against separate columns and ordered Flieden's cavalry in at the decisive moment. So Neustatter was going to make a *lot* of allowances.

"Thought I would spell your medic and Topf for an hour," Neustatter said.

"How many did we lose during the night?"

"Another Fliedener. A couple dragoons." Neustatter shook his head. "All six of those villagers would be alive if I had not ordered a stand here."

"*Might* be alive," Mehler corrected. "The *hauptmann* you captured—O'Brien—would not have savaged this place, but that second *hauptmann*? I saw how O'Brien did not come to his defense when we talked in front of him last night. How is O'Brien, anyway?"

"He should be fine," Neustatter told him. "Ditmar got him with a couple rounds from his .22. The wounds should not get infected, especially since you are taking him back to Fulda. If I may make a suggestion, sir, send him right on to Erfurt."

"I suspect we will, but my *hauptmann*, Major Utt, and *Herr* Jenkins will probably have something to say about that," Lieutenant Mehler returned.

"Sorry, sir," Neustatter apologized. "I am not used to that many links in a chain of command."

Lieutenant Mehler laughed for the first time since arriving in Flieden. "Somehow that does not surprise me, Neustatter."

Neustatter's expression did not change at all.

"Neustatter, people die in battle." Mehler spoke sternly. "You *know* that. You have been in more battles than I have. Six killed and fifteen wounded are remarkably low casualties."

"Mostly suffered by Flieden."

"You have three wounded. I have two wounded. Other villages have two wounded. Flieden has six killed and eight wounded, and that is far less than if they had tried to fend off that second company without your help. I *know* some of them said the village would have been left alone, but we both know that is not true. O'Brien would have ridden until he found whomever he was supposed to find, but that other *hauptmann* . . . His tactics show him to be aggressive and arrogant. You did the right thing."

"*Dank,* LT," Neustatter muttered. "But NESS has only two wounded."

Leutnant Mehler gave Neustatter the sort of skeptical look suited to an exasperated governess. "Were you or were you not bleeding?"

Neustatter snorted. "I have cut myself worse than that shaving. I think he punched me with the hilt and just broke the skin."

Mehler rolled his eyes and continued. "*Und* you took a company of enemy dragoons off the roads. Maybe a few more than that."

"*Ja*, we did. But the victory is going to be hard on Flieden. *Leutnant* Mehler? We captured a dozen horses in the initial ambush. I promised one to the teamsters for the wagon horse that was killed and said we would split the rest with them. Shared ownership with a stables. Does the Fulda Barracks Regiment need the horses captured here in Flieden?"

"I do not think we want to give all of them up," Mehler answered cautiously.

"I know the SoTF and the USE need warhorses. But could we leave some of them here in Flieden? The village is down at least six men, maybe fourteen depending on whether the wounded recover. It would let them keep up with planting and harvest."

"That is a good idea, Neustatter. Come, let us find *Hauptmann* Zeithoff."

* * *

Mehler and Neustatter spotted Zeithoff talking to a few of the villagers.

"*Ja*, I agree—I wish none of it had happened. But once we could not agree to flee, deaths were inevitable. We fought well. We *won*. We will honor those men," the *amtmann* declared.

"*Ja*, we must. A service later today . . ."

Neustatter recognized the short, austere-looking man as Flieden's pastor. He had crossed paths with Franz Struve for only a few minutes yesterday at Hermann Topf's house.

Zeithoff noticed Mehler and Neustatter and beckoned them.

"Pastor Struve has suggested a service later today."

"I think that is a good idea," Mehler said.

Neustatter held out his hand. "Franz Struve, I understand we have you to thank for getting Flieden's women and children out of the line of fire. I asked around last night and found out that you personally led them from houses that were threatened."

Struve looked uncomfortable at that. "Someone had to."

"Most of the brave men I have met say that," Neustatter stated. "My men and I would be happy to attend the service."

When Neustatter returned to where he and his men had slept, he found Ditmar fussing over Hjalmar.

"I am fine, Ditmar," Hjalmar was insisting. "This should not even count as wounded. I got some splinters sliding down roofs."

"What, you slid on your face?" Ditmar retorted.

"Some of them might have been from near-misses," Hjalmar allowed.

Neustatter interrupted. "Can you ride?"

Hjalmar made a dismissive noise. "Of course."

Neustatter nodded and made his way over to Jakob.

"Can you ride?"

Jakob Bracht looked down at the bandages around his upper left arm, then back up at Neustatter. "*Nein*, not on a horse. I will be fine in a wagon, but I do not have the left arm strength to control the reins. It is not deep, just—"

"Deep enough that you will be laid up for a while." Neustatter held up a hand. "I agree, Jakob. If we were still in a life-or-death situation, I would put you back on the line this morning. But we are not. I want you on one of the wagons back to Fulda. *Nein, nein*, do not start. There is a danger of infection, and Fulda can get drugs faster than Frankfurt. In an emergency, they can toss you in a truck to Grantville.

"But I expect all you will do is get to Fulda a week or so ahead of us. *Und* the wagons taking the wounded to Fulda could use an agent with a revolver. Once you get to Fulda, take it easy. Telegraph the office if you need to. I will make sure you have enough money for food and drink."

* * *

At the funeral service, the NESS agents stood with the Fulda Barracks Regiment. The entire village was there, even Hermann Topf. Lieutenant Mehler had sent half a dozen soldiers under the company's medic to care for the wounded during the service.

Struve was not as polished as some pastors Neustatter had heard, not even as much as Pastor Claussen back in the village. But his simple, direct words offered comfort amid Flieden's grief.

Afterwards, some of the men came over and greeted Neustatter, Sperzel, and Mehler. The three of them huddled with Zeithoff, who was back to being the *amtmann*.

"I have to send the men from the other villages home," Zeithoff told them.

"Of course," Lieutenant Mehler agreed. "I will stay with most of my men and the medic. The corporal and three men I sent riding for Fulda after the battle was over should be arriving about now. I requested reinforcements and more medics. Once the wounded dragoons are well enough to move, I will send them under guard to Fulda. *Und* I will send Sergeant Sperzel and a full squad with you, Neustatter, a half-day's ride. I cannot send them far outside the SoTF, but you should be able to reach Frankfurt without further trouble. From what the prisoners have said, there is no enemy army out there. Just a couple companies of dragoons acting like they were going to meet someone."

"*Danke*, sir," Neustatter said.

Friday, September 15, 1634

In the morning, all the NESS agents were eager to continue on to Frankfurt. So were Lorenz and Heinrich. Tobias and Albrecht were noticeably hesitant but not making any verbal protest.

Ernst Wunderlich was. "Neustatter, how do you know the road is safe? A whole cavalry regiment could be out there."

"Could be," Neustatter allowed. "What intelligence we have suggests that the two companies we faced were on their own. But if we run into a regiment, we will come right back to Flieden."

"A couple hundred dragoons could overrun us."

"If they were between Flieden and Frankfurt—but they are not." Neustatter sounded certain. "*Leutnant* Mehler's men will have reached Fulda by now, and as soon as they reported in, a radio message would have been sent to Frankfurt. Any other dragoons out there are going to be busy evading General Brahe's men. Besides, we need to get the machine parts to Frankfurt, *ja*?"

Lieutenant Mehler and *Amtmann* Zeithoff approached.

"*Danke*, Neustatter," Zeithoff said. "Flieden is still here."

"I regret the casualties." Neustatter spoke quietly. "Especially the one pistolier in the wagons."

"But you were right. We probably would have lost that many if we had tried to run." Zeithoff shook his head. "There was no good choice."

"I hope there is no next time," Neustatter offered. "But if there is, you and your families know that you defended your homes."

"If there is, Flieden will be ready," Lieutenant Mehler stated. "We will do some training to make your men even more effective. Get patrols out this way more often." He turned to his sergeant. "Sergeant Sperzel, is your squad ready?"

"*Ja,* sir."

"Safe journey, Neustatter."

Mehler and Neustatter shook hands. Then Neustatter saluted. Mehler returned it. NESS mounted up.

Neustatter turned toward the wagons, grinned, and bellowed, "Wagons, ho!"

The four wagons set out, each trailing a couple horses captured in the initial ambush. All the NESS agents except Jakob were mounted now, as were the ten men in Sergeant Sperzel's squad. Anyone who did not have a revolver or an up-time weapon carried a matchlock or a snaphance pistol captured from the dragoons.

Neustatter figured they were still three days from Frankfurt, and they closer they got, the closer they got to General Brahe's forces. Sperzel's squad rode with them for an uneventful morning. The wagon train reached a village about midday, and those villagers had not seen soldiers of any kind in months.

"This is where we turn back," Sergeant Sperzel told Neustatter.

"*Danke,* Sergeant. I appreciate the escort."

"That was a well-fought battle, Neustatter. You did most of it. We will see you when you come back through Fulda."

Neustatter and Sperzel shook hands and exchanged salutes.

Monday, September 18, 1634

The wagon train met one of General Brahe's patrols on Saturday and arrived in Frankfurt late on Sunday. They were able to get the cargo under lock and key, but missed any opportunity to send a radio message—and

MISSIONS OF SECURITY

the radio operators were not transmitting on Sundays, except for emergencies.

It was Monday morning before Neustatter was able to have two radio messages sent.

> BEGIN: FRANKFURT TO FULDA
> TO: MAJOR UTT
> ADDR: FULDA BARRACKS
> FROM: CPL E NEUSTATTER SOTF NG
> DATE: 18 SEP 1634
> MESSAGE: HIGHEST REGARDS LT MEHLER AND SGT SPERZEL FOR DEFENSE OF FLIEDEN VS MERCENARY DRAGOONS STOP PLS CONFIRM SAFE ARRIVAL OF CASUALTIES TO FULDA BARRACKS STOP
> END

> BEGIN: FRANKFURT TO GVILLE
> TO: ASTRID SCHAUBIN
> ADDR: NESS OFFICE RT 250 EAST
> DATE: 18 SEP 1634
> MESSAGE: ARRIVED FRANKFURT 17 SEP STOP BATTLE VS MERCENARY DRAGOONS 11-13 SEP FLEIDEN STOP JAKOB FLESH WOUND HJALMAR MINOR CUTS SAYS TOO SMALL TO COUNT AND DONT WORRY YOU STOP ESTIMATE RETURN 28-30 SEP STOP
> END

CHAPTER 8: HOME

Monday, September 18, 1634

Those members of NESS left in Grantville were starting the third week of most of the men being away on the Frankfurt mission. Ursula and the babies were doing well. Anna was fretting that she had not gone into labor yet. Agathe was basically running the apartments with some assistance from Astrid.

Karl had been working at the blacksmith on a project for Neustatter. Over the summer, the Grantville Fire Department had rescued a woman partway up the Ring Wall. Neustatter had wondered how, then learned about carabiners. Karl allowed that if he teamed up with a watchmaker who could handle the springs, he could probably make one for each NESS agent.

Today, though, Wolfram, Stefan, and Karl were helping James Ennis and a work crew build the bridge.

Shortly before noon, a messenger came to the office.

"Telegram for Miss Astrid Schäubin, from Edgar Neustatter," he announced.

Astrid paid him and read the message. Hjalmar was hurt? A battle against dragoons? She read the telegram a second time. "HJALMAR MINOR CUTS SAYS TOO SMALL TO COUNT AND DONT

WORRY YOU"—*Ja*, that sounded like Hjalmar. For a moment, she wondered if Neustatter were downplaying the seriousness of Hjalmar's injuries. *Nein*—if it were serious, Ditmar would have added something. Then she recalled hearing something about kidnappings in the Fulda area and decided to leave early for class and read the newspapers at the library.

Astrid noted that the mission was definitely behind schedule and that Neustatter's estimated return date allowed for an equal delay on the return trip. She hoped they did not plan on fighting their way through dragoons again. She also made a note to look up the difference between dragoons and cavalry.

Then she walked over to the work site to bring the men up to date. They were clustered around one of the workmen, an older man, who was pointing something out.

"The bridge will need a support right here, unless you are going to use a rigid metal frame."

"Absolutely," James Ennis agreed. "I'm thinking a pair of pilings here, and a pair on the other side. Metal is out—too expensive."

"How big around?"

"Big," James answered. "Whole tree trunks, not four-by-fours."

"Sturdy," the workman muttered, "but plain. Bridges should be beautiful."

James laughed. "Most of the time, we are just trying to get troops across a creek. It just needs to work."

"What about a carved figure?"

"Wh-what?" James Ennis looked mystified. "Why?"

"Because once you cut a tree down, straight, unadorned wood is *ugly*. It ought to be *art*."

"You are supposed to be a carpenter."

"I carve. My journeyman work was . . ."

MISSIONS OF SECURITY

James Ennis just shook his head. "I forget sometimes. Welcome to the seventeenth century. What do you want to carve, and how much is it going to cost me?"

"I want to carve the support, of course."

Astrid saw James blink. "What kind of art goes under a bridge?" he asked. Then his confusion was replaced by a suspicious look. "You aren't going to carve a troll, are you? Did Julia put you up to this?"

This looked to Astrid like a good time to interrupt. "I just heard from Neustatter!"

Karl, Wolfram, and Stefan clustered around her. She read the telegram to them.

"We should go," Stefan said.

"*Nein*, we need more information," Wolfram said. "Astrid, if the injuries were anything but minor, Neustatter would have asked me about them."

Astrid exhaled. "*Ja*, he would have. *Dank*, Wolfram." She read the telegram yet again. "*Ja*, you are right, Wolfram. I will read the newspapers at the library before class tonight. I heard about something going on in the Fulda area."

At Calvert High School, she looked through the last ten days of newspapers at the State Library. Someone had kidnapped the up-time administrators in Fulda. Some of them had already been found. The mercenaries NESS had fought were probably involved in that. *Well, if I can figure that out, I am sure those on the scene can, too.* Some weeks later, Astrid decided she should have paid as much attention to the discussion about a carved troll as to trying to figure out the details of what had happened out by Fulda.

Astrid had found out how to learn more about cooking: there was a class. It had already started, but she was able to talk her way into joining it in the second week. That gave her two classes this fall. The other was an introduction to business class.

Tonight, the cooking class would be in a classroom. They were learning about nutrition. She found it interesting, but it was easy to get lost in the details of *vitamins* and *minerals* and so on. It was good to know the *why* behind up-timer advice, but it was possible to overdo it, *to miss the forest for the trees*. Sure, she could add up *RDA percentages*, but she also understood why some people summarized all the nutrition advice as "eat more meat and vegetables." Or even simpler: eat more food. Astrid was thankful they had enough.

She *was* going to have to talk to Neustatter, Ursula, and Leigh Ann about having a garden at the Kimberly Heights apartments. It did not need to be complicated, just what they needed most often: kale, cabbage, potatoes, onions, carrots. Up-time carrots were strange. They tasted fine, but Astrid had a hard time getting used to something *orange* tasting like a carrot.

Wednesday, September 20, 1634

Two days later, Astrid was spending a quiet afternoon updating NESS's files when the office door flew open. Agathe Pfeffer burst in.

"Anna has gone into labor!"

"Is Ursula with her?" Astrid asked.

"*Ja.*"

"*Gut.* Go back, *bitte*. She will be nervous. You have children. Tell her everything will be okay. I will send Wolfram and then go get one of those horse litters."

Agathe hurried off. Astrid pulled the door shut and ran off in the other direction, a short distance east on Route 250, left on Riverfront Park Road and down a steep hill. The men were working on the bridge.

MISSIONS OF SECURITY

She skidded halfway down the hill. "Wolfram! Wolfram! Anna is in labor!"

Wolfram's head came up. He set down the timber he was carrying and raced up the hill toward her.

"How is she? How far apart are—?"

"Agathe just ran over and told me. She is on her way back now. Go catch up. I will bring a horse litter so we can take her to Leahy."

By the time Astrid returned to the apartments with a horse litter, Wolfram had eased Anna downstairs and was carrying her *go bag*. Agathe went with them.

"As you say, I have been through this before," she murmured. "You . . ."

"Have not," Astrid agreed.

"Nor anytime soon?" Agathe smiled mischievously.

"Ha! I am nowhere near old enough to marry and start a family."

They got Anna to Leahy. The nurse who checked her in began asking questions. Her eyes widened when Wolfram rattled off Anna's current status in medical language that was only pretending to be Amideutsch. But Astrid could tell that it sped things up. When they wheeled Anna into a delivery room, Astrid excused herself and took little Elisabetha with her. She had a pretty shrewd idea that she was going to be the one responsible for the children and for dinner.

By the time the school bus dropped off Johann and Wilhelm, Elisabetha was up from her nap and watching with interest as Astrid figured out dinner.

"Mutti says not to play with our food," Elisabetha said.

"I am not playing with it. I am cooking it."

"It looks like playing."

"Do you want to help?" Astrid pointed to what would be roast mutton, mashed potatoes, gravy, and, since she had been thinking about them last night, carrots. 'That is for tonight." Then she pointed to a lot of other food that the Pfeffers had bought this morning. "That is for next week."

"Next week? Why?"

"I am going to make something called sauerbraten," Astrid told her. "I have to mix all this up"—she gestured at the vegetables and spices—"and soak the meat in it for a week."

"Ewww! Yucky," the four-year-old pronounced. In no way did this stop her from enthusiastically stirring the mixture as Astrid put it together. She just had no intention of eating it.

Elisabetha took a break from stirring. "This is a lot of food."

"It is for when all the men come home. They will eat a lot."

Later, Elisabetha was skeptical about the mutton, potatoes, and carrots. Astrid got her to eat a small portion by leaving off the gravy. The boys wolfed it down. Astrid had no illusion that that meant they liked her cooking in particular. They tended to eat everything in sight regardless of who cooked it. Hjalmar and Ditmar had been like that, too. The men did the same—they had been working on the bridge all day. But Ursula said Astrid's cooking was coming along, which she took as high praise indeed.

Agathe came in late in the evening.

"Anna had a little girl. She looks just her," she reported. "They named her Kristina, after the princess. They are both well."

Saturday, September 23, 1634

Anna and little Kristina came home three days later. It quickly became apparent that with three infants, no one in that apartment was going to get much sleep. The nearby townhouses looked nearly finished. Astrid made a note to talk to Neustatter about that as soon as the teams returned.

The other thing Astrid had not anticipated was how much laundry three infants produced. That started to take a lot of their time, but she steadfastly refused to shorten NESS's office hours. They did get a couple short missions in the local area. Stefan and Karl were only too happy to take them. Wolfram did not like not being able to fuss over Anna—Kristina had him wrapped around her little finger already—but Astrid thought he needed the break. Then there was a shipment that required four guards, so that day she did close the office and went on the mission. Having four agents was probably an excessive precaution, but the client insisted on it.

Wednesday, September 27, 1634

The following week, a number of prospective clients came to the office, and Astrid added several assignments to the calendar. On Wednesday, one of them let it drop that he'd seen the newspaper article. Astrid made polite noises. As soon as she closed the office for the day, she went straight to the library and searched the newspapers.

It wasn't hard to find. They'd simply been too busy with Kristina's birth to have read the papers. All the papers had articles on the rescue of the administrators in Fulda. The *Grantville Times* had the human-interest stories, including one about the village of Flieden having been attacked. It wasn't clear that this had anything to do with the kidnapping of the up-time administrators in Fulda, but the reporter sure seemed to think so. *Freiheit!* focused on the treachery of some of the *niederadel*. The *Grantville Daily News* concentrated on the big picture. *The Grantville Freie Presse* had the timeline of events and several sidebars, including the Battle of Flieden. Some of the specifics didn't sound like how Neustatter operated at all, so Astrid maintained a healthy skepticism toward the reported details. She shared the information with the others over dinner.

Sunday, October 1, 1634

The same messenger delivered another telegram. Neustatter had sent this one from Erfurt on September 29, and it said he expected the men to arrive in two more days.

After church on Sunday, Karl went to the office while Astrid prepared dinner. NESS wasn't open on Sunday; it was just where the telephone was.

Astrid thought they would probably eat around eight in the evening—NESS seemed to have a pattern of returning from missions or National Guard duty in the evening, and the telegram had said they would need to take care of the horses. She wasn't sure why Neustatter had bothered to include that. It was standard procedure.

Sooner than Astrid expected, Karl burst into the apartment.

"What is it, Karl?"

"Neustatter just called the office from downtown. They came in the west side of the Ring, and they're riding through town. He said we have just enough time meet them at the office in uniform." He dashed next door to tell Stefan and Wolfram.

"I will watch dinner cook," Agathe Pfeffer assured Astrid. "Go."

Neustatter normally did not stand on ceremony. But Astrid was sure he had his reasons. She quickly changed clothes to her tan blouse and skorts, buckled her gunbelt, pulled on the heavy blue coat, and hurried down the stairs while tying her *halstuch*.

"I think we should be in formation," Karl said.

Shadows were starting to lengthen, and a fair number of people were out and about. Some of them were on their way to evening church services. Others were visiting or en route to one of Grantville's restaurants. The NESS agents definitely attracted attention as they marched in pairs up Route 50 to the office. Phillip and Astrid were in front, pistols holstered at their sides. Karl and Lukas were behind them with their rifles at shoulder arms.

Astrid could hear Johann following them, and it sounded like he was gathering up some friends from the Kimberly Heights/Freeman Street/Porter Avenue neighborhood.

Karl wheeled them into line outside the office door. He and Lukas ordered arms, holding the rifles at their sides.

❊ ❊ ❊

A sharp whistle from Neustatter brought the wagon train to a halt. They'd left Grantville twenty-six days ago. They were tired and scruffy and, now that they were in safe territory, had gotten somewhat spread out.

"Let's finish this mission in good order!" Neustatter called. "Team Two, take point. Jakob, do you think you can handle a horse?"

Jakob was already scrambling down from Heinrich's wagon and moving to untie his horse from the back of the wagon.

"Lukas, Phillip, untie the colors from Lorenz's wagon. We will ride next with the four wagons right behind us. Ditmar, Team One has rear guard. Pistols holstered, long arms out and across the saddle.

"Remember it would not have worked if Flieden had not stayed and fought for their homes and if the Fulda Barracks Regiment had not arrived—but y'all done *gut*. Let's go."

They passed through the gap Birdie Newhouse had blasted in the Ring Wall. As they rode down Buffalo Street, a few people waved to them. It was late enough in the day that Neustatter figured they could use Market Street and Route 250.

Ditmar circled his horse back alongside Neustatter long enough to tell him, "Neustatter, there's a rank of Bretagne's Company up ahead. I can see their buff coats and feathers in their hats."

Neustatter was leading his team with Lukas right behind him carrying Anna's SoTF flag. Phillip was riding behind him with the NESS guidon. As they drew even with half a dozen men of Bretagne's Company, Neustatter heard, "Present *arms!*"

"Present *arms!*   " Neustatter ordered.

He saluted, and Phillip dipped the company guidon.

"Order *arms!*"

Neustatter heard one person on the street ask another what that was all about. He knew. It was a professional compliment, and Bretagne's Company had taken the time to find out NESS's itinerary to render honors. Those in the business respected what NESS had done at Flieden.

Well, most of them. Along Route 250, the wagon train passed a couple men from Schlinck's Company.

"Boy Scouts!" one of them called out.

"Well, Schlinck and his men are still pains in the ass," Lukas muttered none too quietly.

Neustatter had to laugh. "*Ja*, they are."

They dropped Ernst Wunderlich off at the machine shop with a round of handshakes and rode out toward home.

Hjalmar turned his horse onto the gravel at the far end of office building and rode back past the office.

His sister ordered, "Present *arms!*" After exchanging salutes with the four NESS agents lined up outside the office, Neustatter ordered, "Dismount and fall out!"

Hjalmar slid from the saddle, and military protocol dissolved into handshakes and backslaps. Astrid ran up and hugged him.

"You look good. Are you really okay?"

"I was just a little cut up. It is mostly healed now." He put a finger to his forehead where there was still a scratch.

'Everyone else?"

"Jakob is getting better. Neustatter has a small cut to the ribs."

Astrid frowned. "That was not in the telegram."

Her brother shrugged. "Everyone else is fine. Tired, of course, *und* we are not done yet. We need to take care of the horses."

"I remember you left here with six. Where did all these come from?"

"We captured them. It is a long story."

"Miss Schäubin!" Neustatter made his way over.

"Neustatter. Welcome home. Is everyone really okay? Hjalmar? You? Jakob?"

"We are. Can you gather the families? We may as well tell the story to everyone at once."

"They are at the apartments. Hjalmar said you need to take care of the horses. Dinner will be ready when you are done there."

Neustatter smiled. "It's good to be home."

The men were at the livery stable longer than Astrid expected, but she did not know at the time that Neustatter and the teamsters were making arrangements for a couple more pools of timeshare horses. The delay was good, though, because it gave Astrid and Agathe time to finish preparing dinner.

Sometime later, the three teams returned.

"Smells good!" Stefan proclaimed. He looked around and did not see Ursula. "Agathe?"

"Mostly Astrid," Agathe told him.

Astrid detected some skepticism, but Stefan did not actually say anything. She was nervous about dinner would taste, so she remained quiet as well.

Once they began eating, though, she could tell everyone liked it. Well, everyone except Elisabetha—she was spending more time telling about how they mixed the ingredients than actually eating.

"I see you made a solid investigation," Neustatter commented.

"I do not know what you were investigating, but this is good," Ditmar declared.

Astrid heard a couple muttered suggestions about making her one of the regular cooks and was horrified.

But Neustatter spoke up before she could. "*Nein*. We need Astrid in the field and running the office. In fact, Miss Schäubin, someone from the National Guard will interview us tomorrow—they call it *debriefing*. I would like you there, taking notes for our files. And Lukas, Wolfram, and Karl, so that we can walk you through what happened."

Later, Astrid spoke to Neustatter privately. "*Dank*, Neustatter. I want to be able to cook, but I do not want to *be* the cook."

Neustatter gave a crisp nod. "I agree. Do we have missions coming up?"

"Quite a few. NESS will be busy," Astrid told him.

"And that is why you are not the cook."

"I had nothing to do with it. The clients read the newspapers. You were mentioned in some of the stories. At least some of the papers think the battle in Flieden had something to do with the up-timers in Fulda being kidnapped."

Neustatter waggled a hand. "Maybe."

"I did not know about the newspaper articles until afterwards," Astrid continued.

"But you still scheduled the missions," Neustatter said. "Is that not how the up-time *PIs* got into trouble all the time? No missions, behind on paying their expenses, and then needing to take jobs even when something about them did not seem right?"

Astrid smiled. "*Ja*, that is what happened. In stories from up-time."

"The important points are that we can avoid that problem, and you are making command decisions."

Astrid frowned. "I will stop if you want, but clients want to hear that we can help them. If we do not put them on the calendar at once—"

Neustatter held up a hand. "I am not telling you to stop. I am asking you to continue."

"Oh."

"At Flieden, Ditmar reminded me not to assume what a prisoner was trying to tell was the answer that I wanted to hear. Hjalmar rode hard to alert the Fulda Barracks Regiment. Both of them fought well, of course. But, Miss Schäubin, I remembered that NESS has three Schaubs, not two. Keep making decisions."

Astrid nodded slowly. If Neustatter wanted her to make those decisions herself, she'd keep doing so. And the form of address he'd used . . .

Astrid figured she ought to just ask. "Neustatter? Do you remember that when you took me to lunch to ask me to be a field agent? You said you had no romantic intentions."

Neustatter gave her a crooked smile. "Still true, Miss Schäubin. And you?"

"The same."

"I think we are too much alike."

Astrid's eyes widened. "Too alike?"

"*Ja*." Neustatter waited a beat. "Ditmar spoke to me about it. I understand you already told him no."

"I did."

Neustatter nodded gravely. "NESS is family, and we are both very decisive. Imagine a husband and wife who are both used to making mission decisions. Now imagine a husband and wife whose approach complements each other."

Astrid smiled. "I see what you mean. Except about me being a leader."

"The rest of us had a six-year head start, Miss Schäubin. In the last two years, you have gained more than two years of ground on us."

Monday, October 2, 1634

The men slept in the next day, getting a well-deserved break. After lunch, they gathered in the office. The SoTF National Guard had sent an older man. He was short and stocky with a lot of gray in his hair. He wore a blue uniform with two silver bars on his shoulders and a satchel slung over one of them.

"*I bin Leutnant* Schmidt," he stated.

"*Leutnant*," Neustatter acknowledged. "Would you like a desk to take notes?"

"*Dank.*"

Schmidt sat at Neustatter's desk. Astrid was seated at her own desk and studied Schmidt as he seated himself and prepared his ink and pen. She knew those bars were a captain's rank. By calling himself a lieutenant, Schmidt had really told them he was with military intelligence. All of NESS's agents were present, seated in chairs or leaning against a wall.

"I would like to begin by updating you on the situation in Fulda. All of the SoTF administrators have been recovered, but the archbishop is still missing. There have been a number of developments on other fronts as well."

"Excuse me, *Leutnant, bitte*," Neustatter looked to Astrid and raised an eyebrow. "What has happened elsewhere that we should know about, Miss Schäubin?"

MISSIONS OF SECURITY

She turned to that page in her notebook. "The Ram Rebellion ended with the capture of *Schloss* Bimbach and von Bimbach himself. General Banér captured Ingolstadt. Well, bribed the garrison, it sounds like, but Banér controls the city now. Emperor Ferdinand II died, and his son Ferdinand III now rules Austria. Prince Fernando of Spain married Duchess Maria Anna of Austria, and they rule the recombined Netherlands. The USE has a peace treaty with them."

"*Dank*. We heard rumors about some of that." Neustatter paused for thought. "Was Maria Anna not missing? How is she in the Netherlands?"

"Colonel Wood flew Prince Fernando to Basel to rescue her."

"Oh. Well done. Good for them. And none of that has anything to do with the dragoons west of Fulda?"

"Not as far as we know," Lieutenant Schmidt stated. "Which brings us to what did happen there. How did it begin? What did it feel like?"

"We were a day's ride west of Fulda. It was cool but not cold. Ditmar's team was in the lead, and there were woods on the right, almost all the way up to the road...."

Schmidt took continuous notes. Astrid did not think he wrote down the entire conversation, but he might have. He asked no questions yet, letting Neustatter and the other NESS agents speak. Sometime later, Neustatter concluded, "We continued on to Frankfurt, delivered the cargo, and reported in at Flieden, Fulda, and Erfurt on our way back. Some of *Leutnant* Mehler's men went with us from Flieden to Fulda with a couple wagons of prisoners who were well enough to move."

"*Dank*," Schmidt said. "A number of questions occurred to me...."

Astrid already had pages and pages of notes. The men's answers to Schmidt's questions added more.

"Is that everything?" Schmidt finally asked and was answered by chorus of "*Ja, Leutnant*."

"Very well. First, *Leutnant* Mehler reported that your defense of the village was outstanding. It was exactly what the National Guard would expect of the men who seem to special in derailing the *Adler Pfeffer* exercise." Schmidt gave a small smile.

"Second, we believe the mercenaries you encountered probably were connected to what happened in Fulda. A unit in support or maybe just working for the same people. I have not received the report itself yet, but a couple of the prisoners you took gave us some useful information."

"If I might make a suggestion, sir, *Hauptmann* O'Brien—the one we captured—should be offered a position," Neustatter said.

"I think you can trust we will make that offer."

At that point, Johann and Wilhelm stuck their heads in the door, having run right over after the school bus dropped them off at the apartments.

"Are all your families nearby?" Lieutenant Schmidt asked.

"*Ja*, they are at the apartments right now," Neustatter answered.

"*Dank*." Schmidt turned to Willi and Johann. "Boys, I have a mission for you—if you are interested."

Two heads bobbed enthusiastically.

"Ask your families to come outside. We will be there in a few minutes."

Astrid was not sure what Lieutenant Schmidt was up to, and she could tell that Hjalmar was wondering the same thing. Neustatter's expression told her nothing, of course.

As we filed out the door, she heard Neustatter quietly ask, "Formation, Sir? Colors?"

"That would be appropriate."

Astrid decided that was the tone of a man who was up to something.

Neustatter raised his voice, but only a little. "Otto, point. Wolfram, rear guard. Ditmar, Hjalmar, colors. Twos."

MISSIONS OF SECURITY

NESS slotted into formation smoothly. Astrid recognized it was a good formation for marching down Route 250. Flanking guards were not necessary; they would just end up in the opposite lane or in someone's front yard. They turned onto Freeman Street. With a sidewalk from Freeman Street to Kimberly Heights, it did not take long to reach the apartments. Agathe and the older children had come downstairs, while Ursula and Anna and the babies were on the landing outside the door.

Neustatter maneuvered them into a single rank.

Lieutenant Schmidt removed something from his satchel before setting it on the ground. He stepped forward and raised his voice to the level of 'official announcement.'

"Corporal Edgar Neustatter, having fought through a near ambush and captured enemy personnel and horses, then led his force to the nearest village where he organized the defense and sent for reinforcements. Under his leadership, the militia repulsed an attack and held until reinforcements arrived. He was then instrumental in defeating two companies of dragoons. His actions reflect great credit on himself, his men, and the State of Thuringia-Franconia National Guard. Edgar Neustatter is hereby promoted to *leutnant*."

NESS uniforms had shoulder straps, so Lieutenant Schmidt pinned the lieutenant's insignia there. Neustatter saluted crisply. Schmidt returned the salute.

For once, Astrid could read Neustatter. He seemed stunned. The rest of NESS started clapping.

"I understand that in the up-timers' civil war, they put the names of battles they fought in on their flags." Schmidt nodded toward where Hjalmar stood with the NESS guidon. "That is . . . unofficial, of course. But unofficially, you might think about adding Flieden.

"If you remember anything else, get word to me at Camp Saale, *bitte*. Excellent work."

With that, not-Lieutenant Schmidt was gone.

NESS agents clustered around Neustatter, congratulating him. Once they had dispersed a bit, Astrid stepped up. With a mischievous smile, she said, "Congratulations . . . *sir.*"

Neustatter just shook his head and gestured at his new rank insignia. "I am sure I do not need this."

"I think the National Guard recognized you *ought* to have it," Astrid told him. "*Und* maybe *they* need you to have it. . . . Neustatter, where they need *you*, that's home."

"Could be." He gave a lopsided grin. "I suppose I have made the occasional comment about what officer ought to do and not do. Reckon I ought to put those into practice, since you are right—we are home."

* * *

The men had a week before the next mission.

Neustatter, the teamsters, and the livery stable worked out an agreement. NESS ended up with a percentage of the ownership in two timeshare pools of six horses each. As Johann put it, they got *first dibs* when they needed horses. Plus, unless all three teams started riding out on missions at the same time, they'd probably make a modest amount of money. The teamsters owned a percentage of the same pools. Since they seldom needed riding horses, they'd probably make a bit more than NESS. But they'd use some of that to buy into a pool of draft horses, which would give their company added stability. The livery stable certainly didn't mind having another dozen trained horses available. It was a good deal for everyone.

The other big project that week was the bridge. The main supports were in, and the main trusses were in place. Karl fashioned the few metal braces required. The planks were next, and the rest of the men could help with that. The carpenter painstakingly made sure they were all straight. He started adding the railings. He had carved them with little figures about six inches high at each pole. Astrid recognized a dwarf, a Brillo, and a mermaid, among others.

She decided to leave those details out of the letter she was writing to Pastor Claussen. It would take pages to explain the relevant parts of up-time culture. This letter was already long, with the births of the babies and an account of the Battle of Flieden. She hoped it wasn't too much trouble for Pastor Claussen to pass their news on to friends and family, especially to Anna's mother and father. They ought to know they were grandparents.

Sunday, October 8, 1634

Kristina was baptized at St. Martin's, too. Eighteen days old was late for a baptism, but Wolfram and Anna had waited for everyone on the NESS mission to return. All (Anna excepted) were at St. Martin's on Sunday. Stefan and Ursula were the godparents, of course.

It was a lovely ceremony.

Astrid stopped in at the other apartment to congratulate Anna.

"*Danke*." Anna grinned. "Now you need to find a young man."

"Ha."

Astrid thought she had better things to do—like finally remembering to take some reloaded brass to Georg Meisner to see if multiple sets of toolmarks really were visible on the casings.

CAST LIST

Augustus – *herr* of Neustatter's home village, married to *Frau* Sophia

Bracht, Jakob – Catholic, a NUS Army recruit looking for another chance, carries lockpicks

Bretagne, Giulio – captain of Bretagne's Company, one of the seven mercenary outfits in the Grantville area, runs a well-trained and well-supplied organization

Brenner, Otto – born 1603, Lutheran, farmed in a village in Holstein-Gottorp, fought at the Battle of Dessau Bridge as part of the village militia, captured and incorporated into Wallenstein's army, NESS agent, the invisible man

Carroll, Sara – an up-timer, a NUS Army recruiter, scheduled to teach horsemanship

Carstairs, Joel – assistant manager, Sommersburg and Carstairs construction

Claussen – Lutheran (Flacian) pastor in Neustatter's home village

Deibert, Johan "Hans" – Lutheran, a member of his village's militia, came to Grantville early on and fought in the Croat raid

Ennis, Leigh Ann Haun – married to James Marvin Ennis, daughter of Fred & Julia Haun, mother of Julia, James Frederic, and Carrie

Ennis, James Frederic – married to Leigh Ann Haun, USE Army Engineering Corps

Felke, Horst – Calvert High school student, Catholic, the leading advocate of the Critical (Alexandrian) text of the New Testament within the *Bibelgesellschaft*

Forster, Josef – a friend of Johann Kirchenbauer, shortstop on his Little League team, lives in Spring Branch

Frost, Dan – up-timer, Grantville Police chief, up-time through March, 1634

Gerhard, Johann – historical down-timer, Lutheran (Flacian), theology professor and dean of the theology faculty at the University of Jena, considered the third most important Lutheran theologian ever (behind Luther and Chemnitz)

Goschin, Ursula – Lutheran (committed Flacian), married to Stefan Kirchenbauer, mother of Johann, a very good cook

Green, Albert "Al" – an up-timer, pastor of First Baptist Church in Grantville, member of the *Bibelgesellschaft*

Groenewold, Gertrud "Trudi" – a prostitute in Erfurt

Grönloh – a sergeant in Schlinck's Company

Haun, Fred – an up-timer, married to Julia Gunderson, owns land east of Calvert High School on both sides of Buffalo Creek

Haun, Julia Gunderson, an up-timer, married to Fred Haun, from Minnesota. Mother of Johnny F.

(Hearts & Minds team in *1634: The Ram Rebellion*), Walter, and Leigh Ann Ennis

Heidenfelder, Lukas - born 1602, Lutheran, farmed in a village in Holstein-Gottorp, fought at the Battle of Dessau Bridge as part of the village militia, captured and incorporated into Wallenstein's army, NESS agent, partier, carries a knife

Heinrich – an older teamster based out of Saalfeld

Holz, Pankratz – Flacian Lutheran pastor holding services in a storefront church in Grantville, critical of the *Bibelgesellschaft*

Hudson, Eric Glen – up-timer, graduated from Calvert High School in 1631, NUS Army assigned to military procurement in Erfurt, then SoTF National Guard stationed in Halle as a railroad scheduler, member of the dinner and a movie club ("Breaking News," Jay Robison, *Grantville Gazette* 5), and occasional 250 Club patron ("The Baptist Basement Bar and Grill," Terry Howard, *Grantville Gazette* 32), dating Gena Kroll

Huffman, Maxwell "Max" – up-timer, NUS drill sergeant, see "Greetings!", Mike Watson, *Grantville Gazette* 68 for his further adventures as an SoTF Marshal

Kellarmännin, Barbara – a Calvert High School student, Brethren (i.e., Anabaptist), a member of the *Bibelgesellschaft*, quiet and observant, see "The Observer," *Grantville Gazette* 78 and "Clique, Clique, Boom," *Grantville Gazette* 82 for her further adventures

Kirchenbauer, Johann – son of Stefan Kirchenbauer and Ursula Goschin, born not long before the Battle of Dessau Bridge in 1626, delighted to be in Grantville, the pessimist

Kirchenbauer, Stefan – born 1593, Lutheran, married to Ursula, father of Johann, farmed in a village in Holstein-Gottorp, fought at the Battle of Dessau Bridge as part of the village militia, captured and incorporated into Wallenstein's army, NESS agent

Kircher, Athanasius – historical down-timer, Catholic, Jesuit, priest assigned to Grantville, omni-disciplinary scientist: Paula Findlen's up-time biography of him (2004) is titled *Athanasius Kircher: The Last Man Who Knew Everything*

Kraft, Heinrich "Heinz" – married to Helene Olbrichtin, a farmer in Kleinjena, Saxon County introducing up-time foods and crops, see "Occupied Saxony," *Grantville Gazette* 55 and "The Saale Levies," *Grantville Gazette* 56 for his further adventures

Kräusin, Anna – married to Wolfram Kuntz, not long before the Battle of Dessau Bridge, Lutheran, several years older than Astrid, a skilled seamstress

Kroll, Gordon – up-timer, married to Maureen, works in military procurement in Erfurt

Kroll, Jennifer "Gena" – up-timer, graduated from Calvert High School in 1634, martial artist—see "American Past Time," Deann Turner and Mike Turner, *Ring of Fire II*, dating Eric Glen Hudson

Kroll, Maureen – up-timer, married to Gordon, mother of Gena, works in the medical clinic in Erfurt

Kuntz, Wolfram – born 1594, married to Anna Kräusin, Lutheran, farmed in a village in Holstein-Gottorp, fought at the Battle of Dessau Bridge as part of the village militia, captured and incorporated into Wallenstein's army, took care of the sick and wounded, NESS agent

Lorenz – a teamster based out of Saalfeld

Mehler, Johann – an SoTF National Guard lieutenant in the Fulda Barracks Regiment

Meisner, Georg – Calvert High School student, Brethren (i.e., Anabaptist), member of the *Bibelgesellschaft*, took the forensics course while his sister stayed late to read Al Green's books, one of the first CSIs down-time

Meisnerin, Katharina – Calvert High School student, Brethren (i.e., Anabaptist), member of the *Bibelgesellschaft*, within it the leading advocate of the Majority (Byzantine) text of the New Testament

Moser, Eberhard – a lieutenant in the SoTF National Guard assigning mercenaries/contractors to supply convoys

Musaeus, Johannes – historical down-timer, with Katharina Meisnerin and Horst Felke becomes one of the leaders of the *Bibelgesellschaft*

Neustatter, Edgar – born 1604, farmed in a village in Holstein-Gottorp, Lutheran, fought at the Battle of Dessau Bridge (1626) as part of the village militia, captured and incorporated into Wallenstein's army, leader of Neustatter's European Security Services

Pfeffer, Elisabetha – daughter of Phillip Pfeffer and Agathe Traudermännin, about 4 years old

Pfeffer, Phillip – married to Agathe Traudermännin, father of Wilhelm and Elisabetha, Lutheran (Philippist—named for Melanchthon, has lived in Grantville since mid-1632 doing day labor

Pfeffer, Wilhelm – son of Phillip Pfeffer and Agathe Traudermännin, roughly the same age as Johann Kirchenbauer

Recker, Karl – born 1600, Lutheran, formerly a blacksmith's apprentice in a village in Holstein-Gottorp, fought at the Battle of Dessau Bridge as part of the village militia, captured and incorporated into Wallenstein's army, NESS agent

Richards, Preston "Press" – an up-timer, Grantville Police chief from March, 1634 on

Rowland, Mimi – an up-timer, one of the Grantville Police Department dispatchers

Rummel, Maria – Wilhelm's sister

Rummel, Wilhelm – leader of a group of thirty-one refugees forced out of their Franconian village in 1633 for supporting the NUS

Schaub, Ditmar – born 1604, Hjalmar and Astrid's cousin, Lutheran, farmed in a village in Holstein-Gottorp, fought at the Battle of Dessau Bridge as part of the village militia, captured and incorporated into Wallenstein's army, leader of NESS Team One

Schaub, Hjalmar – born 1608, Astrid's brother and Ditmar's cousin, Lutheran, farmed in a village in Holstein-Gottorp, fought at the Battle of Dessau

Bridge as part of the village militia, captured and incorporated into Wallenstein's army, leader of NESS Team Two

Schäubin, Astrid – born 1612, Hjalmar's sister and Ditmar's cousin, Lutheran, one of *Herr* Augustus and *Frau* Sophia's maids in a village in Holstein-Gottorp, NESS secretary

Schlinck – captain of Schlinck's Company, one of the seven mercenary companies in the Grantville area, big on brute force

Schrödinger, *Herr* – a NESS client, manufactures something for the USE military that allows him to stay in really good inns

Seidelman, Gottlieb – a NUS Army recruit, went into the Reserves and is taking classes to go into law or perhaps police work, considered an intellectual in the ranks

Sophia – *Frau*, married to *Herr* Augustus

Sperzel, Dietrich – a NUS National Guard sergeant in the Fulda Barracks Regiment

Stroh, Richart – Lutheran (Philippist), a big, unyielding man

Stull, Dennis – up-timer, works in military procurement in Erfurt, Noelle Murphy Stull's father

Thomas, Jr., Harley – an SoTF Marshal, formerly a NUS Army drill sergeant, served with Max Huffman and Archie Mitchell in both jobs

Traudermännin, Agathe – married to Phillip Pfeffer, mother of Wilhelm and Elisabetha, Lutheran

Wesner, Casimir – a library researcher in Grantville on behalf of Saxe-Altenburg and the von Hessler family, see "The Researchers Spiritual and Temporal," *Grantville Gazette* 84) for more about him

Wolf, Hans – a sergeant in Bretagne's Company

Zeithoff, Bernhardt – *amtmann* (administrator) of the village of Flieden

Printed in Great Britain
by Amazon